# Critical Acclaim f

# Also by Leigh Russell

**Poppy Mystery Tales**
*Barking Up the Right Tree*
*Barking Mad*

**Geraldine Steel Mysteries**
*Cut Short*
*Road Closed*
*Dead End*
*Death Bed*
*Stop Dead*
*Fatal Act*
*Killer Plan*
*Murder Ring*
*Deadly Alibi*
*Class Murder*
*Death Rope*
*Rogue Killer*
*Deathly Affair*
*Deadly Revenge*
*Evil Impulse*
*Deep Cover*
*Guilt Edged*
*Fake Alibi*
*Final Term*
*Without Trace*

**Ian Peterson Murder Investigations**
*Cold Sacrifice*
*Race to Death*
*Blood Axe*

**Lucy Hall Mysteries**
*Journey to Death*
*Girl in Danger*
*The Wrong Suspect*

*The Adulterer's Wife*
*Suspicion*

# POPPY takes the LEAD

## LEIGH RUSSELL

A POPPY MYSTERY TALE

cmc

First published in 2024 by
The Crime & Mystery Club Ltd.,
Harpenden, UK

crimeandmysteryclub.co.uk
@CrimeMystClub

A CIP catalogue record for this book is available from the British Library.

This is a work of fiction. Names, characters, places, and incidents either
are the product of the author's imagination or are used fictitiously,
and any resemblance to actual persons, living or dead, businesses,
companies, events or locales is entirely coincidental.

ISBN
978-0-85730-572-5 (Paperback)
978-0-85730-573-2 (eBook)

2 4 6 8 10 9 7 5 3 1

Typeset in 11.1 on 14.85pt Sabon
by Avocet Typeset, Bideford, Devon, EX39 2BP
Printed and bound in Great Britain by
CPI Group (UK) Ltd, Croydon CR0 4YY

MIX
Paper | Supporting
responsible forestry
FSC® C171272

*This story is for Poppy*

*It is also dedicated to Michael, Jo, Phillipa,
Phil, Rian and Kezia*

# 1

TWO YEARS HAD PASSED since I first set eyes on Rosecroft, my very own cottage in the picturesque village of Ashton Mead, a few miles from Swindon in the Cotswolds. It was hard to believe I had been living there for so long, working at the Sunshine Tea Shoppe. I had noticed the brightly coloured café on my first visit to the High Street. To be fair, the café was impossible to miss, with its dazzling yellow and white striped awning and primrose coloured exterior. Inside, the café lived up to its name, the yellow and white tiled floor and lemon walls continuing the colourful theme. Even the table cloths were yellow and white checked gingham, matching our aprons. The cheerful atmosphere of the café was only partly due to the bright decor. The owner, Hannah, loved baking, and I enjoyed serving customers. It was a sociable and generally jolly place to work and, despite my mother's disappointment at my choice of career, I considered myself lucky to have ended up there. It was more varied than any office job I had ever done, and much more fun. As for our customers, only the most curmudgeonly could fail to relish their visits to the Sunshine Tea Shoppe, with its warm welcome and mouthwatering array of cakes. Many of them were regulars from the village, but we also had plenty of visits from people passing through Ashton Mead on their way to some destination rather grander than our small village. So what with locals and tourists, we were kept pretty busy, especially in the summer months.

Hannah laughed at my surprise that two years had passed since my arrival in the village, as she cut the cake she had made to mark the occasion. Her eyes twinkled with glee as she handed me a plate.

'It's chocolate,' she said, knowing that was my favourite. 'I made it especially for you.'

'As long as you don't expect me to eat it all,' I laughed.

Any excuse to scoff her cakes was fine with me, and she was always ready to seize on an excuse to try out a new recipe. As the owner of the tea shop, she knew how important her skill in baking was to the success of her business.

'It's chocolate and cherry, to be specific,' she added, as she manoeuvred a fat slice of cake onto my plate, ignoring my halfhearted protest that I had just had breakfast.

'I still can't believe I've been here two years,' I said, watching her pour the tea.

'You can check your bank statements if you don't believe me,' she smiled.

'I'm not complaining,' I replied. 'It's just that the time has passed so quickly.'

'You're not getting bored with us, are you?'

I shook my head, smiling at the idea, although there was a time when that would have been a fair comment. Before moving to Ashton Mead I had been living in London, and the prospect of moving to such a quiet place would have appalled me. According to my ex-boyfriend, Ashton Mead was a 'Godforsaken hole in the sticks' that no one outside the village had even heard of.

'This place is nowhere,' he had complained. 'You can't spend the rest of your life stuck in this dreary backwater. You'll die of boredom. You might kid yourself it's a rural idyll, but how long is that fantasy going to last? It's a boring place, the people are boring, and you're bored.'

But that hadn't been my impression. I had fallen in love with Ashton Mead and the quaint little cottage left to me in my great aunt's will, and so far neither of them had disappointed. On the contrary, I appreciated my good fortune. I could never have afforded to buy my own property, let alone one with a garden. Apart from any other consideration, the grassy village was an idyllic home for Poppy, the friendly little Jack Tzu who had been left to me by my great aunt, along with her house. Poppy loved going for walks on the wide grassy slopes leading down to the river where ducks scudded about and swans sailed elegantly under the stone bridge.

Coming to live in Ashton Mead hadn't exactly been part of my life plan. In fact, I had not visited the village since I was a small child and had forgotten all about the place until my great aunt had died. At the time, it had made sense to check out my unexpected inheritance, not least because I had just lost my job and was struggling to pay the rent on my flat in London. As soon as I saw Rosecroft, with its trailing plants growing around the door and its soft yellow stone walls, I felt as though I had come home. Used to the noise and bustle of London, I was surprised how rapidly the slow pace of village life had come to seem normal. Working in the café, I got to know the local residents. Compared to the transient population in my area of London, everyone seemed settled and friendly. Even the tourists who stopped off in the village were very welcome, as far as Hannah and I were concerned, since they helped to keep The Sunshine Tea Shoppe in profit. Not all the villagers were happy about so many visitors turning up on sunny days, but all the local shopkeepers were pleased. Hannah's baking had helped to put Ashton Mead on the map.

Never having owned a dog before, I had been nervous about accepting the responsibility unexpectedly thrust on me. But Poppy and I had soon settled down together, and I could no longer imagine my life without her. Fortunately, she seemed content living with me. So when I told Hannah my life in Ashton Mead was perfect, it was almost true. Although I was never lonely with Poppy, I sometimes wished there was a man in my life but, considering how disastrous my last relationship had been, I had accepted I was probably better off single. Even my mother seemed resigned to my situation, although she still grumbled about my single status from time to time. She seemed faintly affronted that I hadn't followed her example, which was to marry and have children at the first possible opportunity. My protestations that life was different for women these days fell on deaf ears, and we had arrived at a tacit agreement to leave the subject alone.

'You're twenty-six,' she had said on her last visit, as though that was positively over the hill. 'Isn't it time you thought about settling down?'

'I have settled down. I'm very happy here. I couldn't be more settled.'

My mother had wisely refrained from persisting in her attack on my way of life, only muttering that she supposed the 'right man' would come along sooner or later. She refused to believe that I liked spending my time in a tiny café, serving tea and cakes to strangers. It was my turn to hold back from retorting that working at the tea shop was my ideal job. There was no point. She would never have believed me. She seemed determined to believe I had taken the job, not to pay my bills, but to spite her ambitions for me.

'You're a clever girl,' she liked to say. 'You could do so much better than a dead end job like that.'

But I wasn't sure what she meant by 'better'. My job might not be one she could boast about, but I was certainly happy. Not long after I had arrived in Ashton Mead, Hannah had offered me a job in the Sunshine Tea Shoppe. Just like my move to Ashton Mead, waiting tables in a café had never been part of my life plan, but I had agreed to work there temporarily, just until I found my feet. As it turned out, the job suited me very well, and Hannah and I soon became firm friends. It only took me ten minutes to walk to the café, my working hours were flexible, and Poppy was happy to be tethered in the yard outside. After a while I had taken to dropping her off with Hannah's mother, where Poppy hung out with Jane's sleepy old dog, Holly, or raced around the garden chasing squirrels and birds, and barking at foxes. At first Poppy had pestered Holly to play. The old dog had patiently tolerated my puppy's energetic attempts to engage her in a game, and after a while they had reached an accommodation. Holly's placid nature had a relaxing effect on my lively little puppy, who had become calmer since she started spending time with her elderly companion. Holly occasionally deigned to chase her young friend around the garden, which they both seemed to enjoy.

Relentlessly cheerful, the café's yellow awning added a splash of colour to the mainly drab High Street. Even the vivid scarlet of the butcher's shop paled beside it. Inside, everything was yellow, like our bright yellow aprons. Statuesque and voluptuous, Hannah even had blonde hair that fell in neat curls, in contrast to my wild red hair. On quiet afternoons, when Jane was unable to look after Poppy, Hannah was happy to let me leave work early. She never docked my pay although, to be fair, she paid me so little it would hardly have saved her much. If my great aunt hadn't paid off the mortgage on Rosecroft, I certainly wouldn't have been able to afford to live in my lovely three bedroomed cottage.

My former boyfriend had tried to persuade me to sell Rosecroft. He couldn't have been more misguided, because I was happy in my new home. It took me a while to discover that he had only ever been interested in how he could profit from my good fortune. Rosecroft turned out to be far better for my peace of mind than my affair with a shallow narcissist had been and, even though I was single, I wasn't lonely.

Walking home from the café that Thursday, stuffed with Hannah's excellent cake, I usually took Poppy across to the grassy slopes that led down to the river. If a bird ventured onto the bank, Poppy would strain at her lead, frantic to give chase, but she had accepted the futility of barking at the ducks and swans swimming on the water. For a change, I took her the long way home, across the village green. Watching her bounding along, pausing to sniff at the ground, I felt utterly content. My great aunt's legacy had brought me a happiness I had never expected.

In an unseasonably dry month, with barely any traditional April showers, the ground had become dry. Now, in May, the rain had returned with a vengeance and after several heavy downpours the grass was looking green and vibrant. Poppy was enjoying herself, searching around for different scents, when all at once she crouched down on her front paws and began to growl softly. She had noticed a figure walking towards us before I was aware of his approach. Seeing who it was, I tensed. I had rarely spoken to Silas Strang, but had heard of his reputation in the village. He waved his walking stick at me. He was barely middle-aged but walked with a stout wooden stick, which he was using to beat the long grass.

'Get that filthy animal off the green,' he bellowed.

His bloated face was crimson with rage, and as he drew near I could see his glaring eyes were bloodshot, and his thick lips wet with spittle. I stood my ground, telling myself that Poppy was entitled to walk on the grass. She was a clean dog, fastidious even, and I always carried bags for disposing of her waste. Poppy's growls broke out in a deep throated barking. A cross between a Jack Russell terrier and a Shih Tzu, she didn't even reach my knees, but she had a surprisingly loud bark for such a cute little dog. Even large dogs could appear daunted by her feistiness, although I suspected they chose to indulge her by pretending she had frightened them off.

Silas came close enough for me to feel a breath of wind as he swung his stick dangerously close to my face, but I refused to budge. If he thought he could intimidate me, he was making a mistake. When I had first arrived in Ashton Mead his truculence would almost certainly have unnerved me, but these days I was not so easily browbeaten. Taking on the responsibility of a house and a dog had boosted my confidence and forced me to grow up. Watching saliva spray from Silas' lips I flinched in disgust and he grinned, mistaking my revulsion for fear.

'I won't warn you again,' he roared, seemingly incapable of speaking at a normal volume. 'You get that brute off this grass if you know what's good for you!'

'Dogs are allowed to walk here,' I replied, resisting the temptation to add that if anyone was a brute, it certainly wasn't Poppy.

We stood for a moment, glaring at one another, until Poppy broke the uneasy silence with a loud bark. Silas spat on the ground, turned and stomped away. Watching his retreat, I felt a sense of triumph, but once he was out of sight Poppy whimpered and I squatted down to pet her.

'It's all right,' I reassured her, scratching under her chin. 'He's gone. He's nothing but a big bully. He can't hurt you.'

But I resolved to be especially vigilant with Poppy. I was afraid she might not be safe with Silas Strang around.

# 2

IT WAS DIFFICULT TO walk quickly with Poppy because of her frequent stops along the way to sniff the ground, or water it. Only in wet weather, when she would whimper to be carried inside my coat, could we make our way quickly along the streets. That evening, Poppy and I took a leisurely stroll to the village pub, as we often did at the end of my working day. One of those glorious evenings in late spring when you can sense summer is on its way, it brought with it a poignant remembrance of timeless holidays spent playing on the beach as a child. The sky was blue and a delicate perfume from nearby hyacinths mingled with the scent of freshly cut grass, as we passed my neighbours' gardens. Poppy trotted along happily, stopping every few yards to snuffle around, but I was keen to reach the pub and tell my friends about my unpleasant encounter with Silas Strang. Hopefully they would at least sympathise with me, even if they had no advice about what to do. I was torn between reporting the incident to the police, and ignoring it. On balance, I thought the police were unlikely to be interested. After all, nothing had really happened. But it was galling to think Silas would get away with his aggressive behaviour.

Cliff, the portly landlord of The Plough, greeted me with his usual smile, and grunted as he bent down to pat Poppy on the head.

'That's not as easy as it looks,' he wheezed as he straightened up.

'If you think you made that look easy, you're deluded as well as overweight,' the barmaid muttered, loudly enough for Cliff to hear.

He ignored her scathing remark. No one paid any attention to Tess, who had treated me with undisguised suspicion on my arrival in Ashton Mead. To begin with, her barely disguised hostility had made me feel uncomfortable, but I soon discovered she was gruff with everyone. After two years, she had grudgingly accepted me as part of the village, and now deigned to serve me without muttering darkly under her breath. Still, she remained anything but friendly, barely glancing at me as she told me my friends were outside. I found Hannah sitting at a table in the pub garden with her boyfriend, Adam, and our friend Toby, who taught science at a school in Swindon. Toby was attractive, with dark hair and blue eyes, and I had once hoped that we might become an item. Eventually, I had accepted that our relationship would never develop into anything more than a sound friendship. Unshakable in her belief that every woman needs a man in her life, my mother had been more disappointed than me.

'It's not the same and you know it,' she had snapped, when I pointed out that I wasn't alone. 'Poppy's just a dog.'

'She's far more intelligent than a lot of people I could mention, and better company.'

Poppy pricked up her ears and wagged her tail, as if agreeing with me. My parents had never owned a dog. Growing up, I had always known that other people became attached to their pets, but until Poppy entered my life I had no idea how strong the bond between a pet and its owner could be. When I tried to explain my feelings to my mother, she just sniffed, which was her sign of disapproval.

My three friends were laughing at some local gossip as I joined them in the pub garden. Taking a seat on the bench beside Toby, I watched him lean down to pet Poppy who lay on her back, her eyes closed in ecstasy at the attention. It was rare that I encountered anyone who hadn't fallen for her. Thankfully, Silas Strang was an exception.

'We were just talking about Maud's romance,' Hannah told me, giggling. 'I know we shouldn't make fun of her but, honestly, she must be seventy if she's a day. Apparently she's found herself a bloke. It's the butcher whose wife ran off with a dentist from Swindon. So there's hope for you yet,' she added, rather unkindly I thought.

I knew she wasn't being malicious, and managed to force a smile.

'You're looking glum,' Adam remarked, looking at me, when I didn't join in with their hilarity.

'That's because I let her leave work early today,' Hannah grinned. 'Never mind, you're going to be rushed off your feet tomorrow and you'll be lucky to get home in time for supper. I'll be in the kitchen baking all day for Saturday, so you'll have to manage the café on your own.'

'Someone needs a drink,' Toby said, rising to his feet. 'The usual?'

I forgot about my encounter with Silas as we talked about our preparations for the May Day festivities, which was a huge annual event in Ashton Mead. The fête took place on the gentle grassy slopes leading down to the river. Near the top of the slopes, where the ground was level, several marquees would be erected for drinks and food and various craftwork. Cliff was providing drinks for those who didn't bring their own, the butcher was arranging a massive barbecue, and Hannah had promised to supply a mountain of cupcakes. Preparations had been going on for weeks, and the excitement was becoming feverish. Everything was supposed to be locally sourced which seemed to work, by and large, although the event inevitably attracted people from further afield, mostly artisans with hand crafted items to sell. The previous year a fortune teller had put up a small striped tent, and a few travellers had turned up, to see what was going on.

Our main worry was that rain might ruin the festivities. The forecast for the weekend was inconclusive, and on Friday we had a heavy shower in the morning. At least the café was fairly quiet, which was a relief, as I was there on my own. The sky cleared in the afternoon and, assuming the local forecast was right, the ground would hopefully dry out overnight. As long as it didn't rain on Saturday the occasion promised to be a success.

# 3

I WAS WOKEN EARLY on Saturday morning, by Poppy nuzzling my cheek. She seemed even more lively than normal, as though she sensed something unusual was going on. Probably all kinds of new scents were in the air, of which I was completely oblivious. After breakfast, we walked down towards the slopes beside the river, and were just in time to see the Maypole arrive, to exuberant cheers from traders who had arrived to set up their stalls. A gang of children materialised as if from nowhere to gaze wide-eyed and shriek with glee as the Maypole was erected. Red-faced and sweating, Cliff was trundling crates of beer around in a cart. Hannah was shouting directions to Adam and they soon roped me in to help fetch supplies from the tea shop.

Adam and I scurried backwards and forwards with trays of cakes and pastries, with Poppy scampering beside me, while an assortment of knitters and jewellery makers, woodworkers and sculptors, painters and antique renovators and other craftworkers, busily arranged their stalls in the shelter of the marquees. Excited children hurtled around, making a lot of noise and generally getting in everyone's way. No one reprimanded them, because this was a joyous occasion and, despite the stress and frenetic activity, a party atmosphere was raising everyone's spirits. Only Tess stomped around looking angry. Children scarpered at her approach.

After an overcast morning, to everyone's relief the weather turned out fine. All the residents of the village turned up. Maud had shut her shop for the day, my friend Toby was there, struggling to push his mother's wheelchair across the grass, and at one point I caught a glimpse of Dana, the reporter from the local paper, in her bright red coat. Throughout the day, groups of pupils from local schools entertained us with their shrill singing, stilted dancing and clunky acrobatic displays, before they ran off to queue for ice creams or chocolate-covered marshmallows on sticks. A local swing band blared out through gigantic speakers, followed by a local choir who sang, mostly in tune. There were Morris Dancers and a giant pantomime horse pulling a wheelbarrow in which the May Queen rode, until she was accidentally tipped out onto the grass. None the worse for her upset, she brushed mud and grass from her gown before tottering on foot to the Maypole, pausing only when one of her high heels stuck in the ground. She was duly crowned by the county Mayor who was paying a fleeting visit before moving on to her next engagement. May Day was a busy time for everyone.

The climax of the day was a dance around the Maypole. Once again, a select cohort of carefully rehearsed school children assembled, with ice cream and chocolate smeared over their faces. Jostling and jumping with excitement, they took their places around the pole. A few of them started running round in the opposite direction to the others, which caused some tripping and tumbling. Before they all joined in a wrestling match that had broken out between two of the boys, a strident woman extracted the offenders and the dance resumed. Already tipsy, I giggled uncontrollably as the children scuttled crablike around the pole, their progress punctuated by intermittent hopping and jumping. When the children had finished, it was the turn of the Morris Dancers, their music punctuated by the banging of sticks which they wielded with gusto.

Absorbed in watching the entertainment, I paid no attention when Poppy growled, and failed to notice Silas until he was standing right beside me.

'You can't bring that animal here,' he snarled.

Poppy barked. He brandished his stick and Poppy snapped at it, uncertain whether this was a game or a threat. Concluding that I needed her protection, she began to bark in earnest. Silas's ruddy complexion darkened and he shoved her roughly with his stick. She yelped and sprang backwards but, trapped by her lead, she couldn't go far. I stepped in between Silas and Poppy, shielding her between my ankles.

'Leave her alone!' I cried out, my indignation fuelled by several glasses of Pimms. 'You know what you are? You're nothing but a coward and a bully. Why don't you pick on someone your own size, instead of attacking a harmless little dog? You're a monster.'

'Shut your gob before I shut it for you!' he snapped, waving his stick dangerously close to my face.

Emboldened by a heady mixture of anger and alcohol, I glared back at him. 'I don't know what that's supposed to mean, but if you think you scare me, you couldn't be more wrong. I'm warning you, if you raise so much as one finger against my dog, you'll be sorry!'

'And what are you going to do to stop me?' he taunted me, thrashing the ground with his stick.

'You're not going to hurt her!' I yelled, my voice rising, as I found it difficult to maintain a lofty dignity after drinking too much. 'You think there's nothing I can do? Let me tell you, there's nothing I *wouldn't* do to protect her.'

'Brave words,' he sneered. 'But you still haven't told me what you're going to do. I'll tell you what. Nothing. You can't stop me doing whatever I want. Who do you think you are, you stupid girl?'

'I don't care what you say, I won't let you get away with threatening me or my dog. If you think you can hit her, you have no idea who you're dealing with. I'll make sure you never lift your stick again. I'll do whatever it takes to stop you!'

Glancing around, I realised that we were attracting an audience. Among the onlookers, I spotted Hannah staring at me, an expression of surprise distorting her features, her blonde curls waving in the breeze. Adam was beside her, with his arm around her shoulders, looking worried. Behind them, I recognised a local reporter holding up her phone. With a snort of disgust, I turned my back on them and hurried home. My day was ruined and my head hurt. Happy to escape from the pandemonium and scrum of the fair, Poppy trotted in front of me. She didn't even want to pause and sniff the different aromas carried on the evening air as we hurried home.

# 4

THE FOLLOWING MORNING POPPY woke me, whimpering beside me on the bed. My head felt heavy and began pounding when I swivelled round to look at my phone. It was only half past five. Before I could settle down again, Poppy scampered to the door and resumed her whimpering. She refused to be quiet, so I finally abandoned all hope of going back to sleep.

'All right, all right, you win,' I grumbled, clambering out of bed.

The view through my bedroom window was obscured by a fine drizzle that formed a veil over my view down to the river. Dimly, I made out the shapes of trees through the mist as Poppy whimpered and scrabbled at the door. Groggily I pulled on my clothes and stumbled downstairs, yawning and muttering imprecations. Yanking the hood of my raincoat up, I stepped outside and paused to gaze along the lane. The rain had stopped, and in the gathering light, branches of trees were emerging from the haze. A shaft of sunlight pierced the mist. I flung back my hood and drew in a few deep breaths of air that were damp but clean and fresh. Feeling invigorated, I let Poppy lead me across the sparkling grass, towards the old brick bridge across the river.

Poppy bounded along, excited to be outdoors, but I was already regretting my rash decision. My feet were damp inside my trainers. Had I been fully awake, I would have resisted her entreaties to run across the grass at that hour in the morning. There was no way this outing was going to set a precedent.

'Don't think I'll be getting out of bed at silly o'clock every day,' I warned her crossly. 'Just because it's stopped raining doesn't mean it's okay to be out and about so early. And don't think that because you got round me once, you can do it again. We should both be indoors, fast asleep.'

Poppy threw me a quizzical look over her shoulder, without slowing her pace.

'I mean it,' I told her. 'You're not going to wake me up so early again. I don't care how desperate you are to go outside.'

Hungover, and distracted by talking to Poppy, I scarcely noticed a pile of old clothes lying on the grass. They must have been left behind after the fair. For once, Poppy wasn't sniffing the ground and, I noted crossly, she hadn't yet stopped to pee, in spite of having insisted she needed to go outside. She trotted determinedly forwards, head raised, nose twitching, alert to the manifold scents in the air that were lost on me. All I could smell was the fresh scent of grass, wet after the rain. Only when we drew close to the heap of clothes did Poppy lower her nose to the ground as though following a trail. Her route didn't zigzag as it often did, when she was following tracks left by birds or squirrels, but she kept going in a straight line, heading for the grey mound. By now we were close enough for me to make out the details of a filthy raincoat lying on the grass. We had nearly reached it, when I saw a large hand with dirty fingernails sticking out of one sleeve. It appeared that the man lying on the ground at my feet had been so drunk, he had managed to sleep through the rain.

Curious to see who he was, yet afraid of disturbing him, I stole closer, tensed to run if he woke up and objected to my peering at him while he was sleeping off the drink. We were almost level with the figure when Poppy made a leap forward, and barked loudly, making me jump.

'Be quiet,' I hissed, worried she would wake the sleeper.

She carried on barking, right beside his ear, but he didn't react. Intrigued, I stepped cautiously around the inert figure and halted in shock when his face came into view. Silas Strang was staring straight at me, with a baleful expression on his face. In the early morning light his skin looked grey. For a moment I thought my legs would give way. He didn't stir, nor did he start bellowing obscenities at me. He was lying on his side in an unnatural position, with one arm reaching awkwardly behind him, as though he wanted to scratch his back, and his coat was open, exposing the front of a grubby white T-shirt. Not until Poppy barked again did it occur to me that Silas might be dead. I nearly turned and fled, but a macabre curiosity had taken hold of me.

'Silas,' I murmured, uncertain whether to hope for a response or not. 'Silas,' I repeated, more loudly. 'Silas, are you all right? Silas, wake up. You're soaking. It's morning. Time to wake up. Silas? Can you hear me? Silas?'

A few moments had elapsed since we had first spotted him lying there, and Silas hadn't shifted position. He didn't even blink when Poppy barked again. It seemed he had lost the power to threaten anyone. But I was no medical expert and he could still be alive, unconscious with his eyes wide open. He might have suffered a stroke, or be having a fit of some kind. Either way, alive or dead, he needed help. Searching my pockets I discovered I had come out without my phone. Pulling myself together with an effort, I spun round on the wet grass and sprinted home, my legs shaking and my feet stumbling over tussocks. Poppy galloped beside me.

Back at home, I raced upstairs to find my phone which should have been on my small bedside cabinet, but there was no sign of it there. I spent the next five minutes searching for it in a panic. Had I known from the outset how long it would take me to find my phone, I would have run next door to my neighbour straightaway. He would have forgiven me for disturbing him at that early hour, given the gravity of the situation. At last I found my phone, which had slipped down between my mattress and my bedside cabinet. Before I could make a call, the sound of distant sirens reached me through my draughty window. I peered outside, my view once more obscured by a fine drizzle. As the sound of sirens grew louder, the air cleared to reveal a car drawing up, its blue light flashing. There was no need for me to alert anyone to my discovery. The police had already arrived. A moment later the first vehicle was joined by two more cars, and a police van.

'It's all right, Poppy,' I told her, with a sigh of relief. 'The police are there. We can leave it to them to sort out the whole messy business. We won't have to get involved.'

In an attempt to calm down, I brewed myself a pot of tea and sat down in my living room. As I sipped my tea, I tried to feel sorry for Silas, and wondered what could have happened to him. Poppy put her head on one side, and gazed at me with a puzzled expression, as if to say that we were already involved. Strictly speaking we were, since Poppy had been first to discover the body, but there was no reason why anyone else need know that. Recalling the odd position in which Silas had been lying, it occurred to me to wonder whether there had been foul play. It wouldn't even have surprised me to learn that Silas had been killed in a fight, given how quarrelsome he was. If that was the case, the less I had to do with the discovery of the body, the better.

'Let's stay well out of it and settle for a quiet life,' I told Poppy. 'This is all becoming complicated, and it could develop into a very nasty situation indeed. We don't want to have anything to do with Silas Strang, alive or dead.'

She put her head down and closed her eyes. '*Now* you want to go back to sleep,' I muttered crossly. 'After you dragged me out of bed so early.'

For an answer, she began snoring very softly. I lay down on my bed, fully clothed, but couldn't get back to sleep. Recalling my last argument with Silas, I shivered, wondering whether anyone remembered what I had said. Living in a small village had its drawbacks as well as its benefits. Soon all my neighbours would know about the argument between me and Silas, just a short time before he died, and speculation would be rife. I just hoped no one would decide to share their suspicions with the police.

# 5

WHERE YESTERDAY A ROW of brightly coloured marquees had stood, festooned with bunting, there was now only one large white tent, and that had been cordoned off by a crime scene tape. A uniformed police officer standing by the barrier appeared to be doing his best to ignore a woman in a startlingly red coat, who was gesticulating at him. From a distance I recognised Dana Flack, a reporter on *My Swindon News* who had once interviewed me. Tall and slender, she would have been elegant if her hunched posture and disproportionately long skinny legs didn't make her look ungainly, like a picture of a giraffe that had been coloured in by a small child fond of bright colours. Drawing closer, I saw that, even at that hour of the morning, she was wearing scarlet lipstick and brandishing her dictaphone, her eyes alert to the slightest movement on the far side of the barrier, while she flapped her hands vigorously in the air to emphasise her words.

The uniformed policeman towering over her striking figure was our local constable, Barry, nephew to the local shopkeeper. Barry had grown up in the village, but had moved away to live closer to the police station in Swindon. Friendly and well-meaning, he had once made a tentative pass at me. After I had rejected him as tactfully as I could, we had become friends. Like Dana, he was tall and slightly bowed, and like her he was almost attractive. Where Dana's looks were marred by a large sharp nose, Barry's were spoiled by a set of prominent front teeth which he frequently displayed in a dopey grin. Not as foolish as he looked, Barry was the kind of man of whom my mother would approve: steady, sensible and good natured. More than that, he was a friend who could be relied on in a crisis.

'Now then, Miss Flake,' he was saying as I approached. 'You know I can't let you through.' His cheerful smile didn't waver. 'We've only just got here ourselves. If a passing patrol hadn't spotted him from the other side of the river and come along to investigate, even we wouldn't know anything about it yet. There's no call to go upsetting yourself. I'm only doing my job.'

'You're the one who's preventing *me* from doing *my* job,' she retorted. 'The public have a right to know what's going on here.'

Despite her badgering, Barry's good natured smile appeared genuine. 'All in good time, Miss Flake, all in good time.'

'This *is* a good time,' she protested, 'and my name isn't Flake. It's Flack. There is nothing more irritating than people who think they know your name when they don't. Now, since you know who I am, perhaps you'll let me through so we can both get on with what we're supposed to be doing.'

'Like I said, Miss Flack, you're going to have to wait for the press release, along with everyone else.'

'That's too late. For goodness sake, don't you understand anything at all? What's the point of being first on the scene if I don't learn what's going on before anyone else finds out? Do you know what time I got up this morning to get here this early? Any minute now, the entire village is going to turn out, and what sort of scoop will that leave me?'

Barry remained firm in his refusal to let her pass and Dana turned away, grumbling that she might as well have stayed in bed. Catching sight of me, she came hurrying over.

'Amelia, how are you?' she cried out, her bonhomie so fake it would have made me laugh had the circumstances of our meeting been less dire. As it was, she made me cringe.

'My name's Emily,' I replied coldly.

'Yes, of course, it is, Emily, Emily. I know who you are. I'm so glad to have caught you.'

Unwilling to engage her in conversation, I turned away without another word. Unlike me, Poppy had no reservations about approaching Dana, and jumped up excitedly when Dana opened her bag.

'She's probably hoping you opened your bag to get out a treat for her,' I explained, yanking Poppy towards me. 'That's why she's getting so excited.'

To my surprise, Dana took a dog treat from a packet in her bag and asked whether she could give it to Poppy, who growled in delight when she received it.

I thanked Dana. 'You've made her day. You must have a dog?'

Dana shook her head. 'Not me. I carry these around with me because, well, you never know when they might come in handy.' She gave a sly grin.

I wasn't quite sure why dog treats might come in handy for someone who didn't own a dog, but I smiled and nodded, pleased that Poppy was having a good time.

'Now,' Dana said, 'you're just the person I want to talk to. My editor is very interested in learning more about your "set to" yesterday.'

With a sigh, I recalled seeing her at the fête, watching my encounter with Silas Strang and taking a picture of us as we argued. She might even have been filming us.

Reluctant to discuss the incident, too late I saw through her ploy to use Poppy in order to gain my attention. Barry was watching us, looking faintly anxious. I gave him a reassuring wave to indicate that Dana was not being a nuisance. Nevertheless he came over to join us.

'Now then, now then,' he called out as he drew near. 'Move along there.'

'I know, I know, nothing to see here,' Dana laughed harshly. 'Do stop interfering, Barry. Two women are allowed to talk without you poking your nose in.' Grabbing my wrist, she tucked my arm under hers. 'Put a man in a uniform and he thinks he can control your every move. Come along, Amelia.'

With that, she dragged me away, leaving Barry standing alone by the cordon.

'Now, you live in the village, don't you, Amelia?' she asked me as we walked away.

I sighed. Having given up correcting her about my name, I wondered how to extricate myself from her clutches.

Her hand was resting on the crook of my arm, long red fingernails glistening like talons.

'Now,' she continued, when Barry could no longer hear us. 'Tell me everything you know about what's going on. And don't leave anything out. It's Silas Strang, isn't it?'

Wondering how she had discovered the identity of the victim, or even that there was a body at all, I insisted I had no idea what she was talking about.

'How did you hear about it so quickly?' I asked her, unable to quell my curiosity.

She tapped the side of her nose and winked. 'A good reporter has her contacts,' she replied. 'I can't reveal my sources, but let's just say no one but the police and me know about this yet. And you,' she added crossly, as though I had deliberately turned up to annoy her. 'I absolutely forbid you to tell anyone else before I've broken the story,' she added, gazing at me with a calculating expression.

'What's that supposed to mean?'

'I'm talking about the body, of course,' she replied impatiently, tapping my forearm with her nails. 'The police only put up those tents when a serious crime's been committed and they need to send in a SOCO team to search for clues. Scene of Crime Officers. Surely you know that.'

As Dana was speaking, the cordon was opened to allow a police van through, and a team of white-coated officers jumped out.

'There they are,' she said, with a complacent smile. 'What did I just tell you? They've come to search the crime scene for evidence. Now, while we're waiting to hear about what's happening in there, tell me all about your altercation with Silas Strang yesterday.'

Mumbling that it was nothing, I pulled myself free of her saying it was time for me to get to work.

'We can walk and talk,' she replied, grabbing at my arm again and tucking it firmly in the crook of her elbow. 'So, what was it all about? Not a lovers' tiff, surely?' she asked archly.

The suggestion was so preposterous it made me laugh.

'Hardly,' I spluttered, struggling to suppress my laughter. 'He must be at least twice my age, and –' I broke off, superstitiously reluctant to speak ill of the dead. 'Why are you so interested in me, anyway? I didn't even know him.'

Before Dana could recover her place on her mental list of questions, I spoke quickly. 'And now I really do need to get to work.'

Forcefully disengaging myself from her grasp once more, I walked swiftly away with Poppy bounding along beside me. I shuddered to think how Dana would have reacted had she known she had been addressing the witness who had found Silas's body. Whatever else happened, my early arrival at the scene of the crime must remain a secret. If it ever came out, questions were bound to be asked about why I had failed to report my discovery of a dead body just a short walk away from my own front door – the body of a man I was known to have fallen out with only hours earlier. The ground underfoot was still damp and muddy; I felt as though I was walking on ice that might crack at any moment.

# 6

ALL THAT DAY I had a peculiar feeling that people were staring at me, dropping their gaze quickly whenever they caught me looking at them. More than once, I saw someone nudge their companion and mutter under their breath, while keeping their eyes fixed on me. It was obvious they were talking about me. Hannah claimed not to notice anything unusual and scoffed at my concerns.

'They're probably looking at you because they're wondering where their order is,' she replied. 'Now are you going to take that tray to table three before the tea gets cold and I have to make a fresh pot?'

On my way home, I called in at the local grocery store for a few supplies. Maud, the shopkeeper, was an incorrigible gossip. Only rarely did I manage to visit the shop without having to listen to some new rumour, generally uncorroborated and usually too far-fetched to be taken seriously. Maud's eyes would light up with glee as she related her anecdotes, and before she took payment she would keep me waiting while she finished her latest story. Her untidy mop of grey hair had been cropped quite short and dyed blonde. To my surprise, she looked at least twenty years younger.

'I like the new hair,' I told her, my compliment genuine. 'It really suits you.'

Instead of launching into a rambling account of where she had gone to have her hair cut and styled, as I expected, she merely nodded, her beady eyes fixed on mine. It was quite unnerving, especially from someone usually as loquacious as Maud. She continued to be oddly quiet when she served me. In place of the obsequious smile she normally bestowed on paying customers, she gazed at me warily. It struck me that I must be the subject of her latest canard. That would explain the strange looks I had been receiving all day. I decided to challenge her.

'Is everything all right, Maud?' I asked, resolved to find out what rumour she had been spreading about me.

She sighed, muttering that my great aunt would be turning in her grave.

'What are you talking about?' I asked, more amused than disturbed.

By the next day, Maud would be spreading a story about someone else. Instead of answering my question, she shook her head and nodded at the card reader. This was the first time she had held back from spreading a rumour, and her reticence confirmed my suspicion that I must be the subject of her latest gossip.

'Is there something you'd like to ask me?' I said. 'Or something you're not telling me?'

She shook her head again. 'My lips are sealed,' she replied enigmatically.

This was so unusual, I laughed, but I couldn't persuade her to talk, so I took my purchases and left. As soon as I was out in the street, a couple of women hurried past me into the shop, staring at me in poorly concealed excitement.

'What did she say?' I heard one of them ask eagerly. 'What did she say?'

Through the open door I could see them gathering around Maud. Resting her elbows on the counter, she leaned forward to address them. This time there could be no doubt they were talking about me. Tempted to return and try to eavesdrop, I decided against it. If Maud *was* talking about me, she would doubtless clam up as soon as she saw me. Thoughtfully, I picked up Poppy and went home. At least she wasn't hiding any secrets from me, other than where she had buried several dog chews in the garden. It was becoming expensive, keeping her in treats.

That evening, I had arranged to meet Hannah and Adam in the pub garden. It was fish and chips night at The Plough, a popular supper at the pub, and every table in the bar was occupied. As I walked through to the garden, I had the uneasy feeling that everyone was staring at me, just as had happened in the café. Whenever I looked up, faces turned away quickly as though no one wanted to be seen watching me. Keeping Poppy on a short lead, I hurried out to the garden to join my friends.

We settled down with our drinks, and Poppy sprawled under the table. She was annoyed with me for keeping her on her lead, but as soon as she was free I knew she would start digging up Cliff's freshly planted display of summer flowers. He had already warned me that he would have to bar her from the pub if she continued to make a mess of his flowerbeds.

'Does anyone know what the police were doing down by the river?' Adam asked. Before Hannah or I could answer, our friend Toby arrived, with a skinny pale blonde girl at his side. When they sat down, he introduced his companion as Michelle. Their relationship wasn't clear. I was wondering who she was, when Hannah began fishing for information.

'Do you work with Toby?' she asked, leaning forward to talk to Michelle, and smiling at her.

The girl shook her head and her fine fair hair fluttered in the evening breeze.

'So, how did you two meet?' Hannah persisted, still smiling encouragement.

Toby answered. 'Michelle's been helping look after my mum,' he explained, adding that they weren't stopping long. 'We just popped in for a quick drink on our way out. We're going to eat in Swindon.'

'Ooh, la-de-da,' Tess called out, walking past and overhearing what Toby was saying. 'Our grub not good enough for you?'

Lifting my drink, I studied Michelle surreptitiously over the rim of my glass. She looked uncomfortable and I guessed she was shy. Toby had told us she helped take care of his mother, who was in a wheelchair, so I asked her if she was a nurse. She shook her head, muttering that she was just a carer.

'Just a carer?' Toby repeated. 'You underestimate how valuable your work is. If you weren't helping her, I don't know how my mother would manage.'

'She could find another carer,' I suggested, rather unkindly.

'You're completely missing the point,' Toby said. 'Carers are the unsung heroes of society.'

I looked down, abashed. Toby and I were never going to be a couple. He was an attractive man, living alone, and I had no excuse for resenting Michelle if she snapped him up. Before I could think of anything to say to mitigate my comment, we were interrupted by a commotion in the bar.

'Where is she? Where's that bitch?' a woman was shrieking, her voice shrill with fury.

A few other voices joined in, shouting incomprehensibly. All we could make out were a few expletives from the woman, and Cliff's calm tones attempting to quieten her down. 'Now, now, none of that language in here.'

Poppy jumped up and began to bark as the door was flung open and a tall woman dashed into the garden. Her red face looked blotchy, matted strands of hair swung around her head like dreadlocks, and her dark eyes glared around with savage intensity. Despite her greying hair and wrinkled face, she appeared to have the vivacity of a young woman. Catching sight of me, she charged over to our table. Pointing a finger at me, she screeched that she would see me suffer in hell. Too shocked to respond, I gaped at her. Across the table from me, I was dimly aware of Hannah's horrified expression. All at once, Tess ran up behind the woman, seized both her arms and held them behind her back.

'That's enough from you,' she roared, dragging the woman away from our table.

'You've not heard the last of this!' the woman yelled as she was frogmarched away.

'Well, we've certainly heard enough from *you*,' Tess retorted, her face twisted with rage. 'Don't you ever dare show your face here again. Next time we won't be so gentle.'

Even though I had done nothing wrong, I felt my face flush with humiliation.

'Who the hell was that?' Adam asked, half laughing in amazement.

Like me, Adam hadn't grown up in Ashton Mead. He had only been living in the village for a year, since he had started seeing Hannah. Toby looked mortified and Michelle sat, wide-eyed, seemingly struck dumb with surprise.

Hannah frowned. 'That was Virginia Strang. Everyone knows she's crazy, but she's lived here all her life so she's accepted as part of village life. I didn't know you'd had dealings with her,' she added, turning to me with a questioning gaze.

'I'm guessing she's related to Silas Strang?' I replied, with a vague feeling of dread.

Hannah nodded. 'She's his mother.'

'Who the hell is Silas Strang?' Adam asked.

'He's a nasty bully,' Hannah answered for me. 'Everyone hates him, except his mother, of course. She's as vile as he is. His latest charm offensive was to have a go at Poppy. He told Emily to get her off the grass and he called Poppy a filthy animal. Isn't that right, Emily?'

I nodded dumbly, trying to look suitably indignant. Mrs Strang's verbal assault had unsettled me so much it was difficult to focus on what Hannah was saying. My friends didn't appear to know that Silas was dead, and I hesitated to admit how much I knew about it. The whole situation was making me feel extremely awkward. I wondered what Michelle was thinking.

'Poppy's allowed to walk on the grass and, besides, she's very clean,' I mumbled, looking down at Poppy and refusing to meet anyone's eye.

'Silas Strang is a bully,' Hannah repeated. 'No one likes him,' she added, turning back to me. 'He has a lot of enemies. Even so, it's probably not a good idea to cross him, especially for someone new to the village.'

'I'm hardly new here,' I replied. 'I've been here for two years. And all I did was tell him there's nothing to stop Poppy walking on the grass. It isn't his place to dictate where my dog can and can't go.'

Hannah whistled. 'Not many people would dare contradict Silas to his face.'

'Still, to say you'll rot in hell is a bit extreme, to say the least,' Adam said.

'He was threatening Poppy with his walking stick,' I said, and Hannah whistled again.

With a solicitous glance at his blonde companion, Toby announced that it was time for them to leave. 'It's not normally so fraught here. We're usually a cheerful bunch,' he added with an awkward laugh, as he and Michelle rose to their feet. She looked relieved to be going, and Toby threw me a baleful glare over his shoulder as they walked away. Clearly, he blamed me for the embarrassing scene, although it was hardly my fault Virginia Strang had yelled at me in front of his new girlfriend. If Tess hadn't stood up for me and thrown Virginia out, the situation might have been even worse. Meanwhile, Adam went to the bar, leaving Hannah and me together for a few moments.

'Michelle seems nice,' Hannah said. Preoccupied by my problems, I didn't answer.

'You must have known Toby wouldn't wait for you forever,' she went on, misinterpreting my silence.

'What? Oh, I'm not upset. And he wasn't waiting for me. We're just friends. There was never anything between us.'

Hannah shook her head. 'If you say so.'

'I'm very pleased for him. She seems nice,' I added.

'If you say so,' Hannah repeated.

My friend's scepticism irritated me, and I decided to leave as well.

'What about your drink?' Hannah asked. 'Adam'll be back in a minute.'

'You can have it. I've had enough.'

Hannah tried to persuade me to stay, but after the fracas I felt uncomfortable and wanted to be alone. This time, there was no doubt that everyone in the bar was watching me as I made my way out of the pub, with Poppy trotting eagerly beside me. I was glad of her company as we walked home. Never before had it seemed to take so long to walk down the High Street, but at least it was still light. As we turned the corner, in the distance we could see the forensic tent. Illuminated by powerful lights, white-coated scene of crime officers were visible, moving purposefully around the tent. Some of them appeared to be examining the grass. From the direction of the tent, a dog barked, and Poppy barked in reply. I pulled on her lead and hurried on, telling myself that Silas had been overweight and unhealthy, and must have died of natural causes. But the police appeared to suspect he had been murdered, and his mother had virtually accused me of killing him.

We turned into Mill Lane and I felt a stab of fear, despite the police presence in the village. With only two properties in the lane, it was an isolated spot. A woman crazed with grief could easily attack me unseen, and Virginia Strang knew where I lived. But Poppy didn't bark or growl in warning, and we carried on undisturbed. Watching her trotting happily ahead of me, I felt more grateful for her company than ever before. It seemed to take us hours to reach home, but at last I closed the front door. Having slid the bolt across and checked that all the windows and the back door were securely fastened, I squatted down to pet Poppy.

'You'd warn me if someone tried to break in, wouldn't you?' I asked her.

She wagged her tail, and trotted into the kitchen to be fed. Clearly, her priorities were different to mine.

# 7

THAT NIGHT I SLEPT surprisingly well and woke the next morning feeling fine until, with a jolt, I remembered Mrs Strang's vicious attack in the pub. Evidently as demented as her son, she had gone to The Plough to single me out for an attack because I had dared to defy him. The memory of her screeching at me in public made me feel hot with embarrassment all over again. Even though Maud hadn't witnessed the outburst herself, no doubt she would gleefully describe the incident to anyone who set foot in the local shop, and before long the whole village would hear about it. There was nothing else to do but carry on as normal, and hope that Mrs Strang's rant would be forgotten by the time the news broke that Silas was dead. I resolved to keep my head down and attract as little attention to myself as possible, but I couldn't help worrying. The police seemed to be investigating his death, which suggested Silas had been murdered, which actually seemed likely. As Hannah had said, Silas had plenty of enemies, any one of whom might have wanted to do away with him.

Having eaten breakfast, I felt a lot better as I set off for the day, but there was another shock in store for me. My front garden had been trashed during the night. For once, it wasn't Poppy who had dug up my flowerbeds. Not only had all my late spring flowers been trampled on, but deep grooves had been gouged out of the patch of grass beside the path, and a message was scrawled on the front of the house: MURDERING BITCH. Rosecroft was situated at the end of the lane. Apart from people coming to see me, and the postman's occasional deliveries, no one walked down that far. Someone had gone out of their way to put the message there just for me. At least very few people were likely to see it.

There wasn't enough time to do much before going to work, so I decided to focus on the graffiti, and leave the garden for later as the less embarrassing aspect of the attack. I found a half empty tin of white paint left over from a time when I had been decorating. It wasn't outdoor paint, but it would have to do, temporarily at least. Poppy frisked happily among the fallen flowers, sniffing and ferreting for insects, clearly enjoying the mayhem, while I covered the graffiti with a splodge of paint. I didn't want to leave the garden in such a terrible state, but it was time to drop Poppy off at Jane's house and go to work.

'I know you're disappointed about Toby turning up with a girlfriend, without any warning. Honestly, I had no idea he was seeing someone –' Hannah began, as soon as we had a quiet moment in the café.

'I'm really not upset about Toby finding a girlfriend,' I assured her. 'Why would it bother me? And I'm sure Michelle's very nice, although it was difficult to tell, she was so quiet.'

'You can't have expected him to wait for you indefinitely,' she went on, stubbornly sticking to her point.

'I told you, it really doesn't bother me,' I said, doing my best to sound completely uninterested in Toby's love life.

In reality, Hannah's accusation irritated me, not least because I actually was a little disappointed. Having resigned myself to being no more than friends with Toby, I was selfishly jealous that he had succeeded in finding a partner while I remained single. Not only that, I had harboured a slim hope that we might one day end up together. Michelle had put the kibosh on that, at least for the time being.

'Well, you don't look as though you're not bothered,' Hannah said, gazing at me critically.

'I am upset, but it's nothing to do with Toby,' I replied.

Hannah struck me as guarded in her sympathy, when I told her what had happened in my front garden.

'It must have been Poppy digging up your flowers,' was her initial response.

'Hannah, are you listening to me? I mean, I know Poppy's clever, but even she couldn't have written on the wall!'

Hannah frowned as I wrote the words down, exactly as they had appeared on my wall, and turned the paper round so the message was the right way up for her. We stared at it together. It wasn't clear to me whether the writer was accusing me or Poppy of murder, or perhaps threatening to kill one of us, so I was dismayed when Hannah shrugged and said it must be kids messing about. Convinced that Virginia Strang was the author of the graffiti, I couldn't dismiss it so easily. Hannah shook her head and advised me to ignore it. Having warned me against doing anything that might upset local residents, she leapt up and ran into the kitchen to try and salvage a tray of scones that were burning. She seemed more concerned about having ruined a batch of scones than the news that a madwoman had taken to prowling around in my garden at night to let me know she intended to kill me.

The morning was quiet, which gave Hannah time to bake more scones, but left me mindlessly wiping tables. With nothing much to do to distract me from my situation, I fretted. More than ever I was glad of Poppy. At least I would be able to sleep at night, confident she would wake me up if anyone tried to break in and attack me. At midday we had a rush of customers coming in for lunch. The village was a small place, and most of them looked familiar, even if I didn't know them well. Once again, I had the impression that everyone was staring at me. I said nothing to Hannah, suspecting she wouldn't take my concern seriously. Taking orders, I smiled at customers, and did my best to pretend there was nothing wrong.

The café was full when Barry came in, looking unusually apprehensive. He made his way over to me and muttered to me to go home, adding that he was surprised to see me at work, given the circumstances. For once, he seemed unable to conjure up his toothy smile.

'What circumstances? What are you talking about?'

'It was on the local news this morning that Silas Strang was murdered.'

Before he could continue, the door flew open and Virginia Strang strode in.

'I tried to warn you,' Barry murmured. 'Can you slip out the back before she sees you?'

But his suggestion came too late.

'Bitch!' Virginia screeched, fixing her blazing eyes on me. 'You'll be sorry!' She pushed her way between the tables, heading straight for me.

'Now, now, Virginia,' Barry said, stepping in front of me. 'You've been warned about this. Losing your temper won't help. You need to leave this matter to the police. Go home or I'll be forced to restrain you.'

'Arrest her!' Virginia shrieked hysterically, waving her arms wildly as though she wanted to claw her way through the air to reach me. 'You know what she did.'

Hearing the commotion, Hannah came out of the kitchen, wiping her hands on a tea towel.

'What's going on here?' She broke off, seeing me and Virginia with Barry standing between us, like an umpire in a boxing match. 'Emily? Barry?' she asked, coming over to us and brushing her blonde curls off her face with the back of her hand. 'What's happening?'

'Virginia is just leaving,' Barry said firmly. 'Come along now. You don't want to be cautioned for causing a public disturbance,' he added in a low voice.

Virginia glared savagely at me. 'You'll rot in hell for what you did!' she cried out. 'If he won't arrest you, I will. A citizen's arrest.' She folded her arms and stood, feet apart, glaring at me.

'Go home, Virginia,' Barry repeated wearily.

'Hang on,' I blurted out. 'Are you going to let her get away with this? You can't just tell her to go home. She's dangerous. She left a threatening message on my house last night. She needs to be locked up. If you don't stop her, I'll press charges.' I turned to face Virginia, refusing to be cowed by her.

Barry muttered that Mrs Strang was very upset because her son had been murdered.

'I'm really sorry to hear that,' I replied, 'but that doesn't give her licence to go around throwing out false accusations at people.'

At the periphery of my vision, I saw Hannah staring at me, aghast.

'You'll be sorry,' Virginia hissed.

She turned and stalked out of the café with Barry following her at her heels. There was a scraping of chairs and a shuffling as two tables of customers rose to their feet and walked out of the café. Others sat openly glaring at me.

I turned to Hannah. 'They don't think – they can't – surely they don't think I had anything to do with what happened to Silas?'

Hannah gazed around and then asked me to join her in the kitchen. To my dismay, she asked me to take a few days off.

'What? Why? I'm fine, really I am.'

The last thing I needed right then was to be sitting at home listening out for a madwoman to break in and attack me.

'Emily, I really think you should take a few days off,' Hannah repeated firmly.

'Are you trying to say you don't want me here any more?'

'It's for the best.'

'The best? What does that mean? Best for who?'

'It's just for a few days,' she muttered.

'But why? Hannah, you know I've done nothing wrong. This isn't fair.'

'Customers don't like to be disturbed when they're out for tea.' She barely had the grace to look shamefaced when she said it.

'If you think it was me who attacked Silas, at least have the courage to say so to my face,' I began angrily, but she interrupted me with an impatient wave of her hand.

'Of course, I don't think you had anything to do with it, but you saw what happened. You know I want to support you, but I can't afford to lose customers.'

'But you're prepared to lose our friendship, throw it away for no reason?'

'Don't be melodramatic,' she snapped. 'What do you expect me to do?'

'I expect my friends to stick by me.'

'I can't watch my business go down the pan. I'm already struggling as it is.'

'Now who's being melodramatic?'

We glared at one another for a moment, and then I walked away. At the door, I turned to look at her. 'You do realise what you've done? I'm innocent, and you know it, but no one else is going to believe that now. Everyone will think you fired me because you think I'm guilty.'

'I'm not firing you,' she replied miserably. 'I'm just asking you to stay away for a few days, until it all gets sorted out.'

She looked wretched, but I felt no sympathy for her. She was supposed to be my friend, but she thought nothing of rejecting me at a time when I desperately needed help. Some friend she had turned out to be! I stormed out, slamming the door behind me, and went to collect Poppy. At least she wouldn't turn her back on me for no reason.

# 8

I WAS EXPECTING THE police would want to speak to me, after Virginia Strang's outrageous accusation. All the same, it was a shock to open the door to a man who introduced himself as Detective Inspector Robert Langdon. Tall and thin, with straw-coloured hair, his pale blue eyes seemed devoid of expression. I wondered whether that was a façade he had developed for work, or if he was naturally aloof and calculating. From his sharp nose and chin and square shoulders, right down to his narrow pointed black shoes, everything about him looked angular and uncompromising. A young woman stood at his side, watching me silently. Plumper than her colleague, she looked as though her stern expression was an accessory she put on with her formal jacket. She wore both with an air of self-conscious dignity. When Langdon introduced her as Detective Constable Crooks, I had to suppress a smile.

Realising that I was reluctant to invite them in the inspector sighed, like a head teacher talking to a wayward child, but they seemed to be genuine police officers, and I wasn't sure whether it was even legal to refuse their request to enter my house. If I appeared to want to obstruct them, he might insist on questioning me at the police station in Swindon, and that would be even more of an imposition than talking to them at home. In any case, I had nothing to hide, in spite of my sudden irrational feeling of guilt. Still I hesitated.

'Do I need a lawyer?' I asked at last.

When the inspector shook his head, I wasn't sure if he was being sympathetic or impatient.

'We just want to ask you a few questions,' he said.

His companion didn't speak, but gazed steadfastly at me, seemingly poised to lunge forward if I tried to run away.

'You'd better come in then. You'll have to excuse the mess.'

Actually, being off work meant there had been time to tidy the place and do some housework, and the living room looked fairly neat, for once, with the carpet hoovered and the surfaces dusted. Apart from making an effort when I expected visitors, my housework was sporadic. I perched on the sofa and gazed around with proprietorial pride as the police officers sat on my two armchairs. The inspector's long legs stretched out in front of him and Poppy wandered over and began busily sniffing at his feet. A friendly little dog, when she took against people there usually turned out to be a good reason for her antagonism. Her response to the inspector was atypical. Neither cordial nor hostile, she seemed to regard him with caution. Sitting down, she watched him warily as though trying to make up her mind whether to trust him or not. I shared her reservations.

Seeming to understand that the inspector was in charge, Poppy ignored the constable completely. This, too, was unusual.

'What do you want?' I asked, nerves making me blunt.

The inspector nodded at his colleague, who showed me a creased printout of a photo. In a surprisingly deep voice, she asked me if I could identify him.

It would be pointless to deny that I knew him, at least by sight. 'That's Silas Strang. He lives in the village. Is it true he's dead?' There was no going back now. 'I – I heard a rumour that he's dead.'

The inspector didn't react, but I knew he had registered my hesitation. As though sensing she had landed me in trouble, Poppy let out a gentle growl and nuzzled his ankles with her nose. But the inspector wasn't so easily distracted. Ignoring her attempts to divert his attention, he continued with his questions.

'I'm afraid the rumour you heard is true.'

'I'm sorry to hear that,' I said, keeping my voice as even as possible and my expression as blank as his.

'How well did you know him?' the detective asked, as the constable slipped the picture back in her pocket.

He spoke quietly but he was watching me closely, a spark of interest in his cold eyes. Meanwhile, I was aware of the constable's gaze fixed on me. I tried not to squirm under their scrutiny, telling myself I had nothing to hide.

'Not well at all. He was just someone who lives – lived in the village. I didn't really know him at all.'

The silence grew uncomfortable and I realised they were waiting for me to elaborate.

'I mean, we met,' I admitted. Forcing a smile they must

have realised was fake, I added that it was impossible to live in the village without coming across everyone who lived there. 'It's a small place. But I wouldn't say I knew him, not exactly. That is, we didn't know each other. He probably didn't even know my name. I only knew his name because he – he had a certain reputation so people talked about him. I've only spoken to him once or twice and then only for a few seconds, nothing of any significance.' Nerves were making me gabble. Afraid of betraying my apprehension by talking too much, I shut my mouth abruptly.

'So, you knew him?' the inspector prompted me.

'Everyone here knows – knew – Silas Strang. He wasn't the kind of person who was easy to overlook.'

'Do you mean to say he was popular?'

'Not exactly. He – he didn't go out of his way to get on with people.'

'What about you? Did you get on with him?'

I hesitated. 'Like I said, I didn't know him. We only spoke once or twice, and then only when he attacked my dog.'

'Silas Strang attacked your dog?' The detective's eyebrows rose sceptically. 'This dog here?'

He looked down at Poppy who put her head on one side and wagged her tail, looking cute.

'Yes, this dog. You can see how friendly she is, and she's very clean, but Silas accused her of being dirty, and he told me to get her off the grass. He had no right to order her about like that. Dogs are allowed to walk on the grass.'

As I was about to start ranting about how harmless Poppy was, and how well behaved, she nudged the inspector's ankles and rolled over on to her back with a playful yelp, waving her little legs in the air. Interrupted by her antics, it struck me that I ought to be circumspect in talking about Silas, especially to the police, so I changed tack and explained that Poppy had adopted a submissive position, and was asking to be petted.

'So, you and Silas fell out?' the detective prompted me, ignoring Poppy.

'Not exactly fell out,' I replied frostily, determined to remain self-controlled and conceal my escalating unease. 'We didn't have any kind of relationship in the first place to fall out of. We scarcely exchanged two words.'

He told me that several villagers had witnessed an argument between me and Silas, at the village fete.

'It was hardly an argument,' I protested. 'I asked him to leave Poppy alone, that was all. There was nothing more to it than that.'

'I wonder what made you speak to him about your dog?'

'Like I said, he went after Poppy.' It was difficult to conceal my indignation when I called to mind what had taken place.

'Not according to our information,' the detective murmured. 'There was no mention of him using threatening behaviour, and a witness has come forward who seems convinced you held a grudge against Silas.'

Unable to control my indignation, I accused Virginia Strang of victimising me, describing how she had verbally assaulted me in public, and scrawled graffiti on my house, accusing me of murder.

'Did you report these incidents to the police?'

'No, but you can ask our local policeman, Barry. He was there when she shouted at me. And I told my boss at work about the graffiti. I should have taken a photo of it on my phone, but I didn't think of it at the time.'

The inspector's eyelids flickered. 'A witness stated she clearly heard you say that there was nothing you wouldn't do to stop him, and several other locals also reported hearing you threaten to "stop him". What exactly did you want him to stop doing?'

'Like I said, he was threatening to attack Poppy. He threatened to hit her with his walking stick.'

'No one claimed to have seen or heard him say or do anything that might have provoked your attack.'

The accusation that I had launched an unprovoked attack on Silas was nonsense, as was the implication that our argument might have led me to behave violently. The detective watched me closely as I refuted his suspicions.

'Tell us how you came to learn about his death.'

Stumbling over my words, I related how Poppy had led me to the body.

'So, you happened to be walking there at six o'clock in the morning?'

'Yes. I was taking my dog for a walk.'

'And do you often walk down near the river?'

'Yes. The grassy slopes are perfect for her.'

'And do you often walk down there early in the morning?'

I hesitated but decided it was best to stick to the truth. 'We don't usually go out so early, but Poppy woke me, whimpering to go out. I couldn't get back to sleep and I didn't want her to have an accident so we went out.'

'So, you came across a dead body but didn't report it to the police?' the sergeant asked me grimly.

'I was going to report it, obviously, but I'd left my phone at home.' I described my panicked search for my phone. 'By the time I found it, I could hear sirens and there were already several police cars at the scene, so there didn't seem any point in reporting it. I thought – I thought it was better to keep out of it.'

The questioning seemed to go on forever. It was impossible to determine what they were thinking, but at last the inspector rose to his feet and thanked me for my time.

'Is that it?' I asked, doing my best to hide my relief.

'That will be all for now,' he replied. 'But please don't leave Ashton Mead. We may want to talk to you again.'

With that, he turned to leave. I was tempted to ask him what would happen were I to disobey him and leave the village. Even though I had no plans to go anywhere, it felt like an unfair restriction on my liberty to force me to stay in the village, and preposterous that I would be unable to go shopping in Swindon, or visit my mother in London. I wanted to know how long this situation would continue, but I didn't dare ask, and showed them out in silence. Poppy gazed at me once they had gone, as though demanding an explanation.

'That was the police,' I told her. 'And they seem to suspect I murdered Silas Strang.'

Poppy let out a single bark. If I hadn't known better, I could have sworn she was laughing. And when I thought about it, the idea was ridiculous. Apart from anything else, there was no way I could have overpowered him. But then

I remembered how he had appeared to be reaching for his back. Perhaps he had been dealt a fatal blow by someone who had crept up and attacked him from behind. My laughter stopped abruptly. The police seemed to doubt my story. Even my best friend had abandoned me.

'It's just you and me now,' I told Poppy, and she wagged her tail.

# 9

THAT EVENING MY SISTER, Susie, rang me. She had recently returned from a holiday in Belgium, and hadn't yet told me about it. As I listened to her news, the world around me seemed to flip back to normal, as though Silas had never existed. When my sister asked me for my news, I replied without thinking, 'Fine, everything's fine.' It was pointless to even attempt to explain my complicated situation over the phone. Susie might easily get the wrong end of the stick. It wouldn't be the first time she had judged me harshly without knowing the full facts. More importantly, she might let something slip in front of our mother and I certainly didn't want *her* knowing the police had been questioning me in connection with a murder. I shuddered to think how hysterical she would become.

Having followed a conventional path herself, my mother was concerned, if not affronted, by my way of life. It seemed to be an article of faith with her that no woman could be safe without a man to look after her. She had fawned over my ex-boyfriend, who had turned out to be a shallow narcissist. Now that I was single, she fussed over me as though I was desperately vulnerable, when nothing could have been further from the truth. I had my own home, a dog who was happy and healthy and, until recently, I had also had good friends and a job I enjoyed. It was not my fault that my friends had let me down, and my job had come to an end, at least temporarily. Still, it was difficult to be angry with my mother because she meant well, even though her comments were generally intrusive and often undermining. So, the less she knew about my circumstances the better, especially when things were going badly. And it couldn't get much worse than being a suspect in a murder enquiry.

'Murder?' I could imagine her pained outburst. 'They're accusing you of murder? That's it, Emily. You're coming home right now. You can't stay in that out-of-the-way village to be treated like a felon.' There would be a lot more along those lines, all completely missing the point, and I would have to argue with her, insisting that Ashton Mead *was* my home now, and her efforts to infantilise me wouldn't deter the police from pursuing their enquiry.

Fortunately, my sister was happy to chat about her holiday, and didn't seem to notice how quiet I was. She told me it was the first time in fourteen years she and my brother-in-law had gone on holiday together, without my nephew.

'Fourteen years. Can you believe it?'

'You left Joel at home on his own?' I asked.

Susie burst out laughing. 'You've got to be kidding. I wouldn't trust him here by himself for a single night, let alone nearly a week. He'd invite all his friends round for a party and they'd trash the place, if not burn it down.'

'He's not that irresponsible, surely?'

'Emily, he's fourteen,' she replied, emphasising each word as though she was talking to someone who barely understood English. 'No, he was staying with a friend while we were away. He had a great time, but Brett's parents were there to keep a close eye on the boys.'

'So how was it in Bruges? Tell me all about it.'

I half listened as she told me about her holiday, sitting in a square listening to a brass band, visiting a museum dedicated to chocolate, going on a tour of a brewery, and taking a boat trip along the river.

'We were really lucky with the weather. It didn't rain once. It's a beautiful town,' she gushed. 'The architecture's stunning. And what makes it really special is that there are hardly any cars, just horse and carriages for the tourists, and people going around on bicycles. There are cobbled streets and no yellow lines. It's like stepping back in time. They do everything they can to discourage people taking cars into the town, and everything's so close, you can walk everywhere. You should go there. You'd love it. It's really picturesque.'

Like Ashton Mead, I thought. Glancing down at Poppy, I smiled. Apart from the fact that my wages scarcely covered my bills, let alone a holiday, I couldn't imagine leaving Poppy even for a few days. Any holiday I took from now on would have to include her. For the first time it occurred to me that if I was arrested and locked up, even assuming a trial would acquit me, it would still mean having to leave Poppy, perhaps for months. Hannah's mother would probably agree to take care of her, but Poppy wouldn't understand why I had gone away without her. In the months before I stood trial, she would languish without me. Worse, she might think I had abandoned her. She might even forget me.

'You know I'd never leave you,' I said and she wagged her tail and nuzzled my ankles with her nose.

'What's that?' Susie asked.

'Nothing. I was just talking to Poppy.'

Susie sighed. 'Seriously, Emily, you should get yourself a boyfriend, then you wouldn't be reduced to talking to a dog. It's not normal.'

'You sound just like mum.'

'Yes, well, perhaps she's got a point. I mean, really, you were talking to your dog?'

I was tempted to protest that Poppy understood everything that was said to her, or at least gathered the gist of it. Not only that, but she rarely argued with me, unless she was trying to investigate rubbish I didn't want her sniffing around in. Her company was preferable to that of many humans. But I kept quiet. There was no point in provoking my sister, who had never owned a dog and would never understand why I loved Poppy so much. Until Poppy entered my life, while I had accepted that other people became attached to their pets, I had never really understood their bond. Poppy's unswerving devotion had swept away my scepticism almost overnight, as fully as a religious conversion.

Reluctant to return to the pub, where I was convinced everyone would be staring at me, I decided to take Poppy for a walk around the village green. It was only seven o'clock and it would still be light for a few hours. Not until we reached the green did I remember that was where Silas had first yelled at me to keep Poppy off the grass. He had lived with his mother in a house on one of the streets leading away from the green. I didn't know which house was hers, and was afraid she would spot me and Poppy out walking. She might come running out to attack me, as her son had done shortly before he died. Keen to hurry away from there, I tried to haul Poppy off the green. She whimpered and lay down on the grass, refusing to budge. It was unfair of me to take her to the green only to drag her away again before giving her a chance to explore, but I was adamant. Scooping her up in my arms, I strode away, back towards Rosecroft and the river.

'I'm sorry,' I muttered, 'it was really stupid of me to take you there. We'll go for a walk on the slopes by the river instead.'

We turned out of the High Street, and looked down towards the river. The forensic tent was still in place, a stark reminder of why I had been avoiding walking there. White-coated officers were moving slowly, seemingly studying the ground. After putting Poppy down on the grass, I stood looking at them from a distance while she snuffled around happily. Absorbed in watching the police activity, I failed to notice someone coming up behind me. Not until my name was murmured very softly was I aware that we had company. Poppy had been happily sniffing around on the grass, but now she jumped up, barking. I had a horrible sensation that Silas had returned and was standing beside me, demanding attention. The speaker was standing so close to me, I felt a faint draft of air on my ear when he spoke. Rigid with fear, I dared not turn round. My thoughts whirled.

The speaker was clearly not Virginia Strang, because it was a man's voice that had called out my name. But there were many other people in the village who distrusted me, and I wondered whether it had been reckless of me to bring Poppy out to this isolated spot. The scene of crime officers were within view, but they would be too far away to hear me call out to them. The irony of being attacked and possibly killed within sight of a team of crime scene investigators was not lost on me.

'Emily,' the voice repeated.

Struggling to control my panic, I turned to face him.

# 10

Speechless with relief, I felt my legs shaking.

'You look like you've seen a ghost,' Richard said, smiling warmly at me.

Richard had been living next door to me for just over a year. As the only two residents of Mill Lane, we had quickly become friends. A retired history professor, he was as kind and amiable a neighbour as anyone could wish for, and our lives had become more closely entwined than ever when his son, Adam, had moved in with Hannah. Poppy jumped up excitedly at Richard and refused to calm down until he petted her. Short and corpulent, he grunted with the effort of stooping down to scratch her under her chin.

'I saw you from a distance and thought it was you,' he said as he straightened up. 'There's no mistaking this little one, is there?' he added, smiling benignly down at Poppy. 'Not at work today?'

Embarrassed to answer his question truthfully, I mumbled about taking a few days off. He gazed sceptically at me, his fluffy white hair bobbing about in the breeze.

'I was sorry to hear someone attacked you at the pub,' he said gently. 'If you ask me, that Strang woman needs to be locked up. She's a public menace. I hope the police are dealing with her. Being accused of a terrible crime when you're innocent is no joke.'

He heaved a sigh and gazed wistfully towards the river. A year had passed since Richard had been suspected of complicity in his wife's murder, and the painful experience clearly still troubled him. He had only escaped arrest when it turned out his wife was still alive. She was the one who had ended up being convicted, having killed her lover's wife. The two women looked so similar, she had attempted to pass her victim's body off as her own, in an attempt to frame Richard for the murder. Probably Richard would never be free of the memory. His other son, Adam's brother, had cut all ties with him after the trial, which had struck me as cruel, given that Richard's only mistake had been to unwittingly marry a psychopath. At least Silas Strang had meant nothing to me. If anything, I was pleased he had gone. But that didn't help me with my current predicament.

'Virginia Strang's upset,' I replied shortly.

Richard's bushy white eyebrows rose.

'She's grieving for her son who was murdered,' I added, trying to feel compassion for the woman who wanted me punished for a crime I hadn't committed.

The eyebrows lowered. 'That's all very well, but I don't see what possible reason that dreadful woman could have for an outburst like that, in public, and against you, of all people. How well do you know her?' He gazed at me anxiously. 'Is there something going on that I don't know about?'

I shrugged. 'She thinks I murdered her son.'

'What rot. The police should lock her away in a secure psychiatric unit. And throw away the key,' he added grimly. 'She probably did away with him herself, and is blaming you to put the police off the scent.'

'They came to see me,' I replied.

'Who did?'

'The police.' All at once, my reserve broke down and I told him about my visit from Detective Inspector Robert Langdon. 'So, the police are looking into it, and they seem to regard me as a suspect.'

Richard let out a bark of laughter. 'Absolute rot,' he repeated. 'I hope you put them straight.'

'It's complicated,' I admitted and blurted out all about my confrontation with Silas at the village fair, the day before he was killed. 'There were any number of witnesses who all heard me say there was nothing I wouldn't do to stop him and, of course, I haven't got an alibi for the time he was killed because it happened during the night when I was at home on my own. If Poppy could talk, she would tell them I never left the house on Saturday night.'

Poppy was nibbling at some moss by my feet. Her ears twitched when she heard her name, but she didn't look up. Richard gazed at me, a frown creasing his plump forehead.

'Without an alibi, I can see how this could be a problem.'

I was grateful to him for not dismissing my concern as nonsense. Instead, he nodded in agreement and his hair fluttered wildly around his head, like a chaotic halo. I wondered why he didn't have it cut.

'Listen,' he said brightly, 'you're not at work today, so why don't you come home with me and have some lunch?

I've got some cold meat left over from last night and there's far too much for me. Come and join me. There might even be a few scraps for you,' he added, smiling at Poppy who wagged her tail and looked up at me eagerly, as if she understood what he had said.

I returned his smile. 'Poppy would never forgive me if I refused.'

At least I still had one friend in Ashton Mead, apart from Poppy. Two days had passed since Hannah had told me I was no longer welcome at the tea shop. I had been waiting for her to contact me to apologise, but had still not heard from her and was feeling quite bereft. So, I was more pleased than Richard could possibly realise when he invited me over for lunch.

We walked slowly back to Mill Lane, stopping every few minutes for Poppy to sniff at the ground or do a little wee. We were in no hurry. Had it not been for the accusation hanging over me, I would have enjoyed the walk. Clearly understanding that I must be feeling tense, Richard did his best to distract me from my troubles by entertaining me with amusing anecdotes from his former life as a history professor. But my mind was only half on his tales. As we entered Mill Lane, I cast my eyes around anxiously, afraid a police car would be waiting to take me away.

Richard was right that he had more left over beef than one person could possibly eat. What he hadn't told me was that Adam was joining him for lunch. When Adam had first visited his father in Ashton Mead, Hannah and I had both found him attractive. Dark haired, lithe and energetic, he was good looking and personable. He had made it clear he was captivated by Hannah from the first time he met her, and I had quickly accepted that he was never going to be interested in me except as a friend. I still felt a faint pang when he smiled at me, but was genuinely pleased that he and Hannah were happy together.

Adam arrived soon after us and looked at me warily while Richard fussed around, preparing us each a tray to take out to the garden table. We had agreed it was too lovely a day to sit indoors. Off her lead, Poppy wandered around happily. Richard's garden was securely fenced in on all sides, a relic from his predecessor in Laurel Cottage. As we tucked into beef sandwiches, it was hard to believe I was currently under suspicion for murder, but the fact that I was not at work was an uncomfortable reminder of my circumstances. All the same, it was encouraging to know that not everyone in the village was treating me like a pariah. When I thanked Richard and Adam for their support, they dismissed my gratitude, assuring me that no one really believed me capable of murder.

'Cliff lost his rag yesterday,' Adam remarked, clearly trying to change the subject.

'You should have seen him.' He chuckled at the memory.

'I've never seen him lose his temper,' I replied. 'What happened?'

'On Monday evening an animal dug up some begonias he'd just planted.'

I smiled wryly. 'At least he can't blame Poppy for that.'

Admittedly Poppy was often guilty of digging around in cultivated flowerbeds, but we hadn't been to The Plough for a couple of days. Had we been there, Cliff might well have believed Poppy was responsible for vandalising his flowerbed. She would have been a likely culprit had she not had an alibi, but everyone knew she hadn't been in the pub garden that evening. I was less fortunate than my dog, having no alibi for the time of the crime I was suspected of committing.

'Cliff's obsessed with finding out whose dog it was. Yesterday he was asking everyone if they know who was sitting in the garden with a dog on Monday evening, but no one seems to remember.' Adam grinned. 'Even Tess says she can't remember, although I bet she does. She was clearing the tables outside all evening. She probably saw who it was and decided not to say anything. I wouldn't put it past her. She's got a sneaky streak.'

'It was probably a fox,' Richard said. 'There are a lot of them about.'

'Don't you think foxes are often used as scapegoats for dogs that misbehave?' Adam asked his father.

'It might have been a cat,' Richard remarked thoughtfully.

They were trying to distract me from my problems but, listening to them discuss Cliff's begonias and how Cliff was searching for the truth, I suddenly realised what I had to do.

# 11

RICHARD AND ADAM LOOKED at me in surprise when I finished speaking. For a moment no one spoke. Richard gazed at the table, as though trying to decide whether to offer to refill the teapot, while Adam stared at the garden, seemingly absorbed in the view. Observing them together, it was hard to believe they were father and son. With his tubby figure and round face, Richard looked like a chubby middle-aged cherub. Were someone needed to play the role of Father Christmas, with the addition of a white beard and red hat and gown he would be the ideal choice. In complete contrast, Adam could have been the romantic lead in an old Hollywood film, with clean shaven, clear cut features and dark eyes, warm with a hint of seduction. But father and son wore similar expressions of bemusement on hearing my idea.

'Don't you get it?' I said impatiently. 'There's only one way I can clear my name.'

I paused, wondering how much to say, as Richard and Adam exchanged a perplexed glance.

'I'm not sure what you mean,' Richard murmured. He looked worried.

'What I'm trying to say is, the only way I can prove my innocence is by exposing the real killer.'

Richard frowned and shook his head, looking exasperated, and Adam gaped at me.

'But first I have to find him or her,' I went on.

Before either of my companions could answer, a squirrel scampered down the fence at the far end of the garden and darted across the lawn. Poppy leapt up and bounded over the grass in pursuit. We watched as the squirrel reached a massive tree in the corner of the garden and disappeared up the trunk, its tail waving as though in mocking farewell of Poppy. Left on the grass, she crouched down, barking in frustration.

'Well, that was a close thing,' Adam said, laughing. 'Has she ever caught one?'

I told him she hadn't. 'She hasn't managed to catch a bird either,' I chuckled.

'I wonder if she'd actually know what to do with a squirrel or a bird if she ever caught one?' Adam asked.

He might have been genuinely interested in Poppy's antics, but it was possible he was deliberately avoiding the subject of the recent murder. I couldn't help wondering whether Hannah had voiced any suspicions of me behind my back. The thought of Hannah spreading negative stories about me made me feel really uncomfortable. I tried to dismiss the thought, reassuring myself that Hannah was my friend, and she couldn't possibly believe anything bad of me. She had only asked me to stay away from the café because she was concerned to protect her business.

Meanwhile, Richard was not so easily distracted by Poppy's frolicking. 'Never mind the squirrels and the birds,' he said abruptly, his plump features still creased in a frown. 'I'm not sure I understand what you mean. How exactly do you propose to find this killer?'

I shook my head; I had no answer to that question. There were people in the village who believed me capable of murder, and the police seemed to consider me a suspect too. But all anyone could say for certain was that someone had killed Silas. It was just bad luck that I happened to have had a row with him shortly before he was killed. But it was clear that only by proving who was guilty would I be free of suspicion.

'You know I don't for one moment give any credence to the notion that you could be capable of murder, and I want to help you in any way I can,' Richard said, adding that he hadn't forgotten the help I had given him when he had been suspected of murdering his wife on first arriving in Ashton Mead.

Much as I appreciated Richard's assurance of support, I decided there and then that my enquiries would need to proceed subtly, without involving anyone else. It was imperative no one else realised what was going on. If the killer ever discovered that I was hunting for them, my own life would almost certainly be in danger. I shook my head at Richard, realising with a pang of regret that my friends could not help me. Someone who had killed once – possibly more than once – would not hesitate to kill again if they felt threatened. This was a felony I had to investigate alone, and in secret. The last thing I wanted to do was put my friends' lives in danger.

Richard continued watching me closely, and repeated his question. 'What are you suggesting?'

'I don't know,' I admitted, honestly. Less truthfully, I added that it was just wishful thinking. 'Of course, I can't find out anything the police don't already know. I suppose there's nothing for it but to leave it to them to sort out this mess. I'm sure they know what they're doing.'

'But they suspect you of murder,' Richard pointed out. 'So, they clearly don't know what happened. They don't know everything.'

'I haven't been arrested. They can't have any evidence against me, because there won't be any, seeing as I didn't do it. I'm going to have to be patient and trust the police to do their job.'

Richard looked sceptical, but he didn't remonstrate, and I looked down at Poppy who had abandoned the chase and was now lying curled up at my feet. Adam looked anxious but he also said nothing. I wondered if he was thinking about my job at Hannah's café. Poppy wagged her tail as I fed her a few scraps from my sandwich.

'This is nice,' Adam said at last, in a clumsy attempt to break the awkward silence. Stretching his long legs out in front of him, he leaned back in his chair to gaze up at the sky.

A few small white clouds scudded across the blue expanse. It was one of those beautiful days of intermittent sunshine when, just as the heat starts to become uncomfortable, a cloud drifts in front of the sun to afford some relief. Then, as the air becomes slightly chilly, the sun comes out to warm everything up again. We finished our lunch and Richard went indoors to put the kettle on. Adam had refused the offer of coffee as he had to return to work, but I had been happy to accept. It wasn't as if I had anywhere else to be. As soon as his father had disappeared into the house, Adam sat up and spoke urgently.

'You know I'll help you in any way I can,' he said quickly. 'But let's agree to leave Hannah out of it.' He hesitated, before adding awkwardly that it could be dangerous if too many people were involved.

Whether his intention was to protect Hannah, or if he was concealing the unpleasant truth that she wanted nothing more to do with me, made no practical difference to my position. Either way, no one else needed to be implicated in my search for the killer.

'Thank you, but there's no need for you to do anything,' I replied. 'None of us are going to risk stirring up trouble. This will just have to sort itself out.'

It was difficult to tell, but I thought he looked relieved. 'Very well. But if you do need my help, in any way at all, you know where to find me. And now, I have to get going. Before I leave, promise me one thing.'

I waited. We both knew he had no right to demand anything of me, but I nodded in a noncommittal way.

'Promise me you'll be careful,' he murmured, seeing Richard emerging from the house with a cafetière and mugs.

Adam rose to his feet in one swift movement, and took his leave. As soon as he had gone, Richard sat forward and gazed at me solemnly.

'Tell me what I can do to help you with your investigation,' he said. 'You can't tackle this alone.'

I gave him the same reply I had given to Adam a few moments earlier, and he reiterated, as his son had, that he would do anything in his power to help me. I thanked him for his friendship but didn't trust myself to say more than that, because I suddenly felt close to tears, knowing that I still had some friends in the village. Richard poured the coffee and handed me a cup. We drank in a silence interrupted only by Poppy's frantic barking as she dashed down the garden in pursuit of a pigeon that rose effortlessly into the air long before she could reach it. I hoped my own endeavours would not prove equally futile.

# 12

HAVING DECIDED TO PROCEED with my plan to unmask the killer by myself, the feeling of liberation on reaching a decision proved short-lived. By the time I arrived home and sat down to make a start, my confidence was wavering. In Richard and Adam's company, the idea of tracking down Silas's murderer had struck me as relatively straightforward, if rather bold. Now, thinking it over on my own, the enterprise seemed fraught with difficulties. Still, I couldn't afford to sit back and wait for the police to arrest me, so I set to work jotting down bullet points for how to go about my investigation. I wrote these on paper, to avoid leaving any electronic record of my notes. Having binge-watched the Geraldine Steel detective series, as well as reading all the books on which the television programmes were based, I knew the police routinely confiscated suspects' phones and computers. It was important to leave no trace of my plans for anyone else to find, in case my notes were discovered and misinterpreted. Still thinking about the fictional detective's murder cases, I began to write.

1) *Leave no one out – the killer could be someone who is easily overlooked*
2) *Suspect everyone – the killer might be the most unlikely person*
3) *Be accurate – don't get dates and times confused*
4) *Pay attention to details – double check everything*
5) *Minimise time wasted on red herrings – try to look out for them*
6) *Work quickly – expose the killer before the police arrest me*
7) *Be secretive – the killer must not suspect what I'm up to*
8) *Be discreet – be particularly careful when Maud is nearby*
9) *Look for information – find out as much as possible, especially from Barry*
10) *Don't do anything to arouse suspicion – appear innocent and relaxed*

While I was writing, everything seemed to be going well, but as soon as I finished I realised how pointless my list was; I still had no idea how to set about looking for the killer. All I had achieved was to waste time procrastinating, fooling myself I was keeping busy. I was wondering what to do that might actually help my defence when there was a loud knock on my front door. Poppy ran to the hall, barking. Doing my best to hide my apprehension, I tried to reassure her.

'You may have to go next door to Richard for a while,' I said, speaking as cheerfully as I could. 'He'll take you to Jane, and she'll take care of you till I come home. It's going to be all right. You'll see. You can stay with Holly. That'll be fun, won't it? Look, I don't like this any more than you do,' I added, as Poppy put her head on one side with a quizzical expression. 'It makes no sense to me either, but the police seem to think –' My explanation was interrupted by another loud knock.

Reaching to open the door, I hesitated, realising it might not be the police. Virginia Strang could be standing on my doorstep, and this time her attack might be physical. Trembling, I ran back to the kitchen and seized my bread knife. Shuddering, I replaced it in the drawer and grabbed my phone instead. Barry had witnessed Virginia shouting abuse at me in the pub and again in the café, where her vicious attack had threatened to cost me my job. To my relief, he answered my call straightaway. Hurriedly I told him who I suspected was outside my house, waiting for me to open the door.

'I'm on my way,' Barry said. 'Wait there. I'm in the village right now. Whatever you do, don't open the door until I get there. That woman's a loose cannon at the best of times,' he added.

He rang off and I sat down in my living room to wait. Barry would be at the pub, or visiting his Aunt Maud who ran the local store, so it should only take him a few minutes to reach Rosecroft. All the same, I seemed to be waiting for a long time until my phone eventually rang. It was Barry, telling me to let him in. Other voices were talking in the background. Opening the front door, I was surprised and relieved to see Hannah and Adam were with him.

'Did you see Virginia Strang?' I asked them, peering out down the path. 'Has she gone?'

'We haven't seen anyone,' Adam replied. 'It's just us.'

'We've been here for ages,' Hannah added. 'Why didn't you open the door?'

Feeling stupid, I stood back to allow my three friends in. Poppy was ecstatic at having so many visitors and she jumped up at each of them in turn, clamouring to be petted.

'For goodness sake, Emily,' Hannah said. 'We were about to give up and go home, when Barry turned up. What's going on? Why didn't you open the door?' she asked, curiosity overcoming her irritation.

I mumbled about not knowing who was calling on me, but Hannah still looked confused.

'Emily thought you were Virginia Strang,' Barry explained.

'What?' Hannah stared at me. 'Why would she be calling on you? I thought she was at loggerheads with you?'

The time had come to take them all into my confidence. We sat down in the living room, where Poppy went to them each in turn to have her neck scratched and her back stroked, while I made them all swear to tell no one else what they were about to hear. Adam already knew what I was about to say, but he kept quiet about that. Hannah would have been furious with him if she'd learned he had known about my plans and not told her. Barry sat with his head lowered. The three of them heard me out in silence.

'Well, that's why we're here,' Hannah said briskly. 'We came to see what we can do to help. No, it's no use arguing. It's obvious you can't deal with this on your own.

No offence, but you must admit you don't always make sensible decisions.'

'What Hannah means is,' Adam interrupted, seeing me about to protest, 'you're not the most rational of people.'

I was on the point of calling him misogynistic when Hannah spoke again. 'It's no criticism of you, personally. No one could sort this out on their own. Stop pretending you can do it all by yourself. You need us, Emily.'

I looked down at Poppy to hide my relief at discovering that Hannah was on my side after all.

'I'll help,' Adam volunteered. 'I'm not sure you should get involved,' he added to Hannah. 'You can't afford to lose your reputation in the village.'

Hannah brushed him aside with a wave of her hand. 'Don't give me that, Adam. If Emily's in trouble, of course, I want to help her.' She hesitated before adding in a low voice, 'If you're quite sure you aren't connected with what happened.'

Bitterly disappointed, I glared at her. 'Do you really need to ask?'

She shrugged, a little shamefaced, but she refused to let it drop. 'Well? Did you have anything to do with Silas's death? It could have been an accident. We'd understand if something happened that was out of your control, but you do need to tell us the truth. Do you have any idea what happened to him?'

'Bloody hell, is this really necessary?' I burst out. 'All right, I promise you I never harmed Silas Strang. I never so much as lifted a finger against him. Imagine how he would have reacted if I had tried to attack him! Can you see me overpowering him?' I added, with a bitter laugh.

'Do you swear?'

'I swear on Poppy's life I never harmed Silas Strang. I never thought about harming him. I never wanted to harm him. I never even dreamed about harming him. I didn't want to have anything to do with him.'

Barry had been listening with a solemn expression on his usually amiable face. Now he seemed to reach a decision. 'I'm in,' he said. 'I'll do everything I can to help find out who's responsible for Silas's death. Whoever it was,' he added grimly.

'No way,' I told him. 'You can't get caught up in an unofficial murder investigation. You're only here because I was afraid Virginia Strang had come after me. It's best if you leave right now. And whatever you do, don't tell anyone what we've been discussing here. In fact,' I went on, looking round at Hannah and Adam, 'you might as well all leave right now. I really appreciate your offering to support me, but I need to do this on my own. I can't let any of you be a part of it.' I didn't add that it could be dangerous.

Barry looked at me speculatively. 'And how, exactly, do you expect to get anywhere without knowing what evidence the police have discovered?'

I frowned. Tempting though it was to try and enlist Barry's help, it had to be against police rules for him to share information with a member of the public.

'Of course, I won't be able to tell you anything,' he agreed cheerfully, when I pointed out that he surely wouldn't be able to share confidential information with anyone outside the police force, let alone with a suspect.

'What *are* you suggesting then?' Adam asked him

impatiently. 'If you can't help, you'd better leave us to ferret around and see what we can unearth for ourselves.'

Barry shook his head and his sandy-coloured hair flopped forward, covering his broad forehead. 'Emily's clever,' he said. 'Too clever for me,' he added, with a touching air of melancholy. Remembering how I had rejected him, I felt a stab of remorse, even though I had done nothing wrong. 'What you're suggesting is risky,' he went on, gazing sternly at me. 'I want to help you, but I think you should leave this to the professionals.'

'I'd like to,' I said, 'but your colleagues suspect me of being involved in a murder. That's how much they know. And besides, I'm living right here in Ashton Mead. With my local knowledge, there's got to be a chance I could find the murderer. I must be in a better position to find out what happened than a team of strangers sent here from Swindon or even further afield. Surely there's no downside to my making a few discreet enquiries.'

Barry looked thoughtful. 'Swindon will be sending out a team, but it's true they won't know the local people, not like we all do, so you could be right that they're unlikely to find out as much information as we can. All right, I'll do what I can to point you in the right direction without saying anything, and I'll keep quiet about what you're up to. But you need to be careful.'

'That goes without saying,' I replied.

Hannah and Adam murmured that they would also do what they could to help.

'I suppose we'll have to be on board, if only to stop you doing anything reckless,' Adam muttered, as he leaned down to pet Poppy. 'Who knows what harebrained scheme you might come up with, left to your own devices.'

And so it was decided. I was relieved to know that I wouldn't be investigating the situation alone.

We started by attempting to list the dead man's enemies, but that got us nowhere at all as everyone in the village had seemed to dislike Silas, including his mother. Barry told us that Silas had recently reported three villagers to the police over petty squabbles. Having hinted there had been several more such cases, Barry refused to reveal any names, insisting that we would need to ask his aunt. Maud knew everyone else's business in the village, but it would probably be impossible for any of us to question her without other people hearing about it.

'We have to be very careful who we speak to,' Hannah said.

'And you have to be careful what you write down,' Adam added, nodding at the names I had been jotting down.

Barry asked me whether there was a safe hiding place in my house. I admitted that there was nowhere completely secure if the police ever decided to search Rosecroft, and in the end we agreed to burn the list. Only Poppy seemed happy when we trooped outside, and she frisked joyfully around our ankles. I scooped her up in my arms as Barry set light to the paper and she barked as it flared up. The flame died away almost as quickly as it started. Barry dropped the charred paper, and we stood watching the flame destroy the last remnant of the paper and go out.

'We can manage very well without an initial list,'

Hannah said. 'We're going to have to speak to everyone. We just need to remember who we've questioned.'

'And we need to be circumspect in making our enquiries,' I added. 'We mustn't alert the killer to our intentions.'

I recalled Richard's suggestion and wondered whether it had been closer to the truth than any of us realised. It was possible Silas's own mother had killed him, and she had tried to frame me in order to clear herself. There was no need to warn my three friends of the danger we might face in trying to track down a demented killer.

# 13

IN ASHTON MEAD LITTLE remained private for long. Neighbours chatted across their fences and in the street, or over a pint at the pub. The local shop was a hub for tittle-tattle, where the owner made it her business to know everyone else's goings-on. While this could be regarded as a drawback of village life, in my current situation I hoped to turn it to my advantage. Hannah had been born in Ashton Mead and had known the local gossipmonger all her life, but we all agreed that Adam was best placed to wheedle information out of Maud. Not only was Adam's connection to me tenuous, but out of the four of us he was the one most likely to charm her. Far from objecting to the idea of pumping his aunt for intelligence, Barry admitted that she could be, as he put it, 'a bit soft' where good looking young men were concerned. So we agreed that Adam should go to the village shop and discreetly quiz Maud for information about Silas.

Initially, Adam was reluctant to accept the role of spy. He was sure Maud would see straight through any attempt he made to coax information out of her. But Hannah persisted, until he caved in and agreed to visit the shop.

'I'd be useless as a secret agent,' he objected. 'I'm bound to bungle it. I have no idea what you expect me to say.'

'You'll think of something,' Hannah assured him. 'All you have to do is find out who Silas's worst enemies were. Anyone who might have hated him enough to do away with him.'

Adam promised to do what he could, but he didn't look very happy. For her part, Hannah volunteered to see what she could winkle out of the barmaid at the local pub. In a position to eavesdrop on all kinds of indiscreet conversations, Tess was another local resident who might hear all the local gossip.

'She's a bit tight-lipped,' I pointed out, and Barry and Adam murmured in agreement. 'You won't get much out of her.'

Hannah grinned. 'Get enough shots in her and she loosens up.'

A slight breeze blew across the garden, sending a few charred vestiges of my list fluttering along the ground. Some tiny blackened fragments rose and vanished in the air. Poppy chased after them and looked disappointed when she managed to trap one in her mouth. Smiling at her antics, we traipsed back inside to advise Adam about approaching Maud. After a lot of discussion, we agreed he would have to pretend he had some interest in Silas beyond mere idle gossip. Improbable though it was, he would have to convince Maud that he had struck up a friendship with Silas. Virginia might be a problem, as she was likely to deny Adam's claim.

'Does it matter what she says?' I asked. 'Surely he was

able to make friends with anyone he wanted. He didn't need her permission.'

He had lived with his mother, who would have known a lot about him. But she couldn't have known everything.

'He might have had friends she never met,' I suggested.

'As far as I can see, Silas didn't have any friends,' Hannah said. 'Plenty of enemies, but no friends. He didn't exactly go out of his way to endear himself to people. He'd argue with you as soon as greet you civilly. Anyone with a modicum of sense wouldn't exchange a single word with him,' she added pointedly, glaring at me.

After further debate, Barry suggested Adam might claim Silas had admired his car. Adam drove a streamlined silver Ferrari, which looked a bit flashy to me. I couldn't see the point in owning a car that could go a hundred miles an hour above the speed limit. But we all agreed it offered a plausible reason why Adam and Silas might have developed some kind of acquaintanceship, unknown to Virginia. We didn't know whether Silas had any interest in cars, but the explanation would have to do, since none of us could think of anything better. Having concocted a story together, we decided we had done enough for one evening. Thanking my friends, I saw them out and bolted the front door behind them.

While I was preparing our dinner, Poppy barked. It was unlike her not to follow me into the kitchen so, putting down the fork I was using to whisk eggs, I went into the living room to see what she wanted and found her sitting on the settee, digging at one of the cushions. As I approached, I noticed the edge of a buff cardboard folder sticking out along one side of the seat.

'What have you got there?' I asked her.

Poppy whimpered and pressed her nose against the folder. It wasn't mine. Wondering what was inside it, I drew it out of the gap beside the cushion and flipped open the cover. What I saw made me gasp. It was a copy of a confidential police report into the death of Silas Strang.

I shut it at once, realising that Barry must have left it behind when he left. But before long curiosity overcame my reticence. Somewhat belatedly fetching a pair of rubber gloves, I closed my living room curtains before opening the folder again. What I read made me tremble: Silas had been stabbed from behind. The missing weapon appeared to have been a long blade, which had been driven in between his shoulder blades. Either by skill or chance, his heart had been pierced. While Silas was undoubtedly strong, a swift and silent killer could have stabbed him without needing to overpower him, which meant that almost anyone could have been responsible for the fatal attack. There were no other injuries to the body to suggest he had been in a fight with his assailant, and no defence wounds. Other details were less specific, notably the time of death which had been estimated at between midnight and four in the morning, possibly as little as five hours after my argument with him.

I was horrified to see my own name at the top of a list of suspects. Flicking through the file, I found reports on the three villagers he had complained about. His next door neighbour, Hetty Mason, appeared to have been engaged in a long-running disagreement with him over the boundary between their properties. The dispute focused on the ownership of a dangerously overgrown tree. The village butcher, Norman Norris, had fallen out with Silas over an alleged gambling debt. Finally, Silas had bought a car from another local resident, Jeff Talbot. According to Jeff, Silas had accused him of concealing the fact that the engine was damaged, making the vehicle potentially dangerous to drive. When Silas had demanded his money back, Jeff had refused and said they had 'exchanged words'. The police had made it clear they were not interested in civil cases, but it seemed Silas had insisted they issue warnings to his antagonists in each instance. When the police had dismissed his complaints as vexatious, he had threatened in every case to 'take the matter to higher authorities'. That appeared to have been empty posturing, since there was no evidence Silas had ever contacted the police authorities, or his MP. There was no mention of Virginia Strang, and I wondered if the police had even considered her as a possible suspect.

Closing the file, I placed it out of Poppy's reach, on the top shelf of my bookcase. Feeling drained, I turned my thoughts to supper. However queasy I was feeling, Poppy still needed to be fed. On my way to the kitchen, I was considering what to do with the police file when someone knocked at my door. Poppy let out a bark and wagged her tail, but I was unnerved. After a moment's hesitation, I called Barry and he answered straightaway.

'It's me,' he said.

'There's someone outside,' I replied, struggling to sound calm.

'I know. It's me. I'm outside. Open the door.'

As Barry entered, I removed my gloves as surreptitiously as possible, hoping he hadn't seen them. He told me he had spoken sternly to Virginia Strang, and was confident she wouldn't bother me again, after which he admitted diffidently that he might have left a file in my living room. He gazed awkwardly at the settee and I wondered whether, far from being an oversight, he had deliberately passed on information to help me in my own investigation. He had pointed out the importance of police evidence, and had undertaken to do whatever he could to help, even though he couldn't actually tell me anything. Besides, it was odd for him to have been carrying photocopies of various relevant reports around for no reason. The more I thought about it, the more obvious it was that Barry had left his file with me deliberately, intending me to read it.

Leading the way into the living room, I pointed at his file, which he retrieved and stuffed quickly into his bag.

'It was Poppy who found it, nearly hidden down the side of the sofa,' I told him.

Barry frowned. 'I left it on the seat – that is, that's where I thought I must have dropped it.'

'I hope Poppy didn't leave traces of her DNA all over the folder.'

'Don't worry, I'll destroy it all. They were just copies. I brought them along in case you wanted to know what was going on. No one knows you've seen them, and we'll keep it between us.'

'Of course. Don't worry.'

It seemed strange to be telling Barry not to worry, when I was the one suspected of murder. He smiled uneasily, without meeting my eye, and said he had to go. Relieved that he had warned Virginia off, I thanked him and he hurried away. Even so, I checked the front door was bolted before taking Poppy into the back garden. Playing with a ball, I tried to make her run around as much as possible. As long as I had an enemy in Ashton Mead, it was too risky to go for a walk in the village at night, and I locked the back door when we went back inside. Trying to resist the impulse to listen out for intruders, I went upstairs to bed, assuring myself that Poppy would bark if anyone was lurking around outside the house.

'What would I do without you?' I asked her, and she wagged her tail.

But even Poppy might be unable to defend me against a maniac. Whether Virginia was intent on avenging her son's murder, or plotting to cover up her own responsibility for his death, there was no question that she was dangerous.

# 14

No one tried to break into Rosecroft during the night, and there was no more graffiti on the front of the house in the morning. With nothing else to do, after breakfast I dropped Poppy off at Jane's house as usual.

'I was wondering when we'd be seeing you again,' Jane said, crouching down to pet Poppy who growled with pleasure. 'Holly's missed you.'

Opening one eye, the old dog thumped her tail lazily on the carpet in greeting, and Poppy trotted over to lie down beside her.

Jane smiled at me. 'Has Hannah come to her senses and taken you back?'

I gave a noncommittal grunt and left, to wander along to the café where I hoped Hannah would be run off her feet and feeling frazzled. If she wasn't comfortable with customers seeing me working there, at least she might agree to let me work out of sight in the kitchen, leaving her free to serve the teas I prepared. But the café was empty of customers. I found Hannah in the kitchen, taking a tray of scones out of the oven and humming softly to herself. My hopes of finding her struggling were dashed. I greeted her warily and she looked round in surprise.

'Emily? What are you doing here?'

It was hardly the welcome I had hoped for.

'How's it going?' I asked her.

'Oh, you know,' she replied evasively. 'My mum's been looking in and lending a hand, and I've been managing. It's fine, really. Thanks for popping by.'

With that, she turned back to the oven and took out another tray of scones. It was obvious she wasn't planning to ask me back yet, but I wasn't prepared to walk away without even attempting to persuade her to change her mind. I asked her outright when she wanted me to return to work.

'Let's wait until the situation is resolved,' she replied.

'You mean you don't want me back until the killer is arrested?'

She nodded.

'But that could take months,' I protested.

'I can't help that.'

'Give me one good reason why I can't come back right now.'

'You know why I can't have you here. It's not good for business.'

'Hannah, this isn't fair. You know I've done nothing wrong. I don't deserve to be punished like this.'

While we were wrangling over whether I could return to work, the bell above the street door jangled and we saw Adam enter the café. There were no other customers so we joined him, and Hannah placed a large pot of tea and a plate of freshly baked scones on the table.

Adam sighed contentedly. 'Is there anything better than taking a break and coming face to face with a plate of Hannah's scones still warm from the oven?'

Tempted to reply that I would settle for not having a murder charge hanging over my head, I merely nodded in agreement.

'If I could stop the world and just live in this moment, I would be happy,' he continued, reaching for another scone.

Hannah laughed. 'Anyone would think you hadn't had a huge breakfast just two hours ago. You want to watch out or you won't fit into any of your trousers.'

Impatient to find out what my friends had managed to discover, and to share with them the details of how Silas had been killed, I interrupted their banter to enquire what they had found out.

Hannah glanced at the door to check no one was about to enter. 'I questioned Tess,' she said quietly.

'And I've spoken to Maud,' Adam added, in a low voice. 'She looked different,' he added, with a puzzled frown.

'Don't tell me you've only just noticed she's gone blonde?' Hannah said. 'Honestly, men! Don't you notice anything? It must be to do with her new beau.' She giggled. 'She's seeing someone.'

Eager to focus on our investigation into Silas's murder, I repeated my question impatiently, only to be disappointed when we were interrupted by a group of noisy hikers who came in, clamouring for tea and cakes. Adam rose to his feet and announced he had to get back to work, and I slunk away out of sight, since Hannah insisted on waiting at the table. Banished to the kitchen, I was nevertheless pleased to be occupied for the rest of the day, preparing tea and scouring baking trays, as I waited to hear what my friends had discovered. We had a steady stream of customers until closing time but at last we finished clearing up and I went to collect Poppy, after agreeing to go to Hannah's house that evening. She and Adam were renting a small house in a relatively new residential estate, on the other side of the river to the picturesque old area of the village. Although she said she was happy living further away from the café, she had confided to me that they were hoping to move back to the centre of the village when a suitable property came on the market.

Whenever I listened to Hannah's plans, I always felt a pang of guilt at my own good fortune in inheriting a mortgage-free property. Most people my age could barely scrape enough together to pay their rent. Saving for a deposit on a home of their own was impossible. Had it not been for my great aunt, I would most likely have ended up going back to live with my parents when I lost my job in London. While I appreciated my luck in having parents who would welcome me back, it would have been difficult to return to my family home, now that I had grown accustomed to my independence. It wasn't that I didn't get on well with my mother, but she did like to interfere in my life and was convinced she knew how I ought to live. Nothing could have been further from the truth. So, my property windfall had been very welcome, as well as unexpected.

My friends and I had all agreed it was important to keep quiet about my friendship with Barry. Not only would he risk getting himself in trouble if he spent too much time in the company of a suspect in a murder investigation, but he wanted to keep the trust of the detectives running the murder investigation. That way, he would be able to find out how the case was progressing, and keep me and my friends apprised of any new evidence that turned up. Recognising the need to be discreet, we had agreed not to discuss our plans in any public place.

Hannah and Adam lived in a neat little redbrick house in a street of identical houses, each with its own paved front yard. There was a large terracotta pot beside their front door, containing a shrub covered in a mass of pink flowers. As I was admiring it, Hannah opened the door.

'That camellia bush was here when we moved in,' she said, by way of greeting.

'It's beautiful,' I replied and we both smiled.

'We can give you a cutting, if you like,' she said. 'I'll ask Richard if that's possible. He's into gardening, isn't he? So, come on in,' she said. 'We've been waiting for you.'

Poppy stepped forward as if in response to Hannah's invitation, and I dropped her lead to let her run indoors. Although they had only been living together for about six months, Hannah and Adam's house gave the impression that they had been there for years. The furniture was worn but comfortable, and there were thick rugs on the floor, and framed pictures on every wall. An untidy kitchen was visible through an open door. This made me smile, because Hannah couldn't bear to leave a single pan or implement out of place in the kitchen at the Sunshine Tea Shoppe.

'If we don't put things back where they belong, we can't work efficiently. Don't forget, time is of the essence when we're serving customers,' she had told me on more than one occasion. 'A tidy kitchen is a well-run kitchen,' was another one of her favourite sayings.

The lounge had a lived-in feel to it, with a few paperbacks on a rectangular wooden coffee table in the centre of the room, and a couple of magazines lying carelessly on the floor. There was a warmth and a homeliness about the place that made me reluctant to return to my empty cottage. Toby was already there, without his new girlfriend.

'How's Michelle?' I enquired politely and he smiled.

'She's fine. She couldn't make it this evening,' he added quietly.

We all understood it would have been inappropriate to invite a virtual stranger to join us, because that evening there could be only one topic of conversation: the recent murder and my prominent position on the list of police suspects.

# 15

ONCE WE HAD SETTLED down, with Poppy contentedly dozing at my feet, I shared what Barry's report had revealed about the murder, without divulging my source. Hannah looked worried.

'You're sure he was stabbed? With a knife?' she asked.

'A knife with a long blade, apparently, according to –' I hesitated. 'Well, we all know where I got this from.'

'Barry told you?' Hannah looked worried. 'He needs to be careful.'

There was no point in equivocating. 'When you left yesterday evening, Barry accidentally left behind a copy of the report on how Silas was killed. Poppy found it under a cushion.'

Poppy lifted one ear but didn't stir.

'Did he leave it there deliberately?' Toby asked.

There was a pause.

'Well, yes,' I replied at last, 'but that's strictly between us. He'd lose his job if anyone else found out.' The others nodded solemnly. 'Thanks to Barry, we now know that Silas was stabbed, just once, with a long sharp knife. It was enough to kill him.'

Hannah cleared her throat and I noticed she looked strained. 'A knife went missing from the kitchen at the tea shop,' she whispered. 'That's why I wanted you to promise me you had nothing to do with what happened.'

'Do you really think I could have done it?' I asked, irritated by her lingering distrust.

'No, I don't, but you might have taken a knife from the kitchen by mistake, and left it somewhere, or you could have left the back door unlocked –'

'Yes, well, so might you,' I retorted. 'Look, I'm positive I never left the door unlocked, and as for taking a knife from the kitchen, that just never happened.'

Hannah nodded. 'Of course, if you say so, I believe you,' she said and I grunted.

Still cross that she would ever harbour such a stupid suspicion, I controlled my irritation and focused on what we had to do.

'Everything we've learned so far could be useful,' I said. 'We're looking for someone who knew about my row with Silas that night, and had access to the kitchen at the café.'

'Assuming it *was* my knife the killer used,' Hannah pointed out. 'That might turn up. It could have fallen down somewhere.'

'You ought to be careful with knives,' Adam told her.

Hannah informed him in icy tones that we were extremely careful with the kitchen knives at the tea shop, and she insisted we had no reason to suppose her missing knife was involved in the murder.

'Maud's been busy telling everyone about your row with Silas,' Adam said. 'So, we can't narrow it down to people who witnessed what happened.'

'The whole village must have heard about it by now,' Hannah agreed.

'Silas was fatally stabbed on the night of the May festivities, just a few hours after I spoke to him,' I said. 'That doesn't give much time for the news of our altercation to spread, so I still think the killer must have overheard us arguing. Even Maud can't spread gossip that quickly, and it can't be a coincidence that Silas was attacked so soon after my public row with him. It looks as if someone seized the opportunity to do away with him, confident that suspicion would land on me. Whoever wanted him dead decided to use me as a convenient scapegoat.'

'Someone clever, who'd been waiting for their chance?' Hannah speculated. 'Or just an opportunist who'd witnessed the row?'

'Or heard about it from Silas,' I added thoughtfully, still thinking about Virginia Strang.

'What about the knife?' Toby asked. 'Who has access to the kitchen at the café?'

'We don't know my knife was used as a murder weapon,' Hannah insisted fretfully. 'Like I said, it might just have been put away in the wrong drawer, or fallen down somewhere. We'll have a thorough search for it tomorrow. I'm sure it will turn up again.'

'After being used and cleaned by a murderer,' Toby said. 'If it reappears, you need to take it straight to Barry and tell him it went missing and was then put back. The police might still be able to detect traces of blood or DNA on it.'

Hannah shuddered, but I nodded, seeing the sense in what he was saying.

'You need to search for it as soon as possible,' Toby said. 'It would be better if the police didn't find it.'

He was right. Discovery of the knife anywhere outside the café would only add to the case against me, since I had constant access to the tea shop kitchen. The police had already placed me at the top of their list of suspects, and I desperately hoped we would find the knife in the kitchen in the café, where it belonged.

'What about Tess?' I asked. 'Was she able to shed any light on all this?'

Hannah shook her head and sighed. 'Poor Tess,' she said. 'She seemed very cut up about Silas. She was crying.'

Having only ever seen Tess dour and hard, I was surprised to hear that she had become emotional.

'She was pissed,' Hannah added, by way of explanation, seeing my expression. 'People say all sorts of strange things when they're pissed.'

Adam nodded. 'Even the most sensible people can become very emotional when they've had too much to drink. In vino veritas.'

He and Hannah exchanged a glance, and I wondered what lay behind his comment.

It was his turn to share what he had learned from Maud. With an embarrassed moue, he admitted that Maud had been telling everyone the identity of the suspected murderer. It was obvious from his prevarication that Maud was talking about me, before he said so.

'And I suppose everyone believes her,' I burst out crossly.

Having listened to Maud's stories with interest in the past, I resolved to treat her tittle-tattle with suspicion in future. Rumours might be entertaining to an audience who were not directly involved, but they were damaging to anyone personally connected to a scandal. When someone was wrongly implicated, such gossip was downright cruel.

'No one takes her stories seriously,' Hannah assured me. 'Everyone knows she embellishes and fabricates.'

'So,' I said, 'where do we go from here?'

'I think I'll go to the kitchen and make us all a cup of tea. Or would you like something stronger?' Hannah suggested brightly.

'Not for me,' Toby replied, glancing at his phone. 'Michelle's waiting for me.'

It struck me that Michelle had arrived in the village at around the same time as the murder. We didn't really know anything about her, other than that she was working as a carer for Naomi, Toby's mother.

'When did you meet her?' I asked him.

'About two weeks ago. She'd been helping my mother and I offered her a lift home, and we just hit it off.' He nodded happily. 'You know how it is, sometimes.'

'She seems very nice,' Hannah said, and Adam and I murmured in agreement.

'Well, I think so,' Toby grinned.

'Has she been helping your mum long?' I asked.

He shook his head. 'Not long. Anyway, I'd best be making tracks or she'll wonder what's happened.'

'Where was she working before?' I pursued my enquiry, doing my best to sound casual.

Toby shrugged, looking faintly puzzled. 'In Swindon, I think. I'm not sure exactly where. Why?'

'Oh, no reason.'

\*

'What was that all about?' Hannah demanded once Toby had gone.

'What?'

'You know what I'm talking about. You were giving Toby the third degree about Michelle.'

I forced a laugh. 'Hardly the third degree. I was just showing an interest, that's all. But doesn't it strike you as a bit of a coincidence, her turning up out of the blue just before Silas was murdered?'

Hannah stared at me. 'What are you talking about? If you think Michelle had anything to do with the murder, that's just bonkers. I mean, why would she be implicated in it, just because she came to the village to help look after Naomi? That's ridiculous.'

'Naomi has different carers, and they must all be vetted. They wouldn't send just anybody to look after someone vulnerable,' Adam agreed.

'Don't let jealousy blind you,' Hannah said.

'Jealousy? What are you on about? Why would I be jealous of Michelle?' I spluttered. 'Now who's being ridiculous. I like Toby as a friend, but there was never anything more than that between us. I never wanted a relationship with him. Why would you even think such a thing? And you accuse me of having an overactive imagination.'

I broke off, aware that I was talking too much, and glared at Hannah. As we stopped talking, Poppy woke up and looked at me as if to ask what was going on. I was wondering that myself.

# 16

WHEN I TOOK MY leave, Adam rose to his feet and offered to accompany me home. I assured him that wasn't necessary, but he insisted it would do him good to stretch his legs by walking with me, at least as far as the bridge. Either he was being courteous, or he was keen to talk to me privately. We walked in silence at first, with Poppy trotting ahead of us. Leaving the estate of neat small red brick houses, we were making our way down the path towards the river when Adam spoke.

'You know Hannah never really suspected you of murdering that creep?'

Uncertain how to respond, I said nothing.

'You know she'd never believe that, don't you? She's been tormenting herself about it ever since you fell out. She's afraid you hate her for not trusting you.'

Disappointed that Hannah had let me down, I spoke more curtly than I had intended. 'Why doesn't she raise it with me herself, instead of sending you as a go-between?'

'She didn't ask me to talk to you.'

'I don't know why we're discussing it then. This is between Hannah and me.'

'I just want you to know she's miserable about what happened.'

'What happened when she suspected me of murder, you mean? Well, I'm sorry *she's* feeling miserable, but I don't know what you expect me to do about it.'

Adam looked so crestfallen that I relented. 'Look, I'm sorry, and you're right. None of this is Hannah's fault. It's over and done with, okay? I don't want to make her miserable, and anyway I'm sure she didn't really mean what she said. We were all confused and shocked by what happened to Silas, and none of us were thinking clearly. I understand if she's feeling guilty for behaving badly, but she needs to put this behind her. I have. Because right now we need to focus on sorting out the mess I seem to be in.'

Adam grinned and told me Hannah would be pleased. He assured me she would talk to me about it and clear the air when we next met, now she no longer needed to be afraid we would fall out. Satisfied, he halted.

'Are you okay to get home by yourself? I can come with you if you like.'

I laughed to cover my apprehension. 'I'm not alone,' I told him. 'Poppy's here.'

'If you're sure?'

'Of course. I'll be fine.'

He turned back and I followed Poppy onto the bridge, feeling slightly bereft. She paused from time to time to sniff the air, before trotting eagerly onwards. All the received wisdom on dog training advised that dogs should be taught to walk to heel. Apparently, allowing dogs to lead the way gave them the false impression that they were in charge of their owners. But despite my efforts to train

Poppy to behave like a model dog, she continued to walk in front of me, sometimes pulling on her lead until she gagged. In every other area she was compliant, obeying a series of instructions like 'sit', 'paw', 'down', 'up', 'wait', and so on. Only when we were out walking was she unresponsive to command. I had all but abandoned my attempts to persuade her to trot beside me instead of running on ahead.

We had reached our side of the bridge, where she stopped to sniff at the ground, when she suddenly turned and darted back the way we had come, barking frantically. I spun round just in time to see a hooded figure racing away across the bridge, back towards the new estate. Whoever it was must have been almost close enough to reach out and touch me. Without pausing to consider what was happening, I gave chase. Poppy ran ahead of me, straining at her lead and barking furiously. Either she believed she was defending me or she thought this was a glorious new game. As we reached the far side of the bridge, I slowed down, wondering whether I actually wanted to catch up with the mysterious figure. If Poppy hadn't alerted me to their presence, whoever it was would almost certainly have caught up with me before I was aware of them. I wondered what would have happened then and shivered, even though it wasn't cold. It might have been a coincidence that another person had been on the bridge at the same time as me, in which case it would have been embarrassing to challenge them. If, on the other hand, they had intended to harm me, I was better off avoiding them. It was growing dark, and there was no one else around. Nervously, I turned and hurried home.

The following day, Hannah and I spent every spare moment looking for the knife, and we both stayed after work to make a thorough search of the kitchen, the yard and the café. In spite of our efforts, the knife was still missing.

'Someone must have taken it,' Hannah concluded grimly.

Reluctant to confirm my reputation for being melodramatic, I made no mention of the shadowy figure on the bridge the previous evening. After all, nothing had actually happened, and my fears had come to nothing. Keen to continue my private investigation until the murderer was found, I invited Hannah and Adam and Toby to Rosecroft so that we could continue our discussion although, so far, my friends hadn't been much help. As before, I said nothing about Michelle and was again relieved when Toby arrived without her.

'So?' Toby prompted us, stifling a yawn, as we sat down in my living room. 'What's the latest? Have you found the knife?'

Hannah shook her head. 'We looked absolutely everywhere. It's not there. Someone must have taken it.'

'Oh well,' Toby said, leaning back in my armchair, 'Silas had it coming. He was a nasty piece of work and no great loss. I don't think any of us need lose much sleep over what happened.'

'The police suspect me,' I blurted out.

As though she understood what I had said, and sympathised, Poppy whimpered. To my annoyance, Toby dismissed my claims with an impatient shrug.

'For goodness sake, Emily. This isn't the first time you've let your imagination run away with you. Of course, the

110

police aren't going to seriously suspect you of murdering Silas, simply because you had a row with him. Just about everyone in the village fell out with him at one time or another.'

Hannah shook her head. 'I'm afraid Emily's right,' she said softly. 'She's a suspect in a murder investigation.'

'My name's first on the list,' I added.

'From what I've heard about Silas Strang, the police have probably got a list of suspects as long as your arm.' Toby said.

I reminded him about Barry's offer to help me in my unofficial investigation into Silas's murder, and how he had left a folder at my house.

'None of us are comfortable with all this subterfuge,' I concluded, 'but it's the only way to protect Barry, and it's necessary if we're to keep up with any new evidence the police find.'

Toby muttered that the police were mistaken in placing my name at the top of their list of suspects. At least he didn't challenge my innocence, as Hannah had done. Listening to my friends discuss the situation made me realise how quickly I had grown accustomed to my predicament. It was only four days since Virginia Strang had first shouted at me in the pub, and just a couple of days since the police inspector had visited me, confirming that I was a suspect in their murder enquiry, and already it no longer felt shocking. Within a few days I had moved on from feeling stunned and helpless to being determined to prove my innocence. Having my friends around me had briefly calmed my anxiety, but now the reality of my predicament hit me once more.

'That's all well and good,' Toby said. 'I get it that Barry's passing on confidential information, accidentally on purpose, and I can see it's intriguing to know what's going on, but what's the point? Barry's risking his job, and for what? I don't see how knowing what the police are up to is going to help you find the killer. What can you do with their information that they can't do themselves?'

'It's not so much what they're doing – which doesn't seem to be very much – it's more what they find out,' I explained. 'We need to know as much as possible about what went on the night of the murder.'

'The police don't know Ashton Mead like we do, and they don't know the people who live here,' Hannah explained.

'Assuming it *was* one of the local residents who killed him,' I muttered.

Hannah scowled at me while Toby insisted that we needed to find the missing knife.

'Yes, we know we need to find the knife, but the police have placed my name at the top of their list of suspects,' I repeated. 'I can't just sit around and wait and see what they come up with next. Of course, I'm hoping they'll discover their mistake, and soon, but what if they don't? Surely you can see I have to do everything in my power to find out the truth? You don't have to be a part of this, if you're not happy about it. I'll understand. You have a responsible job and you have to be careful of your reputation –'

'This isn't about *me*,' Toby interrupted me. 'I'm worried about *you*. As long as you don't do anything dangerous, I'm perfectly happy to help you as much as possible. As your friend, why wouldn't I? But I'm not convinced that what you're proposing is sensible, let alone feasible.'

'Have you got a better idea? I can't just sit around and do nothing.'

Before Toby could answer, Poppy trotted over to him and nudged his hand with her nose. With Hannah, Adam, Barry, Richard and Toby on my side, I felt more confident than I had done for days. But we were still working in the dark, and I had a feeling the killer had not finished yet. Whoever had been following me the previous evening had most likely intended to harm me. Had they caught me unawares, they might have killed me. Aware that I probably owed my life to Poppy, I picked her up and held her close.

# 17

HANNAH REACHED OUT AND took my hand, and I was taken aback to see she had tears in her eyes. Pleased that she regretted her earlier suspicions, I smiled reassuringly.

'Things aren't that bad,' I said. 'Like Toby said, it's not as if I'm the only suspect and, in any case, there's nothing connecting me to Silas's murder. We just happened to have a row a few hours before he was killed, but that doesn't mean anything. He argued with lots of people. He fell out with people all the time. If it hadn't been me, someone else would have been having a row with him just before he died. And as for who might have wanted him dead, well, he wasn't exactly Mr Popular, was he? If the police found out what he was really like, instead of listening to whatever lies his mother concocts, they'd have a much longer list of suspects.'

Even though no one apart from Virginia seemed to have been on good terms with Silas, we agreed that we ought to begin by drawing up our own list of suspects, after which we would proceed with our enquiries into the whereabouts of each of them at the time of the murder. Thanks to the report Barry had shown me, we knew not only how Silas had died, but also the approximate time of the fatal attack. When he had come back for his file, Barry had explained that it was impossible to be precise about the time of death. All the police knew for certain was that Silas had been alive at around eleven, when his mother reported he had gone out for a walk. Following that, he had almost certainly been dead for at least three hours by the time his body was examined at seven o'clock the following morning. That gave an estimated window for the time of death of approximately five hours, between eleven and four o'clock.

'It's all a bit vague, but that's the best they can come up with,' I said. 'According to Barry, they can rarely be sure of the exact time of death when they're investigating a murder. It's not like on the TV where forensic officers come up with more precise times.'

Toby nodded. 'It wouldn't have helped that Silas's body was outdoors for hours, exposed to the elements. Every variable in temperature and humidity would have affected the pathologist's ability to narrow down the time of death.'

As a physics teacher, Toby always liked to express an opinion on anything even vaguely scientific. Adam suggested we focus our attention on Hetty Mason, Norman Norris and Jeff Talbot, all of whom were known to have been at odds with Silas and were on the list of police suspects. Hannah pointed out that Hetty was in her eighties, frail, and reliant on a mobility scooter to get about. I wasn't convinced that necessarily meant she was innocent, and we argued over whether to remove her name from our list of suspects. Adam said the police would almost certainly have discovered tracks from the mobility scooter if Hetty had been there. Not only that, but her scooter squeaked, which would have made it difficult for her to creep up behind Silas unnoticed, even on a windy night. Besides, we all agreed it was virtually impossible for Hetty to have had the strength to deal Silas so powerful a blow. Toby suggested she could have paid someone else to murder Silas, so we agreed to keep her on our radar, but moved her name to the end of the list. That left us with just two names to investigate.

'What about Virginia Strang?' I asked. 'She was very keen to accuse me. What if she was trying to set the police off on the wrong tack, just to divert attention from herself.'

The others were not convinced.

'She was his mother,' Hannah said. 'I hardly think she would have killed him. Besides, no one even suspected her, so it makes no sense to think she was trying to divert attention from herself.'

Adam and Toby murmured in agreement, but I was adamant we ought to consider her as a suspect.

'You can't seriously think she could have killed her own son?' Hannah protested. 'The two of them were thick as thieves.'

'They probably *were* thieves, and they were certainly pretty thick,' Toby muttered, with a little chuckle. 'But you mustn't let yourself be swayed by Virginia's appalling behaviour towards you, Emily,' he went on, becoming serious. 'She must have been in shock, and grief can have a strange effect on people.'

I sighed. My friends were right to view Virginia with compassion, but it was hard for me to feel sympathetic towards her.

'That leaves Norman and Jeff,' Adam said. 'For now,' he added, glancing at me.

'Why are you all so convinced it can't have been some twisted crime of passion, with Virginia stabbing her son?' I asked.

Toby laughed and accused me of indulging my taste for melodrama, but I stood firm. My scenario was no less plausible than the idea of someone stabbing Silas in the back during an argument about a gambling debt or a dodgy second hand car. With a shrug, Adam added Virginia to our list of suspects. With Toby present, I couldn't mention Michelle, but I wasn't ready to dismiss my suspicions of her yet, even though she didn't look particularly strong. It had not escaped our attention that the killer had pierced Silas's heart from behind, which we all imagined would take some skill. It had also been an extremely forceful blow, penetrating the coat Silas was wearing, and a layer of clothes underneath that. Silas had been felled and killed with one thrust of a razor sharp blade. It could have been chance that the stabbing had been so accurate, but it would have taken confidence to hit out at random, hoping that Silas would be unable to turn and defend himself. A minor injury might have left him able to launch a counter attack. It seemed that Silas's killer had been desperate, or skilled, or possibly both. He or she might even have been lucky.

'Or unlucky,' Toby said. 'We don't actually know whether the killer intended the assault to prove fatal. It might have been someone just lashing out in a violent temper, possibly too drunk to know what they were doing.'

'Whatever their motive, they must be strong,' Adam said.

'So, we're saying it can't have been Hetty,' Hannah replied. 'Apart from the problem of her coming up behind him unheard, she wouldn't have had the strength to stab him so forcefully.'

'We'll rule her out for now,' Adam agreed.

Hannah and I were keen for us to begin questioning our new suspects as soon as possible. We both shopped at the local butcher's, but we only knew Norman from our over the counter purchases. A large man, physically powerful and used to wielding a knife, he was definitely a credible suspect. More often than not, Norman's assistant served customers. Billy was an energetic young man, who constantly rubbed his hands together when he wasn't weighing out meat. He didn't strike me as particularly bright. We agreed not to question him, as we weren't convinced he would be discreet. We didn't want some stupid bystander to blab about our unofficial investigation in the presence of the killer.

None of us was particularly friendly with Norman or Jeff, so we had to come up with a reason for approaching them. We could hardly walk up and ask them where they had been between the hours of midnight and four o'clock on Saturday night. This was going to be more difficult than we had initially anticipated.

'What if it wasn't a hate crime at all?' Toby asked. 'What I mean is, who benefits from Silas's death? Perhaps there was a different motive behind his murder.'

This question opened a whole new area of uncertainty. We didn't even know if Silas had left a will, and we had no way of finding out. We needed more information, but we knew we had to act discreetly.

'We don't want to stir up any more trouble,' Hannah said.

I pointed out that my predicament could hardly be much worse, knowing that the police might come and arrest me at any time.

'The fact that they've left you alone since the inspector came to question you shows they haven't found any evidence against you,' Adam said.

'Not yet,' Toby added grimly.

'Of course, they haven't found any evidence against me,' I protested. 'How could they, when I didn't do it?'

But we all knew that my position was precarious. Apart from anything else, Virginia Strang seemed to be convinced I was guilty. She was completely unhinged, shouting about my guilt in public. There was no way of knowing what lies she might tell the police, to see me punished for murdering her son. She might well have lost me my job if Hannah hadn't known me as well as she did. I had to find the real killer, and quickly, before Virginia had a chance to confront me again. It would be pointless to try and speak to Virginia, to protest my innocence, and I wondered why she was so desperate to blame me. There were a number of possible answers to that question. She might genuinely believe I had killed Silas, she might be guilty, or she could be trying to protect someone else, which raised more questions about whom she might be protecting. And a question mark still hung over Toby's new girlfriend, Michelle, who had arrived in the village shortly before Silas was murdered. I had decided against raising her as a possible suspect, as long as Toby was present, but decided to mention my suspicion to Hannah, once he had gone.

Toby was keen to stick to practicalities and draw up an action list, and we all agreed that we needed to allocate tasks. Adam agreed to approach Jeff in the pub and try to strike up a conversation about cars. It made sense for me to visit the butcher, as he occasionally gave me scraps and bones for Poppy. How I was going to worm any information out of him concerning Silas's murder was a problem I would worry about later.

'I'll think of something,' I assured my friends.

'Just be careful,' Hannah told me. 'If Norman *is* capable of murder, you don't want him to think you're poking around in his affairs.'

'Don't worry about me,' I replied, doing my best to sound carefree.

Poppy looked up at me quizzically, her head on one side, as though she saw right through my pretence.

# 18

ON SATURDAY MORNING I was busy in the kitchen when someone knocked loudly and insistently at my front door. It was a sound I had come to dread. *Go away*, I thought. *Just go away.* Poppy began to bark, while I tried to ignore the caller and pretend no one was home. But I couldn't skulk indoors indefinitely. Unless I somehow managed to escape and flee the country, the police would catch up with me sooner or later. It would be as well to face them straightaway, and avoid any suspicion that I was obstructing them.

'All right, all right, I'm coming,' I grumbled.

To my surprise, my mother was on the doorstep, a shiny pink suitcase on wheels beside her.

'At last,' she cried out, grabbing hold of her case. 'I've been knocking and knocking. I thought you were going to meet me at the bus stop. Is everything all right? It's just as well I remembered the way here.'

Not wanting to admit that, with everything that had been going on, her visit had completely slipped my mind, I smiled and said I hadn't been expecting her until after lunch. She glanced at her watch.

'Well, it's nearly midday now. And how are *you*?' she added, leaning down to pet Poppy. '*You* wouldn't have left me standing on the doorstep like that, would you? No, you wouldn't.'

Seizing her suitcase from her, I led her inside.

'How's Dad?'

'Oh, you know,' she replied. 'He's busy with his golf. I don't suppose he's noticed I'm not there.' She smiled and I knew she was joking. 'But seriously, he's fine and he sends his love. Are we going to the pub for lunch,' she asked, 'or to your friend's café?'

Reluctant to admit that neither was a good idea, I hesitated, but with only a packet of cornflakes and a few tins of beans in the cupboard, and a sliced loaf of bread in the freezer, I could hardly suggest we had lunch at home. It would probably be easier to escape attention in the café than the pub. The prospect of Virginia Strang haranguing me in front of my mother was troubling, but with any luck the café would be empty, or occupied by people who were just passing through and knew nothing about the recent murder in the village. There was nothing for it but to brave the High Street and hope we didn't meet anyone from the village who might tell my mother I had been accused of killing one of my neighbours. Although I was confident my mother would never believe me capable of murder, I really didn't want her to hear about my troubles. Much as I appreciated her concern for me was an expression of love, her fussing was sometimes undermining, suggesting she didn't trust me to cope on my own. I saw myself as a responsible adult, but in her eyes I was still mentally a child. What if she was right?

My mother was surprised that we were leaving Poppy at home, but I assured her that she would be fine on her own for an hour or so.

'We don't want to be out for long, do we?' I added breezily. I didn't add that giving us a pretext to hurry home as soon as we finished lunch was my reason for leaving Poppy behind. 'We've got a lot of catching up to do and we can talk more freely here. I don't want everyone in the village knowing our family secrets.'

My laughter sounded fake, and my mother gazed at me inquisitively.

'Are you alright?' she asked.

'Of course, I'm alright. Why wouldn't I be? Never better.' I laughed awkwardly again.

She shrugged and said she would leave her unpacking until later. Right now she was hungry and ready for lunch. 'My treat,' she added, leaning down to pet Poppy. 'Are you sure she'll be okay?'

I felt guilty leaving Poppy behind, but it seemed like the best option. There was not much point in trying to hide my face when we left Rosecroft, but all the same I put on sunglasses and positioned my mother on the outside of the pavement. Anyone driving past might not notice me as we made our way towards the High Street in the centre of the village. We didn't see anyone out walking, and only a couple of cars went by. Neither of the drivers stopped. Reaching the café without incident, I took a deep breath and went inside. As I had hoped, there were no local residents having lunch, only two tables of strangers. One couple looked like hikers, and the other table was occupied by a family group of two adults and three young children. I breathed a sigh of relief and led my mother to a corner table where I could sit facing the wall. So far so good. Now I just had to ensure Hannah didn't spill the beans about my run in with the police, and all might yet go smoothly.

After lunch, I could rush my mother home and, while she was unpacking, I would book a taxi to drive us into Swindon for supper. On Sunday, we could go for a walk out of the village, and avoid meeting anyone from Ashton Mead until it was time for my mother to leave on Sunday evening. It wouldn't be too difficult to find an excuse for not accompanying her to the bus stop. She might not be pleased, but she knew the way by now. Probably I would have to say that Poppy was unwell. I felt guilty at using Poppy as an excuse again, but had she understood what was at stake, she would have supported my subterfuge. It was preferable to my mother finding out I was suspected of murder.

Hannah came over to serve us, smiling warily. 'Mrs Wilson, how lovely to see you.'

'It was very kind of you to let Emily have the weekend off for my visit,' my mother replied.

'We can't stay long,' I blurted out. 'We've left Poppy at home. She was feeling tired. So, we'll have to go home soon.'

Hannah raised her eyebrows at my stilted excuse, and I wondered if she understood what lay behind my remark.

'I'm planning to take my mother into Swindon this evening,' I went on brightly, hoping Hannah would realise that I was keen to keep my mother away from local residents and their wagging tongues. 'I thought she might like to see something of the area outside the village for a change,' I added, staring at Hannah, as though I could force her to read my mind. 'I thought it would be a good idea to take her away from the village,' I ploughed on.

Hannah nodded.

'So, could you look after Poppy for me this evening?' I asked. 'I can drop her off here or at Jane's, before we go out.' I turned to my mother. 'There's no need for you to walk here again later on. You've spent time in Ashton Mead before.'

My mother laughed uncomfortably. 'Anyone would think you were ashamed of me, you seem so keen to hide me away,' she said bluntly.

'Not at all,' I replied. 'It's just that there's nothing new going on, nothing at all. Just the same old, same old.'

Hannah smiled and nodded, convincing me she had finally understood my concern. 'Of course, no problem,' she said. 'Tell you what, why don't we all come over to Rosecroft this evening and Adam and I can pick up some Chinese on the way?' She looked at my mother. 'There's a new takeaway opened across the river and it's really good. That way, we can all spend time together.'

'That sounds perfect,' I said gratefully.

'I'm sure Toby will come,' Hannah added.

'Toby?' my mother repeated, with sudden interest.

'And he can bring Michelle,' I added quickly.

'That's settled then,' Hannah said. 'Now, what can I get you?'

Before we could place our order, the bell above the door jingled and Hannah stiffened, pen poised over her notepad. 'You haven't seen the kitchen here, have you?' she asked my mother suddenly. 'It's this way. Come on.'

Either she wanted to conceal me from whoever had come in, or she wanted to prevent them from speaking to my mother. Terrified of being seen, I dared not turn round as Hannah ushered us into the kitchen.

'Wait here,' she told us, and she dashed back into the front of the café.

'Well, really,' my mother burst out. 'What on earth's going on? First you behave very strangely, and now your friend is being decidedly odd.'

'What do you mean?' I blustered. 'She thought you might be interested in seeing the kitchen, that's all. There's a new oven, but it's not big enough. What she really wants to do is extend out the back and build a kitchen in the yard, and make room for more tables –'

'Emily,' my mother said severely, 'I didn't come all this way to hear about your friend's plans for a new kitchen. Now, are you going to explain what's going on or do I need to go out there and ask Hannah to spell it out in front of all her customers?'

While I was professing not to understand what my mother meant, Hannah joined us again.

'What do you think?' she asked, gazing around with proprietorial satisfaction, while I breathed a silent sigh of relief. 'Why don't I box you up some sandwiches and scones, and you can take them home with you? That way the two of you can have a good long chat before we all come round this evening?' As she was speaking, she began packing a box of food with swift deft movements.

'Do you mean you want us to leave?' my mother protested. 'We've only just got here.'

'Emily will explain,' Hannah replied testily.

To be fair, this was my mother we were dealing with, and the situation was hardly Hannah's fault. She hadn't invited us to the café, and our presence had placed her in an awkward situation. She was already uneasy about my being seen there.

'Can you give us some milk?' I muttered as she put the food box in a bag.

With a nod, Hannah told me to help myself. Just then, Adam came into the kitchen. He looked surprised to see us, and glanced back towards the front room.

'We're just leaving,' I said.

With a warning frown, Adam stepped sideways, blocking the way back to the café.

'We'll go out this way,' I said, opening the back door. 'Come on, Mum, I'm starving. Poppy's going to be pleased to see us back so soon.'

My mother glanced irritably from me to Hannah and Adam and back again, before following me out across the yard and back along the High Street. As we passed the front of the café, I lowered my head. Out of the corner of my eye, I saw why Hannah had been so keen to hurry me out of the café. Virginia Strang was seated near the window, looking around. Through the glass, I caught a glimpse of a fierce gleam in her eyes as I scurried past.

# 19

'SLOW DOWN,' MY MOTHER complained. 'I can't keep up with you. What's the mad hurry? Really, Emily, I sometimes wonder what on earth goes through your head.'

She was still grumbling when someone yelled my name. I tensed, recognising the voice. Taking hold of my mother's arm, I tried to hurry her away down the High Street.

'Go on, run away, like the coward you are, but you can't run forever! I'll see you go down for what you did, bitch!'

There was more along those lines, but I was too mortified to listen closely. As though in a daze, I was aware only that Virginia Strang was yelling at me in the street, and my mother was beside me, listening to the abuse being hurled at me. Suddenly, my mother halted, resisting my efforts to propel her forwards.

'Is that woman shouting at you?' she asked in surprise. 'Well, I knew there was something going on.'

'She's just some drunk,' I replied. 'It's nothing to do with us. Don't take any notice of her.'

'You'll burn in hell, Emily Wilson!' Virginia continued, sounding increasingly hysterical. 'The police will track you down and lock you up for the rest of your miserable life. And if they don't get you, I will! You won't get away with it!'

'Just ignore her, mum,' I pleaded. 'She's drunk, or drugged up to the eyeballs. You can hear she's unhinged. Let's get away from here before she decides to come after us.'

My mother's eyes widened in astonishment. To my dismay, instead of walking away she spun round to face Virginia.

'Go home, you foul-mouthed harridan,' she shouted. 'If you don't stop screaming at my daughter, right now, I'm calling the police. This is completely unacceptable,' she added, turning to me. 'It's certainly not what I expected to hear on the streets of Ashton Mead. Who *is* that cow?'

By now, Adam had emerged from the café and was standing in front of Virginia, blocking her way. The sun had come out, and a group of customers had abandoned their tea and cakes and spilled out onto the pavement to watch the fracas. Hannah was talking animatedly to the onlookers while Adam remonstrated with Virginia. We couldn't hear what he was saying but he was gesticulating and it was clear he was trying to calm her down. A few other shopkeepers had come out to see what was going on. The large-framed butcher was standing beside his assistant, who was rubbing his hands eagerly, and behind them the local hairdresser was watching with interest. Next to her, a woman in rollers was peering round to see past the butcher.

'Come on,' I urged my mother. 'Let's get away from here.'

As we hurried away, a police car came speeding past us down the High Street and screeched to a halt in front of the café. Glancing round I saw two uniformed figures jump out. One of them was Barry. Then we turned the corner and saw no more of the scene unfolding outside the café.

'Well,' my mother said, stopping to catch her breath, 'I think it's high time you told me exactly what's going on.' She frowned at me and I saw that beneath her make-up she looked pale. 'As for running around like this on such a hot day, I think we must be as crazy as that woman who was yelling at you. At least she had the excuse that she was drunk, although that's hardly acceptable at this time of day. I hope she apologises to you once she sobers up, although I dare say she won't remember anything about it.'

I nodded miserably. 'Let's get home and make a pot of tea, and I'll tell you what that was all about.'

There was very little shade to protect us from the early summer sun which beat down on us as we made our way back to Mill Lane. We walked in silence, my mother breathing heavily beside me.

'I haven't run like that in years,' she muttered when she had recovered her breath.

I wasn't sure if she was complaining, or admitting she didn't exercise enough.

Poppy was really happy to see us. We made a fuss of her, and took her out in the back garden while the tea was brewing. By the time we sat down to eat our club sandwiches at the kitchen table, I had worked out how much to tell my mother, who insisted that she be told everything about the madwoman and her appalling abuse.

First of all, I thanked my mother for defending me. She shrugged off my gratitude.

'You're my daughter,' she replied. 'Of course, I want to protect you. Whatever you've done,' she added pointedly.

'I haven't done anything.'

'You must have done something to set that woman off, even if she was drunk.'

'She wasn't drunk,' I replied. 'She's a maniac.'

Putting down my sandwich, I told her about Silas, and how he had been murdered just hours after I had rowed with him in public. His death so soon after our encounter had been an unfortunate coincidence, leading some people to suspect me of being implicated in the murder.

'So, that crazy woman is accusing you of murder?'

I nodded. 'All I did was argue with him, and it wasn't my fault. But he was her son, and she's desperate to find someone to blame.'

Whatever I did, I never seemed to satisfy my mother's expectations. But this time, she was the one who confounded *my* expectations. Having criticised me for leaving London, rejecting an offer of marriage from my narcissistic ex-boyfriend, and working as a waitress which she regarded as unworthy of my education and natural abilities, she took Virginia Strang's animosity in her stride.

'None of this was my fault,' I assured her.

'What did you argue about with the man who was murdered?' she asked, tucking into an egg and cress sandwich.

'He threatened to hit Poppy with a walking stick.'

Poppy growled softly, as though she understood what we were talking about.

'Well, he sounds like a nasty piece of work,' my mother said, reaching down to stroke Poppy's head. 'As if anyone in their right mind would want to hurt you. That's appalling.'

'He is appalling. That is, he was. But I had nothing to do with his murder.'

'Well, of course, you didn't,' she replied, feeding Poppy a morsel of egg. 'No one in their right mind would think you killed a man just for being mean to your dog, even if he did deserve it. He must have upset a lot of people, if he was capable of being cruel to a dumb animal like Poppy.'

Poppy looked at my mother reproachfully, as though she was offended at being called dumb. But I felt a wave of gratitude for my mother's support. Having resolved to say nothing about the covert investigation my friends and I were conducting, I hastened to reassure her.

'The police will get to the bottom of this,' I said, forcing myself to sound confident. 'We just have to be patient. There's nothing to worry about really, and I didn't want you finding out about all this nonsense in case it upset you.'

My mother grunted. 'So, now you expect me to thank *you* for wanting to protect *me*? If you ask me,' she went on, looking thoughtful, 'that lunatic who screamed at you in the street committed the murder. Talk about unhinged! I wouldn't put anything past her.'

'She's his mother.'

'That doesn't mean she's not guilty. I've sometimes been tempted to do away with you, and I'm your mother.'

Poppy watched her closely as she took a bite of her sandwich.

'Thanks, mum,' I smiled.

She might be disappointed in me but, reckless of the risk to herself, my mother had faced up to a maniac to defend me. What was more, she had done so without any hesitation, before she even knew what was going on.

'Have a scone,' I said.

She smiled at me and reached for the little pot of cream Hannah had packed for us. 'I suppose living in Ashton Mead has some good points,' she said. 'These are without doubt the best scones I've ever tasted. You should ask Hannah for the recipe.'

Content to bask in my mother's unaccustomed approval, I didn't let on that I had been trying to bake scones as good as Hannah's for two years, so far without success.

# 20

ON SATURDAY AFTERNOON, AFTER the embarrassing scene in the High Street, we headed out of the village, keeping close to the river so we would be able to find our way back easily. I regretted not having done that when my mother first arrived, but it had been nearly lunchtime and she had been hungry. We followed the river for over an hour, gossiping about the family. It felt good to get out of the village, and I enjoyed chatting with my mother as we took Poppy for a long walk. My mother spoke at great length about my father's bunions, which seemed to occupy an inordinate amount of her time and attention. I wondered if she was transferring her anxiety about a different condition onto his relatively minor issue with his feet, but she assured me he was otherwise fine.

Reaching the next village, we had a late tea in the afternoon sunshine at a pub overlooking the river. Tired after our long walk, Poppy fell asleep under the table. It was relaxing sitting in a pub where no one recognised me and no one talked about Silas Strang. Much as I loved Ashton Mead, I resolved sadly to leave the village more often. Hannah, Adam, Toby and Michelle had arranged to join us at Rosecroft that evening. Toby and Michelle picked up a Chinese meal on their way over from Swindon, and we spent a convivial evening together.

My mother left on Sunday after tea, and although it was a relief no longer having to guard my words, in some ways I was sorry to see her go. That evening, my friends came round to Rosecroft again to share what they had discovered. As usual, Poppy was thrilled to have so many visitors and circulated busily among them. She would have been a perfect hostess had she been bestowing attention on our visitors, rather than demanding it from them. Although I was the reason for our investigation, I alone had nothing to report, having spent the weekend with my mother. I promised to go to the butcher's the following morning and try to speak to Norman Norris. It wouldn't be easy for me to question him without arousing suspicion, since by now everyone in Ashton Mead knew that Virginia had accused me of murdering Silas, but I had to do something to further our enquiries.

Meanwhile, Adam had fared quite well, having engaged Jeff in a long conversation about the merits and disadvantages of a sports car.

'He seems like a nice enough guy, if slightly dodgy,' Adam reported. 'I rather liked him, actually, although I wouldn't buy a car from him.'

'No one's asking you to buy a car from him,' Hannah pointed out, a trifle sharply. 'Now, can we focus on him as a possible suspect?'

Adam frowned. 'I'm not sure we should consider him a suspect.'

'What are you basing that on?' Toby asked. 'Vague

impressions are not necessarily helpful.' As a science teacher, Toby always liked to stick to facts. In this instance he was right to dismiss speculation.

Adam shrugged. 'It's difficult to be certain, but he didn't strike me as a violent man. The police have no record of him getting in fights, or being drunk and disorderly, or anything like that. It just seems a bit random for him to have suddenly stabbed someone.'

'Did you mention Silas?' I asked.

He nodded and we all sat forward. Poppy, noticing our interest, sat up and pricked her ears.

'I asked him outright who he thought had murdered Silas,' Adam said.

Toby whistled.

'I mean, it's a hot topic of conversation in the village, so it didn't exactly come out of the blue,' Adam went on. 'It seemed quite natural to talk about what's going on.'

'And?' I prompted him. 'What did he say?'

'He knows Virginia Strang's convinced you did it. In his opinion you're an unlikely suspect, but he also said that, if the police think you're guilty, he's got no reason to think otherwise. He doesn't know you. When he asked me for my view on the case, I said I had no idea. He didn't really have anything much to say about it, but he seemed perfectly at ease with the subject. He even volunteered that he'd had a run in with Silas himself over an old banger he sold Silas. That's what made me think he's a bit dodgy, because he said once the money had changed hands, there was nothing Silas could do. According to Jeff, Silas was livid, and shouted and swore at him a bit, but that was it. Jeff flatly refused to give him his money back. If Silas was too stupid to have the car properly checked out before he paid for it, that was his hard luck, was what Jeff said. He told me Silas had let greed blind him, because the car appeared to be a bargain. Silas thought he was getting one over on Jeff, getting the car for a knock down price, when in fact it was the other way round. The engine gave up the ghost the day after Silas bought it. Something to do with a botched job on a blown head gasket.'

'Did Jeff know the car was faulty when he sold it?' I asked.

'We didn't get that far but I suspect he must have done. Either way, Jeff refused to give the money back.'

'Caveat emptor,' Toby muttered. 'Let the buyer beware.'

'Jeff said he was satisfied with the deal, and claimed he had made the sale in good faith. He seemed pleased to have got rid of the car.' He frowned. 'I would have thought Silas was more likely to be angry with Jeff than the other way round. So, I can't think of any reason why Jeff would have killed Silas. If anything, it would have been the reverse.'

'Perhaps Silas was angry and attacked Jeff, who ended up killing him in self defence?' I suggested.

But Silas had been stabbed in the back, at some point between midnight and four in the morning, and there were no other injuries on his body to indicate he had been in a fight. Jeff was hardly likely to have been sufficiently angry or frightened to attack Silas from behind, and if they had chanced to meet at night and exchange angry words, Silas was not a man to turn his back and walk away from an argument. We agreed that, while Jeff remained a possible suspect, he was an unlikely one.

Having finished with Jeff, we moved on to consider Norman, who seemed a more likely suspect. There were several indications that he might be guilty. He was powerful enough to have given Silas a fatal stab wound, and they had a long-running feud that could conceivably have come to a head at any time. Although we had no evidence that they had been arguing recently, it was no secret that the two of them used to meet to play poker, or that they had fallen out over money. We didn't know which of them was supposed to owe money to the other. According to local gossip a substantial sum was involved, although the amount had doubtless been exaggerated as the rumour spread.

'I'll see what I can find out from Maud,' Adam said.

Over the weekend I had been preoccupied with my mother, but I now asked Hannah whether she had found the missing knife. She shook her head and said we would postpone our weekly cleaning the following morning, to give us time to search the kitchen again. Finding the missing knife had become a priority.

As far as I was concerned, there were two further suspects. I refrained from mentioning Michelle in front of Toby, but there was still Virginia Strang to consider. Choosing my words with care, I put forward my case, which was largely based on her eagerness to blame me. Hannah dismissed my suggestion, insisting that everyone knew Virginia had idolised her son, and she would never have harmed him. People could become deranged when they were grieving, she argued, and Virginia was unhinged to begin with.

'Exactly. The woman's completely mad. Surely that proves my point?'

Hannah was intransigent. 'I don't believe she would have killed her son.'

Adam agreed with her.

'Why is she so desperate to blame me then?' I demanded. 'It must be because she's trying to cover something up. That has to mean she's guilty, or she's protecting someone else. Either way, she knows who killed Silas.'

'Perhaps she genuinely believes you're guilty,' Hannah suggested softly.

'But why would she think that? Why pick on me?'

'Someone must have done it, and she's desperate to blame someone,' Toby said.

That was hardly the answer I wanted to hear, but it made a kind of sense.

'The woman's lost her son,' Hannah said.

'So, you think we ought to make allowances for her, and let her go around telling everyone I murdered Silas?' I asked angrily.

My three friends looked uncomfortable. For a moment no one spoke. At last Hannah pointed out that we couldn't control what Virginia said, but I shouldn't take it to heart. No one would believe her wild ranting.

'That doesn't help,' I grumbled. 'I should sue her for slander.'

But I knew Hannah was right. There was no way we could silence Virginia. My only hope of clearing my name was if we found Silas's killer.

# 21

AFTER DROPPING POPPY OFF at Jane's house the next morning, I went to the café and found Hannah busy emptying cutlery drawers onto the worktop in the kitchen. There was still no sign of the missing knife. Leaving her to continue searching for it, I went next door to look for Norman Norris, the butcher who was on our list of suspects. It was imperative I speak to him discreetly, without arousing suspicion. Luck was on my side, because his assistant, Billy, was talking to a customer. From what I could make out, they were engrossed in discussing the virtues of mutton as opposed to beef, taking into account the relative cost and how the meat was to be cooked. This was my opportunity to speak to Norman, but I hung back and pretended to study the display on the counter.

The overhead light gleamed on the butcher's bald head, and his brawny arms and huge shoulders reminded me that he had the strength to fell Silas with one blow, even though he must have been in his sixties. Summoning up my courage, I approached him.

'I was wondering,' I began in a nervous squeak. I cleared my throat and started again, and this time managed to keep my voice under control. 'I was wondering whether you had any leftovers that no one wants, that might be suitable for a small dog?'

Behind me, I heard a woman's voice murmur that I was a scrounger as well as a murderer. I ignored her. We had never met, and she didn't know anything about me.

'Leftovers?' Norman repeated in ringing tones that would have found him employment as a town crier in olden days. 'For your dog?'

Overwhelmed by the impossibility of quizzing him discreetly about his alibi for the night of the murder, I nodded dumbly.

'Wait there,' Norman said. 'I might just have something for that dog of yours, poor little blighter.'

Behind me I heard the woman muttering about my being unfit to keep a dog. She made her purchase, plumping for mutton, but lingered, no doubt eager for a snippet of gossip that she could pass on to Maud.

'You'll never guess who I saw in the butcher's,' I imagined her saying. 'She was in there, bold as brass, begging for scraps for that dog of hers.'

'Talk about a cheapskate,' Maud would respond. 'I sell perfectly good tins of dog food.'

As I was speculating, Norman returned with a bag containing a bone which he passed to me across the counter. Thanking him, I turned to leave. Seeing that I had finished, the other customer scurried out of the shop and hurried towards Maud's Village Emporium. It was tempting to follow her and eavesdrop, but Hannah was busy ransacking the café for her missing knife and I needed to get back to help her. Just at that moment, Billy went out to the back room, leaving me alone with Norman. Without stopping to think, I seized my opportunity.

'You've heard about Silas Strang?' I ventured.

Norman's grey eyebrows shot up and his florid cheeks darkened.

'I didn't know him,' I ploughed on, 'but I gather he fell out with a lot of people. Still, it was a terrible thing that happened to him.'

Norman grunted. 'It was a terrible thing to happen to anyone,' he agreed, staring at me with glittering eyes. 'The sooner the police catch his killer and lock them up, the better.'

'That's what I think,' I agreed, hoping my sincerity would be obvious. 'Like I said, I didn't know him, but anyone could see he was no pushover. If you ask me, it must have been a man who attacked him, because I don't think a woman would have the strength to kill a powerful man like Silas just with a knife.'

'That depends on the sharpness of the blade,' the butcher replied. 'My cleaver here could slice a man in two without any effort.'

To demonstrate, he picked up a shiny knife and slashed right through a side of beef with one blow. The blade hit the metal tray with a loud crack that made me start, and the butcher grinned. His display of brute force shocked me; it seemed he was warning me to leave him alone.

'Razor sharp, see?' he said, holding the implement up. 'It's necessary in my line of work. Saves me a lot of effort. A bad workman blames his tools and so on. But the right tools make all the difference.'

I nodded. Taking a deep breath, I pressed on. 'You knew Silas, didn't you?'

He grunted. 'Feckless bastard,' he replied. 'It's no secret he owed me money. He liked his game of poker, did Strang, even though he was completely useless.' He grinned mirthlessly. 'It was like taking money off a child. Some people never learn. The more he lost, the more he wanted to play. He was convinced he could win it back. He was an imbecile. Oh well, it's my bad luck because he's never going to hand over what he owes me now.'

'Won't his mother pay his debts?' It was a halfhearted suggestion.

Norman scoffed at the idea. 'The minute I heard what happened, I said to Maud, that's that then. He's gone, and my money's gone with him. Bastard.'

Billy came back and Norman turned to speak to him. There wasn't anything more I could say, so I muttered my thanks again and left, clutching the bag he had given me. On my way back to the tea shop, I thought about my visit to the butcher's, and the more I thought about what Norman had said, the more uneasy I felt, because something didn't add up. He hadn't seemed at all uncomfortable speaking to me about the recent murder in the village. If he was deliberately using me as a scapegoat for a terrible crime he had committed, surely he would have seemed rattled when I raised the subject. In any case, if he was guilty he would hardly have been so ready to admit there had been bad feelings between himself and Silas. He had also made the point that he had lost any hopes of Silas paying his debt. Not only had he gained nothing, he was actually out of pocket as a result of Silas's death. Our list of likely suspects was shrinking.

Returning to the tea shop, I found Hannah in the kitchen. Normally she was tidy and ruthlessly organised, even when she was in the throes of baking and the table was covered in flour. In my absence, she had emptied all the kitchen drawers and cupboards, and oven trays filled with cutlery were precariously piled up on every available surface. And she still hadn't found the missing knife. Ignoring the chaos, we went and sat in the front room where I related my encounter with the butcher.

'So, he's actually worse off now that Silas is dead, because he's never going to get his money back,' I concluded.

'He's worse off financially,' Hannah pointed out. 'He might not have thought of that when he killed Silas. He could have stabbed him in the back in the heat of the moment, overcome by rage.'

'If he acted without any planning, wouldn't he feel awkward talking about the murder? I mean, he didn't hold back telling me there was bad blood between him and Silas, and he was quite happy to demonstrate how easily he could slash through a lump of meat.' I shuddered at the memory. A thought occurred to me. 'The knife that's gone missing from the kitchen here, that wouldn't have been very sharp, would it?'

Hannah frowned and admitted the knives had all been sharpened only a few days before the murder took place. I grunted, remembering she had mentioned it to me at the time. It was not unusual for a few itinerant craftsmen to turn up in Ashton Mead around the time of the May Day festivities, and one of them had called at the café offering to sharpen our knives.

'Who else knew about that?' I asked her.

'Only you and me,' she mumbled. 'But I suppose anyone could have seen the knife sharpener going in and out of the café.'

We gazed at each other. It would be easy enough to conceal a stolen knife among other knives, and the butcher was next door. Everything now pointed to him once again, but we had no way of proving our suspicions.

# 22

WHEN I RETURNED HOME after work, Poppy was reluctant to enter the house, although she had trotted back to Mill Lane quite happily. Instead of following me to the door – or leading me there, as she normally did – she hung back, whimpering. For a moment I thought there might be an intruder inside and faltered, but it seemed that she wanted to drag me sideways across my narrow area of grass towards the strip of a flowerbed at the edge of my property. I let her lead me and she went straight to a patch of earth that looked as though it had been recently turned over.

'Oh, Poppy, what have you been burying now?' I asked her.

Poppy sat back on her haunches and looked at me askance, seeming to invite me to unearth her buried treasure. As a rule she guarded her hidden treasures jealously. Intrigued, I scuffed at the soil with my toe and let out a faint gasp, hardly able to believe what had been buried there. As soon as Poppy and I were safely back indoors, I called Hannah and Adam who came round straightaway. Leading my friends into the living room, I carefully unwrapped the earth encrusted knife which had been buried just below the topsoil in my front garden. It lay on the sofa in front of us, on the towel that I had used to pick it up. We stared at it in horror.

Adam was first to recover his wits. 'Is that your missing knife?' he asked.

Hannah nodded slowly. 'It looks like it,' she whispered.

'We have to hand it to the police,' Adam said, with a worried frown.

'No,' Hannah replied. 'We can't do that. It might have Emily's fingerprints on it.' She turned to me. 'Have you used this knife recently?'

I stared at it. 'I don't know,' I muttered. 'I might have. We both used it all the time. Someone's setting me up. They stole the knife from the café and buried it in my front garden to make it look as though I killed Silas.'

'I wonder if this knife was the actual murder weapon?' Adam said.

I shuddered, gazing at it lying on my sofa. Poppy whimpered.

'I'm never arguing with anyone in public ever again,' I said.

'Give it to me,' Hannah said, suddenly decisive.

'What are you going to do with it?' Adam asked her.

'I'm going to scrub it and put it through the dishwasher and put it away in the drawer where it belongs.'

'You can never clean it completely,' Adam objected.

As we were arguing about what to do with the knife, Poppy barked a warning. A second later we heard a loud knocking, and a man's voice shouted 'Police!' Throwing a frightened glance at my friends, I went to open the front door. Inspector Langdon was standing outside.

'We've received information that a murder weapon has been concealed on your property. We have a warrant to search the premises.' He sounded almost apologetic as he added that they were going to have to dig up my front garden.

By now Hannah and Adam had followed me into the hall. Hearing what the inspector was saying, Hannah began to protest. Adam reminded her sternly that this had nothing to do with either of them, and they should leave and let the police do their job. I did my best to maintain a semblance of composure, but was bitterly disappointed by the way he was distancing himself from me and my plight.

'Do you *have* to make a mess?' I asked the inspector, trying to sound weary rather than terrified. 'I mean, you will put everything back afterwards, won't you? And leave the garden looking tidy?'

The inspector looked grim. 'That depends on what we find. Let's hope for your sake that you're still here to put everything back to rights when we've finished,' he added quietly.

'You say you received information,' I went on. 'What were you told exactly, and by whom?'

The inspector shook his head. 'I can't share our source with you.'

'Do my girlfriend and I have to stay?' Adam asked. 'We just popped in to see Emily, and we would rather like to get home now. We'll stay if you think there's any point in our hanging around, but we do have plans.'

'Yes, you can go,' the inspector replied. 'You'd only get in the way here.'

As the inspector stepped aside to let my friends pass, Poppy darted outside with a dog chew between her teeth. I chased after her with the inspector following close behind me, as though he was afraid I might try to run off. Poppy dashed over to the flowerbed and began digging a hole where the knife had been hidden, so she could bury her chew there.

'We noticed the earth had been recently dug over just there,' one of the search team told the inspector. 'That was one of the spots we earmarked to take a look at.' He shrugged. 'I guess we don't need to look there now.'

'Check everywhere,' the inspector said.

'I'm not sure what you expect to find there, other than a lost dog toy,' I said, adding untruthfully, 'it's one of my dog's favourite places to dig. I've no idea why. I'm trying to train her to restrict her digging to the back garden, where no one can see the mess she makes.'

If the detective realised that I wouldn't leave Poppy alone in the front garden in case she ran off, he would suspect she never had an opportunity to dig there. Afraid that I was talking too much, I called her. For once, Poppy obediently abandoned her digging and trotted over to me. Leaving the police to search the front garden, we went inside and I shut the door. Trembling, I went into the living room. The knife and its muddy towel covering had vanished. Hannah and Adam had managed to smuggle them out. Breathing a sigh of relief, I settled down to wait for the police to finish. They had a job to do, but it felt to me like a disturbing intrusion of my privacy. At last the inspector knocked on the door to tell me they had finished outside and to ask if they could take a look around the house.

'We can come back with a search warrant,' he added, seeing me hesitate.

It seemed best to let them in. After all, I no longer had anything to hide. With a fleeting panic I pictured the stolen knife, wrapped in a muddy towel, lying on the sofa, in full view of anyone who entered the room. I remembered Adam asking if they could go home, and how I had thought my friends were abandoning me. Now I appreciated the risk they had taken to protect me. Eventually, the police left. The inspector merely nodded at me when he informed me they were leaving. He didn't even have the grace to thank me for my cooperation. As they were trooping out of the house, I overheard one of the search team complain about wasting their time, as though it was my fault they hadn't found what they were looking for. In a way, it was. Before the inspector strode away, I made one last half-hearted attempt to discover who had sent him to search my garden.

'Isn't it odd?' I suggested clumsily. 'Someone's very keen to point suspicion at me, for no good reason. Don't you think they might be trying to divert your attention away from someone else? Whoever sent you here must know more than they're letting on.'

I couldn't disclose that someone had buried a stolen knife – quite possibly a murder weapon – in my garden. The inspector didn't reply. Shutting the front door behind him, I turned to sort out the mess they had left behind. Starting in the kitchen, I began stacking my pots and pans and cutlery in the dishwasher. It probably wasn't necessary to clean everything, as the search team had worn plastic gloves, but everything felt contaminated. My anger at the invasion of my privacy was soon overwhelmed by relief at my narrow escape. If the police hadn't witnessed Poppy digging up my flowerbed, a forensic examination of the soil might have revealed all kinds of suspicious evidence, proving that my dog was not the only one to have turned the earth over in that particular spot. In all the upheaval and alarm of the search, it only now struck me that Poppy had never before shown any interest in that flowerbed. It was almost as though she had understood what was happening, and had appreciated that my liberty was under threat.

Once the dishwasher was full, I sat down for a moment to scratch her neck.

'You know you saved my bacon this evening,' I told her.

At the mention of bacon she pricked up her ears and looked at me hopefully. There was no bacon in the house right then and, in any case, it was too salty to be good for her. Instead, I found a tin of her favourite dog food and she wolfed it down while I finished tidying the kitchen before making myself something to eat. It had been a long and stressful day. There was no longer any doubt that someone was trying to frame me for murder, but I didn't know who it was. With the help of my friends, I had succeeded in thwarting them for now. Next time I might not be so lucky.

# 23

THAT NIGHT I LAY awake, mulling over everything that had happened. While wondering how Hannah and Adam had taken the knife without the police noticing, it occurred to me that someone else must have known Hannah's knife had been sharpened. With a number of unanswered questions whirling around in my head, it took me a long time to fall asleep. I was woken the next morning by Poppy barking at me to get up. Feeling groggy, I stumbled out of bed. My heart raced as we stepped outside, but nothing had been disturbed, and there was no graffiti on the wall. Not only that, but my garden looked a lot tidier than it had done for a while, as the police had taken the trouble to replace all my plants neatly after their search.

As soon as we had a quiet moment in the café, I asked Hannah about the knife sharpener, and learned that he was a stranger.

'I didn't take much notice of him, to be honest,' she added. 'It's not unusual for a small rabble of tinkers and peddlers and so on to turn up around the time of the May Day Fair. Hangers on, you know? So when he came to the café, I didn't really think about it. The knives needed sharpening and he was there with his gear, offering to do it.'

Frustrated, I urged her to try and remember as much as she could about the knife sharpener.

'Yes, well, it was a man, and he looked a bit disreputable. I mean, I wasn't sure whether to invite him in. In the end I opened the gate to the yard and took the kitchen knives out to him, so he never actually came inside. He didn't seem to mind,' she added, a little defensively. 'It was a nice day. He probably preferred being outside. But I didn't stop to chat. I never asked his name, or where he was from, or anything like that. I just gave him the knives and he knocked on the back door when he'd finished and asked for his money and left. I locked the gate behind him and that was it.'

'What happened when you paid him?' I asked, not really expecting to hear he had given her a receipt.

'He asked for cash and it was so cheap, I just paid him without a second thought. I could see he'd done a good job.' Hannah looked puzzled. 'I can see you think this is important, but I'm not sure what you're getting at.'

'It just seems a bit of a coincidence, that's all. A stranger turns up out of the blue to sharpen a knife which is then used to kill someone.'

'We don't know the knife that's gone missing from the tea shop is the one that was used to stab Silas,' Hannah protested. 'If you're trying to make something out of this, I really think you're on the wrong tack. Just because we've mislaid a knife, that's no reason to go jumping to conclusions and linking it to the murder. Anyway, there's nothing strange about random tradesmen coming to the village when the fair's on. We've had knives sharpened before. It's just a coincidence that it happened when it did.'

'But what if it isn't a coincidence? What if the knife sharpener was deliberately approached by the killer, and paid to come here and sharpen all your knives? Someone might have wanted to make sure our long knife was razor sharp, so it would be effective as a murder weapon, and suspicion would fall on one of us.'

We agreed we needed to trace the knife sharpener and ask him whether anyone had sent him to the café. We could only hope that someone more businesslike than Hannah had requested a receipt. Leaving me to look after the tea shop, Hannah scurried off to ask the other retailers along the High Street if they had any information that might help us trace the knife sharpener. After about half an hour she came hurrying back, breathless, and led me into the kitchen where she told me no one else had seen a knife sharpener recently. She had even drawn a blank with the butcher and the hairdresser, who would have been obvious prospects for a knife sharpener. If the police had found the knife buried in my garden, they would easily have been able to tell that it had been recently sharpened. If they had also detected traces of Silas's blood on the blade, the evidence would have appeared conclusive. I shuddered to think what might have happened if Poppy hadn't found the knife. I could think of only one person who might target me in this manner to draw attention away from themselves but, yet again, we had no proof.

'You don't know Virginia Strang's responsible,' Hannah said, when I shared my suspicions with her.

'It could be her, or it could be someone else,' I agreed. 'But whoever is behind it, I have to expose them before they fabricate any more evidence against me.'

With my name on the police list of suspects in a murder enquiry, Barry was understandably reluctant to speak to me at The Plough, so Hannah invited us all to meet at her house that evening. A light rain had been falling steadily for over an hour when Poppy and I left Rosecroft. She disliked going out in the rain and I ended up carrying her most of the way to Hannah's house, tucked inside my jacket. It was still raining half an hour later when Toby joined us, eager to hear our news. He draped his coat over a chair and patted his wet hair before settling down in an armchair to stroke Poppy. Shortly after Toby arrived, Barry slipped in, wearing a dark hoodie.

To my relief, without anyone mentioning her name, Toby seemed happy to exclude Michelle from our discussions about the murder. He was probably trying to avoid her discovering that one of his friends was involved in sinister goings-on, and was hysterically paranoid. Whatever the reason for his decision, Toby seemed keen to keep Michelle away from me. Realising I found it easier to speak to my friends without a stranger present, I wondered if I was turning into a stereotypical villager, wary of anyone who might be regarded as an 'outsider'. It wasn't long since I myself had been treated with distrust by the established residents of the village. Some, like Tess, still seemed to resent my coming to live in Ashton Mead. Admittedly Tess had banned Virginia Strang from the pub for haranguing me so publicly, but she might have done that to keep the peace, rather than to protect me. After we had all greeted one another, and Barry had petted Poppy, we addressed the subject that had brought us together on that wet evening.

Barry shook his head when we asked him to update us on the police enquiry. 'I've no idea what's going on,' he admitted miserably. 'No one will tell me anything. It's very frustrating. All I know is the DI's furious, and the investigating team has gone all cloak and dagger on us. No one else is supposed to know anything, so I'm not sure I'm going to be much help to you any more.'

Quickly I told him and Toby about the sharpened bread knife that had been buried in my garden, and how Poppy had fortunately discovered it before the police turned up.

'Someone must have arranged to have Hannah's knife sharpened before they stole it and hid it in my garden, and then told the police where it was,' I concluded.

'If it turns out to be the murder weapon –' Hannah began and broke off, too upset to complete her sentence.

Toby whistled. 'If it wasn't for Poppy –' He frowned. 'It doesn't bear thinking about.'

'Can't you find out who gave that information to the police?' I asked Barry. 'Whoever it was, they must have deliberately set out to incriminate me by burying the knife in my garden, and contacting the police to tip them off about where to find it. You need to discover the identity of that informant. If he or she didn't murder Silas, they must know who did.'

Barry looked thoughtful. 'Not necessarily,' he said.

'Why else would someone be so keen to frame me, if they're not trying to protect the actual killer?'

'Perhaps they're convinced you murdered Silas, and they think police are dragging their heels over making an arrest,' Toby suggested.

'Exactly,' Barry said.

'Is there any way you can find out who called the police station and gave them that information?' I asked.

'Virginia has been to Swindon nearly every day, badgering the desk sergeants,' Barry said. 'They keep telling her we can't proceed against you without any evidence, but she refuses to listen. She's fixated on seeing you behind bars which, according to her, would be justice for her dead son.'

'What happened to innocent until proven guilty?' Adam protested indignantly, and Hannah murmured in agreement.

I stared at Barry, willing him to answer my next question. 'Was it Virginia who told the police about the knife hidden in my garden?'

Barry shook his head mournfully, and repeated that he didn't know. He promised that he would try to find out, and then he slunk away, his face concealed in the shadows beneath his hood. Hannah, Adam, Toby and I stared at each other in dismay. I had escaped being arrested for murder, for the time being at any rate, but we were no further ahead in our investigation.

'You need to be careful,' Toby warned me.

Hannah nodded. 'Someone's out to get you.'

'Well, they haven't succeeded yet,' I replied, with fake cheerfulness. 'Thanks to Poppy,' I added.

Hearing her name, Poppy jumped up and came over to nuzzle my legs, and I leaned down to pet her.

'That's all very well,' Adam said, 'but you can't rely on a dog to save you from a vindictive and cunning human adversary.'

Poppy turned to him and let out an indignant bark, and we all laughed.

'Even a dog as clever as Poppy, who seems to understand every word we say,' Adam added.

'Seems, Adam, nay it is,' I murmured to myself and Poppy wagged her tail.

'So, what next?' Toby asked.

Once again we stared at each other, at a loss how to answer that question. Only Poppy seemed perfectly content. She rolled onto her back and lay with her little legs in the air, waiting to be petted. Even with all my troubles, it was hard not to smile as she growled with happiness when Toby reached down to rub her belly.

# 24

IT WAS NEARING THE middle of May, and summer had arrived early that year. One evening I spent an hour storing my thick winter jumpers and fleeces on the top shelf of my wardrobe, along with the thick blanket that had lain on top of my duvet all winter. After that, I fiddled about with the thermostat, turning my heating down. With the milder weather, the tea shop was increasingly busy with people stopping off in the village. All of them were on their way to other destinations, because no one ever stayed long in Ashton Mead. The pub had a couple of rooms for travellers passing through, and there were one or two holiday cottages on the other side of the river, but in general none but local residents stayed in the village overnight. With the brisk uptick in trade, Hannah was glad to have me back at work, although she still asked me to remain out of sight in the kitchen. Only when we were too busy for her to keep up with the demand did she forget, and send me out to serve customers.

We kept a couple of old garden chairs outside in the backyard, under a brown awning which was nothing like as smart – or as clean – as the brightly striped yellow and

159

white awning at the front of the tea shop. Although it was faded, the cover in the back afforded the chairs – and Poppy – some shelter from the wind and rain. When it was stormy, the chairs would be blown over, and were sometimes sent hurtling across the yard, so their legs had become slightly wonky from the battering they received. On wet days when Poppy wasn't with Jane, she was allowed to stay in a corner of the kitchen beside the door, out of sight of customers. She seemed to understand that she was only permitted to stay indoors if she kept still and quiet, and she caused us no trouble. But as long as the weather was dry and there were no gales blowing, she preferred to be left outside, pottering around in the yard.

When the café wasn't busy, I escaped from the heat of the kitchen and sat in the yard, waiting for Hannah to summon me back to work. One sunny afternoon I was sitting on a wobbly chair out there, by myself, kicking my heels, when Hannah called out that someone was asking for me in the café. Warily, I stood up to find out who it was. Steeling myself to hear that the police had come to arrest me, for a panicky instant I considered running out through the back gate. The bus stop wasn't far away, but my bag was in the kitchen and I didn't have the money for a bus fare on me, let alone the means of survival on the run, even for a day. Besides, if I became a fugitive, I might never see Poppy again. As these frantic thoughts were whirling through my mind, Hannah poked her head out and told me that two old ladies were asking for me. She added that they looked vaguely familiar, but she didn't know who they were.

'That is, I *think* I've seen them before,' she concluded, with a bemused frown, 'but I couldn't say for sure.'

Peering round the edge of the kitchen door, I recognised the old women. They had both scraped their curly white hair into small buns at the nape of their necks, and despite their uneasy expressions, their blue eyes twinkled as they gazed around the tea shop, seemingly delighted by the cheery décor.

'Do you know who they are?' Hannah whispered.

I nodded. Nearly two years had passed since I had last seen these elderly sisters. Close friends of my Great Aunt Lorna, when she died they had looked after Poppy until I arrived in Ashton Mead. We had parted on bad terms, after my ex-boyfriend had attempted to blackmail them for a crime they hadn't committed. I had no intention of confessing that embarrassing faux pas to Hannah, and wondered why the sisters would want to see me again, after what had happened. It could only be because they wanted to be reassured that Poppy was all right. There were no other customers in the front of the café, so I went through to greet them.

'Are you still with that boyfriend of yours?' Denise demanded sharply as I approached their table.

She looked as frail as her older sister, but while Catherine was meek, Denise was forthright and could be quite ferocious, for all that she was tiny. Catherine sat hunched over, staring down at her lap, as I explained that Ben had left Ashton Mead shortly after they met him.

'Oh dear, I hope it wasn't anything we said,' Catherine murmured, looking stricken.

'I hope it was,' Denise retorted.

'But poor Emily,' Catherine said.

'Don't be ridiculous,' Denise snapped. 'Honestly, Catherine, I do wonder about you sometimes. That young man had trouble written all over his pretty face.' She snorted. 'If you ask me, Emily's had a lucky escape.'

'It's quite alright,' I hastened to reassure them. 'It was my decision to split up with him.' I explained that we had fallen out because he had wanted to sell Poppy, and it suited me perfectly, because he was now out of my life. 'I'm glad I finally saw him for what he was, a parasite, and a narcissist. That's why I threw him out.' I smiled. 'And it's not as if I'm on my own anyway.'

'How is Poppy?' Catherine asked eagerly, straightening up and breaking into a smile.

Just then the bell rang as another customer entered the café behind me. At once, Hannah darted out of the kitchen and hissed at me to go out into the yard.

'We're talking to Emily,' Denise protested.

'Follow me if you want to talk to her,' Hannah urged them, and she ushered them through the kitchen and out into the yard behind me.

Denise and Catherine looked bemused by Hannah's insistence on our going outside, via the kitchen. Instead of sitting down on the wobbly chairs in the yard, they decided to stay and enjoy an afternoon tea, before coming along to my cottage to see Poppy. In the meantime, while they were at the café, I went to fetch Poppy from Jane's house. Used to my irregular hours, Jane made no comment when I arrived early to collect her. We hurried home and arrived not long before Denise and Catherine who had clearly rushed their tea in their impatience to see Poppy.

She was ecstatic at seeing her old friends again. They both commented on how healthy she looked, and how much she had grown. They spent nearly half an hour making a fuss of her, and laying out an assortment of treats for her. Finally Poppy settled down with a new chewy toy, and Catherine drew her crocheting out of her bag and started fiddling with it.

'Well,' Denise said, leaning back in her chair and looking at her dainty gold watch, 'we mustn't miss the last bus home. Before we go, perhaps you'd like to tell us what that was all about earlier on?'

Catherine's crochet hook seemed to twitch more rapidly as she listened.

'What do you mean?' I asked, although her meaning was perfectly clear.

'Your manager at the tea shop seemed very keen to whisk you away out of sight when another customer arrived,' Denise said.

Gazing into my interlocutor's shrewd eyes, I could tell there was no point in trying to fob her off with vague excuses. With a sigh, I explained that her impression was right. Hannah didn't want customers to see me.

'She thinks it might put people off coming to the tea shop. Local people, that is,' I added wretchedly.

'But why?' Denise persisted.

Catherine looked up from her crocheting and watched me with a worried expression.

'I'm – I'm not very popular in the village.'

Denise made a spitting sound. Catherine's fingers stopped moving.

'I know a lot of people distrust newcomers, but you're

Lorna's great niece. You're hardly a stranger,' Denise protested.

Catherine had been watching me closely. 'What's happened? Tell us. We can't stand by and do nothing if Lorna's great niece is being mistreated,' she added fiercely. 'She would turn in her grave if she thought we had failed to help you if you're ever in trouble.'

It was farcical that two such frail old ladies were poised to spring to my defence, but I appreciated their support and thanked them.

'Well?' Denise followed up her sister's question. 'What's going on?'

I heaved a deep sigh and Poppy looked up from her chewing and whimpered. 'They think – that is, some people think –' I hesitated.

'Yes?' Denise prompted me. 'What do some people think?'

'Some of the villagers think I murdered someone,' I blurted out.

The two old ladies looked startled. Then Denise burst out laughing, while Catherine dropped her crochet. Poppy darted across the room and seized it between her teeth. It took me a few minutes to coax her into dropping it. I returned it to its owner, slightly damp, and Catherine waved my apology aside.

'You mustn't miss your bus,' I said as she stuffed it back in her bag while Poppy watched mournfully.

'There's always the taxi,' Denise said briskly. 'Now, suppose you tell us exactly what's been going on?'

The two old ladies settled back in their seats, their gnarled hands folded in their laps, their bright eyes fixed on me, inquisitive and concerned. Catherine's fingers twitched once, but she didn't take her crochet out again. All her attention was focused on me.

# 25

RELUCTANTLY, I TOLD THE two sisters the whole worrying tale. As it turned out, I was pleased to have confided in them, because their support was reassuring, even if they weren't able to offer to help in any practical sense.

'That awful, awful man, Silas Strang,' Catherine said, making a tutting sound with her tongue. 'We heard about him, you know. This is dreadful, just dreadful. I can't believe anyone would believe you had anything to do with him, dead or alive.'

'He was a vexatious person,' Denise chimed in. 'We know all about him. He was very rude to your Great Aunt Lorna. She had taken it upon herself to weed the green – dear Lorna was very public spirited, you know. Anyway, there she was, pulling up weeds, for the benefit of everyone who walks there, when this foul-mouthed oaf accosted her, quite out of the blue, and accused her of taking over common land. What a ridiculous thing to say.'

Catherine took up the tale. 'He seemed to be suggesting she was scheming to stake a claim to that patch of green, to claim it for herself, just because she was doing some weeding. What would Lorna have wanted with a piece of the green? It's nowhere near here.'

'Not even close,' Denise chimed in.

It was only a short walk away, but I let that pass.

'He really was a most unpleasant character, from what we've heard.'

'He certainly was a vile man,' I agreed. 'But I never assaulted him.'

'Of course, you didn't,' Catherine crooned, her bright eyes soft with sympathy. 'We know you would never do anything so dreadful. A lovely girl like you.'

'Although no one would blame you if you had,' Denise muttered, scowling. 'That man deserved to be punished. Lorna told us how obnoxious he was.'

'Oh, how could anyone be so horrible to poor Lorna?' Catherine cried out, shaking her head again.

'Or to dear little Poppy?' Denise added.

'He was horrible to everyone,' I assured them. 'Not just my great aunt and Poppy.'

The two sisters nodded their heads, their expressions dark. Anyone who had crossed their friend was wicked in their eyes.

'What else did my great aunt tell you about him?' I asked. 'Can you remember any details about him at all?'

I didn't hold out much hope that they would be able to tell me anything that wasn't already common knowledge. The sisters didn't even live in Ashton Mead, and it was unlikely they had ever met Silas. They had probably only heard his name mentioned by my late great aunt. It was all rather tenuous, and while I was keen to find out as much about him as I could, it seemed impossible that these two kindly old ladies would be able to tell me anything new. So, Catherine's next words surprised me.

'Only that he was disappointed in love,' she said, frowning and shaking her head. 'Lorna told us all about it.'

Denise scoffed as her sister's eyes filled with tears, but I was intrigued and asked her to tell me more. Shaking her head at Catherine, Denise told me that Silas had embarked on a passionate love affair. That amazed me. Silas had never struck me as the romantic type.

'It was years ago,' Denise said. 'The girlfriend was a few years younger than him, according to Lorna.'

'It was his mother who put an end to it,' Catherine added.

Denise nodded. 'They were planning to elope. They had it all worked out. They were going to Gretna Green, Lorna said.'

Catherine giggled.

Denise silenced her sister with a glare, and continued with her story. She told me Silas and his girlfriend were already in his car with their overnight bags when his mother came out of the house, brandishing a carving knife. By the time Silas started the engine, Virginia had slashed his two front tyres. While he was clambering out of the car, fuming, she hacked his back tyres too. His girlfriend ran off wailing as his mother marched him back home, screaming at him that he had betrayed her by plotting with a hussy behind his back. It was a dramatic tale, and very romantic. Some of the details had no doubt been embellished as the tale went from one telling to another, but it was probably based on a kernel of truth. There was no reason why my great aunt would have fabricated such a story.

'What happened after that?' I asked.

Denise shrugged. 'We don't know what passed between Silas and the girl, but that seems to have been the end of the affair.'

'If he'd really loved the girl, he would have run away with her,' Catherine sighed. 'Nothing should stand in the way of true love.'

'My sister is an incorrigible romantic.'

'So, who was the girl?' I asked, intrigued.

The sisters both shook their heads. 'Lorna never told us her name. You could ask Maud,' Denise added. 'She would know.'

'I can't talk to Maud, especially not about Silas. She thinks I murdered him.'

'Of course, she doesn't think you murdered him,' Catherine bleated.

'It's what she's telling everyone.'

'I know these gossipy women,' Denise said sourly. 'They don't believe half of what they say and nor does anyone else. According to your Great Aunt Lorna, this Maud is the worst gossip you could ever wish to meet. She spreads all kinds of stories just to make herself sound interesting. People like her are a menace. They use other people's misery to attract attention to themselves.'

'That's not quite the whole story,' Catherine corrected her. 'At least not according to Lorna. She told us Maud confided in her that gossip is good for business. Everyone loves to hear about a scandal, and Maud exploits her customers' curiosity. She said a lot of locals go to the grocery shop just to hear the latest rumours. Keeping abreast of all the local news is Maud's way of attracting customers.'

I thought about all the stories I'd heard from Maud. She couldn't possibly believe half of the rumours she spread, but that hadn't seemed to matter much, until now. On the contrary, I had often been happily entertained by her tittle-tattle. Only now that I had become the victim of her gossip had I come to realise that there was a cruel aspect to it.

At last, Denise and Catherine left, promising to return to see Poppy again soon. Rosecroft felt empty when they had gone, and I decided to accept an invitation to go and see Hannah. With Poppy pausing to sniff at every patch of grass and weeds, and lifting her leg at frequent intervals to water the ground, we made slow progress. I was in no hurry, having decided I would accept Adam's offer to walk me home this time. It was still daylight when I arrived, but I was dismayed to find Hannah alone. I would have to make my way home by myself. When I told Hannah that I wouldn't be able to stay for long, she looked surprised.

'You've only just got here,' she said.

Although we saw one another almost every day at work, she added that we rarely had a chance to chat undisturbed, just the two of us, and admitted that she had taken the opportunity to invite me over while Adam was spending the evening with his father. She was so keen for me to stay that I just smiled and said nothing about being followed after my last visit to her house. I had probably imagined my mysterious stalker anyway. There was no reason for me to rush home early and ruin the evening. After petting Poppy, Hannah opened a bottle of wine and brought out a fruit cake that was still warm, and we settled down to have a natter. Over a glass of wine, I told Hannah that Catherine and Denise had suggested Maud knew more about Silas than she had let on, and it might be a good idea for Adam to pump her for information again.

'Why not ask her yourself?' Hannah said. 'I know Adam wants to help you, but is it really necessary to drag him into this?'

I didn't blame Hannah for wanting to protect Adam, and wondered if she knew he was doing the same for her. Their concern for each other was touching, but also a little annoying, because I desperately wanted them to pursue our investigation with unflagging dedication.

'I'm going to be honest,' Hannah went on, refusing to meet my gaze. 'The fact is, I'm not very happy with the current situation. I've been discussing it with Adam, but I still don't know what to say to you. I'd really like you to come back to work properly, without having to keep you out of sight, but that's going to be awkward as long as your feud with Virginia continues. You must see that it's getting out of hand.'

For a moment I was too shocked to respond.

'My feud with Virginia?' I spluttered at last. '*She's* the one who's been attacking *me*. I never started anything with her. You can't say this is down to me.'

Hannah reminded me of Virginia's bereavement, and suggested I might be more compassionate.

'Yes, yes, I know all that,' I said. 'I'm perfectly well aware that the poor woman lost her son in the most dreadful way, but that doesn't give her the right to accuse me of having anything to do with his murder.'

With a sigh, Hannah suggested we leave Adam out of it and approach Maud through Barry, and I agreed to call Barry the next day. But it was clear that Hannah was distracted.

'So, how's things with you?' I enquired, wondering what was on her mind.

Lately we had seemed to talk exclusively about my troubles, but my friend admitted that she had problems of her own. At first, she tried to play her worries down, but I persisted and, after pouring us both another glass of wine, she began to explain how she was feeling. When the daylight began to fade, I knew it was time for me to leave, but once my friend started unburdening herself to me, it was difficult to interrupt and say I was going home.

'The trouble is,' Hannah was saying, 'I'm just not sure if he really wants to settle down. We're happy enough together, but I think it might just be that it suits him for now, being near his father.' She paused and took a sip of wine. 'The thing is, if he doesn't want to be with me for the long haul, then I'd rather know now. I mean, of course, there's no guarantee any relationship's going to last, but I just don't know what his plans are.'

'Hasn't he said anything at all? Not even hinted?'

She shook her head. 'We've been living here for nearly a year, and he hasn't said a word.'

'You could ask him?'

She gave a wry smile. 'Believe me, I've tried, but he just brushes aside any mention of the future. I don't want to force the issue and end up pushing him away.'

'It's hardly pushy, wanting to know where you stand. But I know what you mean.'

'I don't suppose you could say something?' she asked.

To my relief, she agreed that could be awkward and, as I was at pains to point out, Adam would suspect the question came from her anyway. I wished there was something I could do to help her, but this was between her and Adam. It wasn't my place to step in like some kind of amateur relationship counsellor. I offered her what reassurance I could, which was basically a few clichés to the effect that everything would work out for the best. At last I took my leave, insisting the wine was making me sleepy and by the time I reached home I'd be ready for bed. Adam still hadn't returned, but in any case he could hardly be expected to accompany me home when he had just walked back from his father's house, right next door to mine.

Doing my best to feel bold, I listened out for footsteps and kept Poppy close, but this time no one appeared out of the darkness to follow me home. I was finally satisfied that I had imagined someone pursuing me after my previous visit to Hannah. It was probably stress that had made me imagine something so frightening. Other than the recent murder, atrocities simply didn't happen in the peaceful village of Ashton Mead. Meanwhile, Poppy sniffed her way back across the bridge to the old part of the village where we lived, and I strode beside her, constantly looking around so no one could creep up on me unawares. Nothing happened and I saw no one else out walking. Nevertheless I was relieved to reach home without encountering any danger on the way.

# 26

Poppy woke me from a deep sleep where I was dreaming about sailing on the open ocean in a worryingly small boat that rocked precariously on high waves. It took me a few moments to wake up fully, only to realise that I was not lying on a rocking vessel but in bed at home, and the roaring of the waves was the sound of Poppy growling repeatedly. Squinting at my phone, I saw that it was ten past four. Groaning, I shut my eyes, and would probably have drifted back to sleep had Poppy not barked again. Drowsily I pulled myself up on one elbow. My love for Poppy had completely overwhelmed me right from the start. Even so, there were moments when her presence seemed more of a liability than a blessing, and this was definitely one of them.

'What is it, Poppy?' I grumbled. 'Just go back to sleep. It's the middle of the night, for goodness sake. You're the only dog in the village who insists on making a racket every time a fox goes past. No one else cares. It's not as if we keep chickens. There are always foxes out there, day and night. Now shut up and let me get some sleep.'

As though she understood exactly what I was saying, Poppy stretched out at my feet, gazing at me mournfully.

About to lie down and try to get back to sleep, I paused and sat up, hearing an unfamiliar scratching sound. My bedroom was at the front of the house, facing the river, and the noise seemed to be coming from directly underneath the window. Listening intently, I heard more scratching and Poppy let out a single bark. Jumping down from the bed, she dashed over to the window. By now fully awake, I scrambled out of bed after her. Pulling open a slit between my curtains, I looked down. There was nothing to be seen in the darkness, but I heard what sounded like the soft thudding of rapidly retreating footsteps, as though someone was running away. Wondering if I had imagined hearing the footsteps, I crawled back into bed, but couldn't get back to sleep.

In the morning, I set off for work feeling tired and grumpy after my disturbed night. Unusually for her, Poppy resisted going for a walk. Where normally she was eager to drag me through the gate, this morning she tugged at her lead to stop me from leaving Rosecroft.

'For goodness sake, Poppy, what is it now?' I demanded crossly. Much as I wanted to be gentle and understanding with her, there were times when she tried my patience. 'Isn't it enough that you woke me up in the night? You know I have to get to work. So come on. We need to get going or I'll be late.'

Poppy let out a curious little yap and pulled me over to the narrow flowerbed under my bedroom window. She darted forwards, and I noticed something dangling from her jaws, gleaming with a metallic lustre. Puzzled, I bent down to retrieve what she had found, and discovered she was holding a watch between her teeth. The watch face was quite large and it had a leather strap, and probably belonged to a man. I was fairly certain it hadn't been there the previous day, which could only mean that a stranger had been hanging around in my front garden during the night. Poppy's barking at four o'clock strengthened my conviction. Feeling increasingly uneasy, I slipped the watch into a dog poo bag to protect it before setting off for work.

For the first hour after the café opened, we were kept busy serving breakfasts, and there was no time to tell Hannah about my night time intruder. At last we had a quiet interlude and sat down together with a pot of tea. But before I could say anything about what I had heard, and Poppy's subsequent discovery, Hannah told me that Adam had lost his watch. For a moment I was too taken aback to speak. Gathering my wits, I realised that this must be a coincidence. All the same, I had to be sure what was going on, and asked what the missing watch looked like. Hannah promptly described the watch Poppy had discovered outside my house, and showed me a photo of Adam wearing his watch. There was no doubt he was wearing the watch Poppy had found in my garden.

'Did Adam stay out late last night?' I asked, doing my best to sound indifferent.

Hannah glanced at me curiously. 'I mean,' I went on hurriedly, 'perhaps he was drinking and didn't notice when his watch fell off?'

'I doubt that very much,' she replied. 'He was out with his father.'

'Oh yes. You told me. I hope they had a good time.'

'I think they had a great time. Richard is so sweet and

he's been very kind to us. It was Adam's mother's birthday yesterday, and Richard finds that difficult, so Adam wanted to take him out, just the two of them.'

'That's nice.'

'They went into Swindon for a meal, but he wasn't home late. Richard insisted on paying for a cab back to the village.'

Before we could continue, a couple of customers came in and the moment passed. I promised to look out for Adam's watch and slipped into the kitchen, leaving Hannah to take the order. The more I thought about what Hannah had told me, the less sense it seemed to make. While Adam had probably accompanied his father home, it was hard to see why he would have dropped his watch outside my house and, in any case, I couldn't imagine Richard would stay out until four in the morning. I needed to find out whether Adam had returned to Mill Lane to snoop around outside my house in the middle of the night.

That evening, I met Hannah and Adam and Toby at the Plough. We had agreed it was time to revert to meeting there. We all felt it would be perfectly safe, as long as we couldn't be overheard discussing our investigation into the murder. Poppy settled down under my chair and fell asleep as I asked Adam how his father was.

'Dad's fine,' he replied, smiling. 'We went out last night.'

I nodded. 'Hannah told me.'

After wracking my brains to think of a subtle way of discovering the information I wanted, I blurted out a direct question.

'Did you go home with your dad after you got back from Swindon?'

Adam shook his head, looking faintly bemused. 'No. Should I have done?'

'I was just wondering, because you might have popped in to say hello if you were in The Lane.'

'It was nearly eleven when we got back to the village,' Adam said, half laughing but clearly surprised by my suggestion. 'We dropped Dad off and then the cab took me home.' He gave a sheepish grin. 'I could have walked but we'd been drinking and to be honest, I was half asleep. And I wanted to get home.' He smiled at Hannah.

Concerned that my comment might have come across as an inappropriate invitation, I forced a laugh which I hoped didn't sound fake, and muttered that I hadn't realised it was so late when he and Richard had returned to Ashton Mead. Clearly, Adam hadn't dropped his watch outside my house on his way home from Swindon. The noise outside my house had woken Poppy at around four in the morning, five hours after Adam had returned with his father. I desperately wanted Adam to tell me more, but the situation was awkward, and I decided to wait until the next day and see what Hannah might let slip.

It would be difficult to question her directly about her boyfriend's movements. Somehow I had to come up with a plausible excuse for my interest in Adam's watch. It would be tricky. If Adam had been lurking in my garden at four in the morning, his motive couldn't have been honest or upright. On the other hand, it was possible there was an innocent explanation for the watch turning up in my garden, even though it was difficult to imagine what that could be.

# 27

ALL THROUGH THE FOLLOWING day, I wondered what to do about Adam and his watch. The tea shop was quiet after lunch and, as it was sunny, Hannah and I took a couple of chairs outside so we didn't have to perch on wobbly ones. We sat down for a break during the lull, propping the kitchen door open so we would be sure to hear the bell tinkling should any customers arrive. With Hannah's mother out for the morning, Poppy had come with me to the café and had been dozing happily in a sunny spot while we were busy indoors. Since I had started working at the Sunshine Tea Shoppe, the yard at the back had been improved by the introduction of some large flowerpots and hanging baskets. The introduction of a few colourful flowers had been my suggestion. Hannah had responded enthusiastically so that we now had, if not quite a garden, a pleasant area at the back of the kitchen in which to sit and enjoy the summer weather. We had discussed laying a patch of grass there, but Hannah thought that would feel too permanent. She still hankered after extending the kitchen at the back of the premises and was reluctant to expend too much time and money on turning the area into a garden. Still, the flowers brightened it up considerably.

Poppy was excited when we joined her, and rolled onto her back, growling with happiness when I leaned down to tickle her. I spent a few moments making a fuss of her to hide my perplexity from Hannah who was amused by Poppy's noisy expression of her appreciation.

'She sounds more like a cat than a dog,' she laughed. 'She's definitely purring.'

I was still wondering how to broach the subject that was uppermost in my mind when Hannah leaned back in her chair and raised the issue herself, launching into a complaint about the loss of Adam's watch.

'When did he first notice he wasn't wearing it?' I asked.

If it had been missing for more than a day, that would mean he couldn't have dropped it outside Rosecroft the previous night. I waited, hoping Hannah's reply would help, but she merely shook her head and said he didn't know.

'He must know when he last saw it?' I persisted, doing my best to hide my frustration.

'Are you listening to me?' she replied. 'I just told you, he doesn't know. He can't remember where he last saw it, and that means he could have dropped it anywhere. The point is, I don't know what to do. I can't press him to discuss whether or not we have a future together while he's stressed about his watch.'

Hannah was clearly upset, but I had my own reason for feeling agitated, and it made me answer sharply. 'It's only a watch. It's not like someone's died.'

'I know it's only a watch, but he's very upset about losing it because it belonged to his grandfather and so it's irreplaceable.' She sighed. 'It's the sentimental value rather than the value of the watch itself. I don't know that it's even a particularly expensive one.'

Aware that Adam's watch was hidden at the back of a drawer in my bedroom, I was growing increasingly uncomfortable. The longer I remained quiet about it, the more difficult it would be to confess that Poppy had discovered the missing watch in my garden. As though she could read my thoughts, Poppy jumped up and gazed at me enquiringly. In the past, my friends had often dismissed my suspicions as unfounded paranoia. Sometimes my friends had been right to be sceptical, yet quite often my suspicions had been borne out by the facts as they emerged. But regardless of what had happened in the past, I could hardly confess to Hannah that her boyfriend had dropped his watch while he had been prowling in my front garden at night. There was no way that could be explained away as an innocent caper. Usually I discussed my difficulties with Hannah. Unable to share this particular problem with her, I was feeling stranded.

Desperate to discuss the situation with a friend, I was really pleased to see Toby sitting on his own in the pub garden that evening. While he petted Poppy, I blurted out a garbled account of how Poppy had found Adam's watch. Toby straightened up abruptly and stared at me.

'You are joking, aren't you?'

'Toby, I'm being completely serious.'

I wondered whether it had been wise to share my problem with him. Like me, he hadn't known Adam for very long, but he had known Hannah since they were children. If he were ever forced to take sides, his loyalty would lie with her and so, by association, with Adam.

'What are you talking about?' he demanded. 'Honestly, Emily, if you're going to start suspecting your friends of – well, of I don't know what, exactly – for no reason, then no one's safe.'

'I'm only saying it's possible he dropped his watch in my garden during the night. He could have been trespassing –'

Toby interrupted me. 'In that case, we might as well all hand ourselves over to the police and insist they lock us up, in case we might turn out to be criminals.' He laughed, but he seemed angry.

His response irritated me, and I answered crossly. 'I just told you, I found Adam's watch. He dropped it in my front garden at four in the morning.'

Toby shook his head at me and scowled. Poppy whimpered when he stopped scratching her neck, then settled down under the table.

'For a start, you don't *know* it's Adam's watch,' Toby said, with exaggerated patience. 'It could be anyone's watch. Secondly, if it *is* Adam's watch – which seems pretty unlikely – you don't know who left it outside your house. If it really *is* Adam's watch, the chances are it was stolen, and the thief dropped it in your garden when he heard Poppy barking. And finally, don't you think it's possible you're letting your imagination run away with you again? It wouldn't be the first time.'

There was nothing more to be said. Muttering that I would take the watch to the police the next day, and let them deal with it, I let the matter drop. It was lucky we had reached a conclusion, of sorts, because a moment later Poppy stirred and we saw Hannah and Adam approaching our table. As if by a tacit agreement, neither Toby nor I mentioned what we had been talking about before they arrived. Adam looked dejected, and it wasn't long before the subject of the lost watch cropped up, with Hannah telling Toby about it.

'Maybe someone found it?' Toby suggested, glaring at me. 'And they'll return it to him once they know whose it is.'

Hannah nodded. 'I was thinking of putting up a few notices around the village.'

'Tell Maud,' Toby suggested. 'She'll make sure the whole village knows about it. But hopefully whoever found it will return it very soon, before it becomes a talking point round the whole village.'

'It's possible I have it,' I murmured, and immediately regretted the admission.

Whichever way I spun it, there was no hiding the fact that I had kept quiet about Poppy's discovery all day, while Hannah had been bemoaning Adam's loss. There was nothing for it but to tell a craven lie and claim to have only just spotted it, outside my house, when I arrived home after work.

'I thought we'd be seeing each other this evening,' I added awkwardly, smiling at Adam. 'Otherwise I'd have called you straightaway. Actually, we don't even know if it's yours. If you hadn't been here, I would have phoned you.' I babbled on, not meeting Toby's eye, and trying not to sound apologetic, as though I had done nothing wrong.

'Where is it?' Hannah demanded.

'At home,' I admitted.

'Why didn't you bring it with you?' There was a fierce light in Hannah's eyes, and her lips were pressed together as though she was making an effort to control herself. 'I told you Adam had lost a watch.' She didn't add that she had talked about little else all day, but we both knew that was the case.

Hannah was furious with me for failing to pay attention to her, and Toby despised me for lying. Only Adam wasn't upset with me, and I had suspected him of being responsible for skulduggery behind my back. Poppy let out a whimper and I reached down to pet her. She wagged her tail as though to reassure me that at least she wasn't angry with me.

# 28

ADAM WAS IMPATIENT TO see whether Poppy had found his watch, so he and Hannah walked back to Rosecroft with us. It was a beautiful evening. The day had been mild, the heat of summer not yet fierce. The sun would soon set, and the moon was already clearly visible in a cloudless sky. According to Adam, it was going to be a starry night. We chatted in a desultory fashion about the weather, and which stars I might look out for when taking Poppy out before we went to bed. Adam was surprisingly knowledgeable about the night sky. Meanwhile, Hannah maintained an air of silent disapproval on our walk back to Rosecroft. My friends waited in the living room when I ran upstairs to fetch the watch. It felt heavier than I remembered it as I ran back downstairs.

As soon as he saw the watch, Adam's face broke into a broad grin and he seized it with a cry of pleasure, confirming that it was indeed his.

'I thought I'd never see it again,' he said, as he thanked me. 'Did Hannah tell you it was my grandfather's?'

Hannah nodded. While Adam examined the watch for any sign of damage, I told him where Poppy had discovered it. Adam looked up in surprise and asked me what his watch had been doing in my front garden. I confessed to having no idea how it had got there. I had assumed he must have dropped it on his return to Ashton Mead the previous evening. There was no need to add that I had suspected him of lurking outside Rosecroft at four in the morning.

'Someone must have stolen the watch and dropped it in Emily's garden by mistake,' Hannah said.

'Whoever it was, presumably they were up to no good,' I added. 'Could you have dropped it in the village on your way home? Someone must have picked it up somewhere. Try to remember where you might have dropped it.'

He looked perplexed. 'I don't remember losing it, but I was a bit pissed, so it's possible I was careless.' He frowned. 'We took my dad home first and then the taxi dropped me home. I remember reaching through the window to shake my dad's hand when he got out of the car, so I suppose my watch could have fallen off then. It could have scraped against the edge of the window, or something. To be honest, I've been meaning to get the strap fixed for ages. It's my own stupid fault. I knew it was broken.'

He held the watch up and showed us that the buckle tongue was wobbly and would no longer engage properly with the notch in the frame. It would be relatively easy for the buckle to come undone. It made sense that the watch had fallen off and a thief had chanced on it lying in the road at four in the morning, only to drop it by mistake while checking out my house. Poppy's barking must have sent him scurrying away, the only sign of his presence the sound of footsteps receding into the night, and the watch he had left behind as he made his escape.

'Perhaps Poppy scared a burglar off?' Hannah suggested, evidently thinking along the same lines as me.

Bending down to pet Poppy, I decided it was time to tell my friends everything that had happened. Hannah looked alarmed on hearing there had been an intruder in my garden at four in the morning. When I protested that nothing had actually happened, Hannah insisted that other residents be alerted to the fact that a burglar had been prowling in the village. We talked round in circles for a bit, while she tried to persuade me to report the incident to the police.

'You keep saying nothing happened, but if Poppy hadn't barked, whoever was hanging about outside could have broken into your house.'

'But they didn't.'

'The fact is, someone was in your garden at four in the morning. You can't ignore it. You have a responsibility to report it. They might still be hanging around. It can't have been anyone local, because they would have known Poppy would wake you up,' she pointed out.

Aware of her feelings about my suspicions of Virginia, I merely nodded.

'I wonder why the burglar went for Rosecroft and not The Laurels?' she went on thoughtfully.

'He probably tried Dad's house first and couldn't get in, so he went on to Emily's,' Adam suggested.

'Or she. It could have been a woman,' I said, and Hannah grunted. 'There is another possibility,' I added. 'What if all this was more calculated than that? I mean, it's a bit of a coincidence, isn't it? Adam drops his watch in the lane and a few hours later a random burglar happens to come along and find it. Adam, could someone have stolen your watch at any time during the evening?'

He frowned. 'I don't follow you.'

That was understandable. My thoughts weren't clear in my own mind yet. But I had a vague suspicion and it was making me uneasy.

'What if someone deliberately dropped your watch outside my house?' I asked.

Adam and Hannah both looked baffled.

'Why on earth...?' Hannah blurted out. 'What are you talking about? Why would anyone...?'

It had occurred to me that Virginia Strang might be setting me up to suspect Adam of snooping around my house. If she could isolate me from my friends, I would become an easier target for her attacks. It was a nasty idea, and too embarrassing to suggest, in case my friends were shocked at me for thinking of it. If it was true, it had very nearly worked.

'I don't know,' I muttered anxiously, forcing an awkward laugh.

Hannah peered at me, and I wondered if she had guessed what I was thinking. On balance, we all agreed that Adam must have lost his watch when the taxi dropped Richard home, and a passing thief who chanced to find it had then dropped it in my garden. It was the simplest explanation, and the only one that appeared to make sense. But I knew that I had an enemy in the village, and I had a horrible suspicion that something more sinister lay behind the theft of Adam's watch, and its subsequent discovery outside my house. From now on, I resolved to be even more vigilant than before.

When Hannah announced it was time to leave, Adam stopped polishing his newly returned watch with the sleeve of his shirt and slipped it in his pocket.

'Make sure you get that strap fixed,' Hannah said, and he nodded.

'Don't worry, I'll get onto it first thing tomorrow.'

Closing the front door behind them, I checked it was securely shut. As though sensing my fear, Poppy trotted over to me and nuzzled my ankles with her wet nose but, for once, even her presence failed to reassure me. Poppy was fiercely loyal to me, but she was very small. If my suspicions were right, having failed to drive a wedge between me and my human friends, it was terrifying to think what Virginia might do to Poppy.

'From now on, you don't leave my side,' I told her as I scooped her up in my arms.

Aware that it would be impossible to keep her with me at all times, I shuddered to think how vulnerable she was. As though she knew exactly what I was thinking, Poppy growled.

'That sort of bravado is all well and good,' I told her, 'but we might be up against a devious lunatic. We both know who I'm talking about. If that's the case, then I'm afraid you're not going to be able to protect me. You may be intelligent for a dog, but there's no way you can hope to stand up to someone like that.'

Poppy squirmed out of my arms and jumped to the floor. Scurrying to the door, she looked over her shoulder and glared, before turning her back on me and running out of the room.

## 29

THE FOLLOWING MORNING, AS soon as I entered the café Hannah burst out of the kitchen and greeted me with a broad smile. Expecting her to be annoyed with me for having kept the discovery of Adam's watch a secret from her for so long, I was pleasantly surprised. Her welcome was all the more unexpected because I was late. When I began to blame Poppy for stopping repeatedly on the way to Jane's house, Hannah dismissed my excuse with a wave of her hand.

'It doesn't matter. You're here now,' she beamed.

'Where do you want me to start?' I asked, looking around.

On Mondays we usually remained closed until mid-morning, allowing us to spend a few hours cleaning. Baking trays, crockery and cutlery, and other small items were cleaned as we went along, but bigger tasks we tackled on Mondays. Having wiped the yellow oilcloth table covers and mopped the floor in the front room where customers sat, we would roll up our sleeves and turn our attention to the kitchen. We scrubbed the worktops and the inside of the ovens, before washing the floor. If it had been left to me, the ovens would probably have only been cleaned occasionally, but Hannah wanted to scour the ovens, inside and out, as part of our weekly routine. Together with all the food preparation that went on behind the scenes, we barely managed to stay on top of our work, however hard we tried. There was always a lot to do after the weekend, and we tended to leave the ovens until last. If we ran out of time, we sometimes didn't get round to doing them at all, and hoped no one else would find out. So far it had never been a problem, but Hannah lived in fear of the hygiene inspectors turning up and scrutinising every inch of the café.

We routinely devoted a few hours each week to keeping the café looking spotless, at Hannah's insistence. So, I was surprised when she suggested that we forget about the cleaning, for once, and have a chat. We sat down with tea and a couple of thick slices of chocolate sponge. Happily tucking in, I murmured that she really had to stop letting me scoff so much cake. Tall and statuesque, Hannah seemed able to eat as many cakes and buns as she wanted, without any problem, although she was constantly complaining that she was putting on weight. I was shorter than her, and slight. With the frequent addition of Hannah's cakes and scones to my diet, most of my trousers were becoming a little too tight for comfort, and I was afraid of growing tubby. Hannah laughed at my fears.

'Tubby? You?' she replied. 'You mean you're unhappy because you don't look like a scarecrow any more?'

According to Hannah, gaining weight suited me, but I wasn't convinced. The trouble was, her cakes were irresistible.

'It's Adam's birthday next weekend,' Hannah told me, as she poured the tea. She giggled with anticipation. 'That's what I wanted to discuss with you. We're going to throw a huge party for him!'

I hesitated to share her excitement before hearing her plans. First of all, I wanted to know whether Adam knew about the party. In my experience, the subjects – some might say the victims – of surprise parties weren't always pleased to be caught off guard. But when I voiced my reservations, Hannah fluttered her hand at me and accused me of being a killjoy. Still, her party plans certainly helped to take my mind off Silas Strang. For the remainder of the day, we were kept busy plotting, between customers. Hannah wanted to invite just about all the residents of Ashton Mead. I did my best to rein her in, reminding her that this was supposed to be a party for Adam who had been living in the village for less than a year, and only knew a limited number of local residents.

'Don't you think this would be a good opportunity for him to meet everyone?' Hannah asked, a trifle wistfully.

It seemed to me that, far from hoping to be introduced to a roomful of strangers on his birthday, Adam might prefer to take the opportunity to relax and enjoy himself. I didn't add that he might want to go out with Hannah on their own for a romantic evening. Even though I was convinced that was the case, Hannah was clearly too excited about organising a party for him to listen to my objections. I decided it would be unkind to point out that the party was more about satisfying her own wishes than his. So, the preparations for Adam's birthday continued, with extra baking in the kitchen at the Sunshine Tea Shoppe, and at Jane's house. Every evening after work I was sent home with a bag packed with cakes and scones to be stored in my freezer, since the ones at the café and Jane's house weren't enough for all the supplies and, of course, Hannah couldn't hide any party food in her own house without arousing Adam's suspicions.

'It was you, wasn't it?' Hannah demanded furiously as soon as I arrived at work on Friday morning.

For a moment, I thought she was accusing me of killing Silas.

'What? No, no,' I stammered, backing away from her and knocking over a chair. 'Of course not. How can you think I would do something like that? Surely you know me better than that.'

'All right, calm down,' she replied, catching my horrified expression as she reached forward and set the chair upright again. 'It wouldn't have been the end of the world. It doesn't matter.'

'But – but – what made you say that? How could you?'

'Well, someone must have spilled the beans,' she said calmly. 'Because he knows.'

'Who knows?'

She frowned. 'Adam, of course. Who do you think I'm talking about?'

'Adam knows? What does he know?'

'About the party. What do you think I mean?'

She had a point. For a week, she had talked about little else. Laughing with relief, I sat down. 'I thought – I thought –' I began, and stopped.

'Now come on,' Hannah said. 'It's gone eight thirty. We need to get ready to open up and get breakfast going soon. 'Where's your apron?'

In spite of Hannah's efforts to keep her plans from Adam, he had discovered what she was up to on the Thursday before the party. I didn't confess that I wasn't sorry he had found out. Springing a party like that, as a surprise, had never struck me as kind or sensible. But, of course, I kept my opinions to myself. We never did find out who had told Adam about the party. I suspected Maud had let it slip, although Adam claimed no one had told him, and he had just guessed from all the unusual excitement and activity he had observed at the café.

# 30

WE WERE BUSIER THAN usual that Friday, which was probably just as well since we were closing early on Saturday, to give us time to prepare the café for the party. By the time we finished for the day we were both worn out. My mood didn't improve when it started to rain as we turned the sign around and locked the door against latecomers hoping to persuade us to serve one last tea. Pulling up my coat collar, I set off for Jane's house. Poppy was pleased to see me and frolicked happily at my feet, but she was reluctant to walk home. She never liked going out in the rain, and it had turned a little chilly. In the end, I had to carry her most of the way, tucking her inside my jacket to shelter her from the drizzle that was falling steadily. By the time we reached our front door, I was feeling damp and thoroughly disgruntled.

Poppy ran into the living room, while I hurried upstairs to change out of my wet clothes before going to the kitchen to heat up a tin of soup. My freezer was crammed with cakes and buns and other provisions for the party, and when I opened the door to take out a sliced loaf for toast, a small avalanche of rock hard scones tumbled out of a bag that was not properly sealed. Swearing, I gathered the scones up from the floor and, after a brief deliberation, threw them away. No one would know. There were plenty more. It was lucky that none of them had fallen on Poppy who was on self appointed guard duty by the patio door in the living room, where she often stood watching out for foxes in the garden.

Having taken out a carton of frozen soup to heat up for my supper, I carefully repacked the freezer, wedging everything in closely. Hannah had invited me to taste so many cake samples during the day that soup was all I could manage that evening. Mug in hand, I turned on the television and settled down to watch a film. I must have dozed off eventually because, when Poppy woke me, the film had finished and another one had started. Switching off the television, I cleared away my few supper things and turned to go upstairs. Poppy whimpered and began scratching at the front door.

'Poppy it's late,' I grumbled. 'Come on, it's time for bed. What is it? Do you need to go out? Come on, then.'

The sun had just set, so I decided to take her for a very short walk along the lane, just as far as the main road and back again. For some reason, Poppy was happy to run out into the front garden, but she balked at going out into the street and I had to drag her through the gate. Her shenanigans annoyed me, and I told her so. After all, she was the one who had wanted to go out in the first place. Feeling cross, I picked her up and carried her a few yards, thinking she would soon change her mind and want to jump down to run around on the grass verge. But she seemed quite happy to stay where she was, snuggled inside my jacket.

Focused on Poppy, I was only dimly aware of a car parked across the road. As we drew closer to it, the engine revved and a blaze of lights sped towards us. There was an acrid smell of burning rubber, and a fine drizzle began to fall, looking like sparks of light in the beam of headlights. Terrified, I hurled myself into the hedge at the side of the road. I was dimly aware of clutching Poppy to my chest while the side of my face brushed against sharp twigs. A gust of air whooshed past us as the car sped away. Racing along the lane, it turned the corner, tyres squealing, and was gone. The whole incident could only have lasted a few seconds.

Had I flung myself flat on the ground, the car would almost certainly have run me over, and Poppy would have been crushed beneath me. As it was, I had thrown myself sideways and downwards to avoid the car, and she had miraculously ended up nestling in my arms in the angle between the hedge and the grass verge. Everything seemed to be happening in a dream, but there was no mistaking the smarting of my grazed cheek, or the clammy sensation of wet grass against my legs, while a faint smell of burning rubber lingered in the air. Shaking, I clambered to my feet, still holding Poppy close to my chest. I had to force my legs to move, but it didn't feel safe staying where we were. Whoever had tried to run us over might return at any moment. As I hurried back home, it was hard to believe what had just happened. But my cheek stung where the hedge had scraped my skin, and I distinctly recalled hearing the car engine rev and the smell of burning rubber as the bright headlights hurtled towards me.

'You'll have to go in the back garden,' I told Poppy as we reached our front gate. I was strangely composed, but as soon as the front door slammed behind us, I began to shiver. Seeing my face in the hall mirror made me feel sick. My left cheek was dotted with tiny scratches, a few of them flecked with minute beads of blood. Upstairs in the bathroom, I examined my face more closely. Once I had gently washed away the specks of blood, it was clear that my injuries were superficial. I rubbed some Savlon on my cheek and went back downstairs, feeling calmer. After letting Poppy out in the back garden, I made myself a mug of tea before phoning Hannah to tell her what had happened. She was sceptical on hearing that someone had deliberately tried to run me over. Although I was struggling to believe it myself, it was still disconcerting to have my account doubted.

'They probably didn't see you,' she said. 'It's dark out.'

When I insisted the car had driven straight at me, she suggested I report the incident to the police.

'It sounds like the driver was pissed,' she said. 'If someone's driving around the village in that state, they need to be stopped before they cause some real damage. Did you get their number?'

Sheepishly I mumbled that the incident had been so unexpected, and had been over so quickly, that I hadn't registered anything about the car.

'You must remember what colour it was?'

'It was dark – black or dark grey, I think, but I didn't really see. It all happened so fast.'

We discussed whether or not I should report the incident to the police, but given that I didn't know the colour or the make of the vehicle, there seemed no point. Hannah grew impatient when I asked if she knew what car Virginia Strang drove, and she scolded me for persisting in what she called my 'paranoid obsession'. When the conversation ended, I hung up feeling decidedly disgruntled. I had at least expected some sympathy from my best friend. Instead, she had dismissed my experience as though it was insignificant.

To my surprise, I slept right through the night. I woke feeling sweaty, with a vague recollection of dreaming about a car racing towards me out of the darkness, tyres squealing. The noise was not a dream. Coming to, I realised the squealing was the sound of Poppy whimpering to be let out. It was already an hour past the time we usually left the house. In my agitation the previous evening, I had forgotten to set my alarm, and was going to be late for work. As I tumbled out of bed, my phone vibrated. It was Hannah, calling to ask if everything was all right. Jane had called her to enquire if I was going to work, as I was late bringing Poppy to her house and hadn't answered my phone when she had called me a few moments earlier. My day was not off to a good start.

'It's just as well you woke me up,' I told Poppy as I dressed hurriedly. 'If you hadn't been making such a racket, I'd still be fast asleep. I'm going to be really late as it is.'

Poppy wagged her tail.

# 31

IN MY HURRY TO take Poppy to Jane's house and then get to work, I had forgotten to bring the pastries and scones which were stored in my freezer for the party that afternoon. Hannah sent me straight home to fetch them so they would have time to defrost and would only need warming up for a few minutes later on. By the time I returned to the café, it was packed. A coach load of American tourists had made a stop in the village for morning coffee on their way to Bath. Rushing between the kitchen and the front room, Hannah was red-faced from her exertions. The café was full of boisterous Americans, enthusiastically discussing our menu offering tea cakes and crumpets.

'I just love their quaint little cookies,' they were telling one another, and 'Their scones are so gorgeous!'

'Thank goodness you're back,' Hannah burst out when she saw me. 'Get them settled and take the orders as quickly as you can while I get things started in the kitchen. I swear they've only come here to use the toilet, but they're not leaving until they've all paid for breakfast.'

'Nothing to do with the village being so picturesque,' I agreed, laughing. 'And certainly nothing to do with the reputation of your baking. The only attraction of Ashton Mead is the toilet at the Sunshine Tea Shoppe.'

I didn't remind her that, in her haste, she had completely forgotten that she had banished me to the kitchen.

'Just take the orders,' she hissed. 'If we need to use some of the scones I made for this afternoon, go ahead. We can't afford to lose paying customers, and we've got loads of scones.'

She didn't know about the bag of cakes that had split in my house and been thrown away.

We were busy all morning, so Hannah decided to close at midday to give us time to clear up before the party. We had still exceeded her target for our takings that day. It was going to be a quieter affair than she had originally intended, but even so we spent a few hours rearranging the tables and putting up bunting left over from the May Day celebrations, along with a massive shiny banner wishing Adam a Happy Birthday, and were only just ready at four o'clock, when the guests began to arrive. Adam's father, Richard, turned up first, followed by Jane and Poppy.

Maud appeared next, wearing a ghastly cerise dress with frothy sleeves, pink shoes and a matching handbag. She would have looked only faintly ridiculous had she not chosen to complete her ensemble with a crimson fascinator that perched at a jaunty angle above her left eyebrow. With bright red nails and lipstick, she had evidently taken a lot of trouble over her appearance. In my view, she had looked far better when her hair had been naturally grey, and she had worn sedate skirts and twin sets appropriate for a woman of her age. The reason for her extravagant outfit soon became obvious. At her side, Norman, the butcher, took her hand and leaned towards her, listening attentively as she chattered. The pair of them looked radiant, and seemed oblivious of other people staring at them.

After Maud and Norman arrived, there was a sudden influx of guests. Cliff, the landlord of The Plough, beamed at everyone, shaking hands and clapping people on the back as though he was hosting the party himself, while the barmaid, Tess, glared around with her usual cantankerous expression. My friend, Toby, joined me and for an instant I hoped he was on his own. It was a selfish wish, soon dispelled as Michelle joined us. I had to admit that Toby looked happier than I had ever seen him, although I struggled to understand what he saw in Michelle. She was pretty enough, but I never heard her speak. She seemed to me to be really boring company. I had intimated as much to Hannah, who had refused to criticise Toby's new girlfriend.

'What do you think of Hannah's cakes?' I asked Michelle, determined to initiate a conversation. If she and Toby were going to be an item, I wanted to make friends with her.

She smiled feebly and muttered evasively she didn't really have a sweet tooth.

'Are you a good cook?' I tried again.

Toby answered for her. 'She's fantastic,' he said, smiling at her.

Before we could continue the conversation, Hannah summoned me. After that, Hannah and I were kept busy all afternoon, pouring drinks and brewing tea and replenishing plates of cakes and buns and scones. At last it was time to cut the birthday cake, and a hush fell as Hannah carried it from the kitchen. Decorated with chocolate and cream, it looked luscious. Adam stepped forward. He picked up a long knife, and raised it in the air with a dramatic flourish.

'Make a wish,' Hannah cried out, clapping her hands.

Other voices echoed her words in an ebullient chorus. 'Make a wish, make a wish, make a wish!'

Glancing at the circle of villagers gathered around Adam, my attention was caught by Tess. Unlike the other guests, who were all talking and smiling, Tess appeared to be glaring balefully at Adam as he lowered the knife to make the first cut into the cake.

'I see Tess is her usual cheerful self,' I muttered to Toby.

'Not sure what you mean,' he replied, sounding puzzled.

I looked round and saw that Tess was chatting to Maud. They were both laughing.

'Nothing.' With a shrug, I dismissed my concern about Tess.

After we had all spent a couple of hours gorging ourselves on cake, a few of the guests drifted away, but many of us trooped to The Plough for supper. Hannah insisted we leave all the clearing up for the next day.

'We'll open in time for lunch,' she said. 'We can afford to miss one Sunday breakfast after the day we've had.'

We were a cheerful crowd, calling out and joking as we made our way along the High Street to the pub. Hannah was in particularly high spirits after the success of the party she had thrown for Adam. Poppy trotted beside me, seemingly unfazed by all the activity around her. Once, she let out a loud bark for no apparent reason; in all the throng of people it was impossible to see who or what had provoked her.

At the pub, Cliff and Tess ran around serving food and clearing plates. Poppy snuggled down under the table and waited patiently for scraps and we passed an enjoyable evening. Adam seemed genuinely pleased that so many people had come to the party Hannah had thrown in his honour. Whether most of them had come for Hannah's mouthwatering spread, rather than to celebrate with Adam, was a moot point. Toby and his new girlfriend didn't come to the pub, which gave me an opportunity to ask my friends for their impressions of Michelle. Afraid of being accused of jealousy, I was cautious in my criticism when they threw the question back at me.

'She seems very quiet,' I said.

'That's not a bad quality in a woman,' Adam teased us, yelping as Hannah kicked him under the table.

'She seems nice,' Hannah said. 'I like her and Toby's happy with her, which is more important.'

Most people had gone by the time we were ready to leave. It was already dark and I was pleased to be walking back down the High Street with Adam and Hannah. When we reached Mill Lane, they kept going towards the bridge while Poppy and I turned off into the lane where we lived. Recalling what had happened the last time we had walked there after dark, I hurried towards Rosecroft. We were halfway along the lane when Poppy barked. At the same moment, I heard footsteps behind us. I walked faster. Whoever was following us sped up as well. They were gaining on us. Alarmed, I broke into a run. Poppy raced ahead of me, barking loudly. Breathless, more from fear than exertion, I reached our front gate and fumbled with the latch. Hearing a rustling, I glanced over my shoulder and saw a shadowy figure raise its arm as though to strike me. Poppy leapt up, growling ferociously. There was a sound of snapping jaws, and a strangled yell as the figure fell to the ground.

A light came on in The Laurels next door, and I heard Richard call out. Looking round, I saw my assailant scramble to their feet and flee. An instant later they had vanished in the direction of the river.

'Is that you, Emily? Everything all right?' Richard called out.

'Yes, yes,' I lied. 'Everything's fine. Did you see who it was?'

'Who what was?' he replied, hurrying to my gate. 'What's all this noise about, eh?' he asked, leaning down to pet Poppy.

'There was – someone here,' I stammered, shaken by the mysterious encounter. 'Did you see who it was?'

Richard shook his head and his fluffy white hair fluttered around his pudgy face. 'There's no one else here,' he assured me, gazing around and yawning. 'Just you and me and little Poppy. So, what was all the barking about? Another one of your night time prowlers?'

She wagged her tail and he reached down to scratch her under her chin. I shook my head, uncertain what to say. Unlike some of my friends, Richard had never accused me of being paranoid or melodramatic. I suspected he shared their view, but was too polite to say so to my face.

'Well, as long as everything's all right, I'll say goodnight.

I was just off to bed when you started barking,' he added, addressing Poppy in mock admonishment.

With that, he patted her on the head and walked away. I wanted to call him back so I wouldn't be alone, but there was no good reason to do so, unless it was to tell him that someone had just tried to attack me outside my own house. But whoever it was had disappeared without trace into the darkness of the night. Back in the warmth and comfort of my own home, I started to wonder whether I had imagined that Poppy had thwarted an attacker. Even if it was true that she had barked at someone passing by, there was no reason to suspect they had been stalking me, intending to harm me. To be fair, I had drunk quite a lot during the day.

'Do you think I imagined it, Poppy?' I asked her.

As though in answer to my question, Poppy wagged her tail and dropped a scrap of blue fabric at my feet. On examination, it proved to be a small piece of denim she had picked up from somewhere. I was almost sure she hadn't found it before we left the pub, and we hadn't stopped on the way home. I wondered where she had picked it up, and whether she might have torn it from my attacker. Remembering that I had an enemy in the village, I tried to recall whether Victoria Strang had been wearing jeans the last time I saw her.

# 32

'Jeans?' Hannah repeated. 'What are you on about? Why do you want to know who wears jeans? Just about everyone wears jeans, don't they? Except Maud,' she added thoughtfully. 'I've never seen Maud in jeans. But why the sudden interest in who wears jeans?' Her eyes narrowed. 'You're not thinking of changing jobs, are you?'

'What? To conduct market research into who wears jeans in Ashton Mead?' I couldn't help laughing.

Hannah stopped stacking the dishwasher and frowned at me. 'What on earth are you talking about?'

I put down a baking tray and cleared my throat.

'It's just that something happened last night, in Mill Lane, after you and Adam went off home. You know someone tried to run me over the other night? They were waiting for me again, and I think they tried to attack me on foot this time.' I didn't mention the figure I had seen on the bridge just over a fortnight before.

Hannah straightened up and stared at me. A few drops of water dripped from her hand into the open door of the dishwasher without breaking the silence between us.

'You *think* someone tried to attack you?' she repeated

at last. 'Emily, what's happened? Do you mean an actual physical assault?'

I nodded miserably. 'An attempted physical assault, yes. At least, I think that's what it was.'

'Well, were you attacked or weren't you? You must know. I mean, either someone attacked you or they didn't.'

She sounded impatient. While I had to concede it was unlikely anyone could be uncertain about whether or not they had been assaulted, the reality was that I just didn't know. It was a pity Poppy couldn't talk. She had been the only witness to the incident. Hesitantly I described what had happened.

'You think I imagined it, don't you?' I concluded anxiously.

Having listened to my stumbling account, Hannah scowled.

'This has happened before when the fair passes through the village,' she said grimly.

It was my turn to feel confused, until Hannah explained. Once a year a fairground was set up in the village, as it passed through on its way to Bristol. She thought it likely one of the itinerant fair workers had tried to rob me. When I suggested it might have been Virginia Strang, Hannah waved the idea away, and muttered that I was irrationally paranoid about her. I was fed up with hearing that accusation levelled at me.

'Irrational?' I protested. 'Paranoid? You heard her yelling obscenities at me in the street and accusing me of murdering Silas. It's hardly irrational paranoia if I think she's out to get me.'

Annoyingly, Hannah brushed off my suggestion, telling me that everyone was fed up with my obsession with Virginia Strang.

'What obsession?' I snapped. 'And who, exactly, is everyone?'

I was gutted to hear that she and Adam, together with my other friends, Toby and Barry, had discussed my allegation against Virginia and agreed that I was allowing my imagination to run away with me. According to Hannah, they all thought it understandable that a mother would go a little crazy following the murder of her son, and start hurling abuse at anyone who might or might not have been responsible for his death. When I tried to present my point of view, Hannah frowned.

'If you ask me,' she said, 'you're still upset about Virginia yelling at you in front of your mother, and now any time anything untoward happens, you immediately blame that poor woman. Not everything that happens is her fault. I mean, honestly, do you really believe she would want to run you over?'

When I pointed out that recently both she and Adam had agreed that Virginia might be trying to frame me for Silas's murder, she shook her head again, saying they had just wanted to be supportive since I was so obviously upset. But it was time to put it behind me, she added.

'You can't hold onto a grudge forever.' She looked straight at me. 'You're always talking about yourself. You're not the only one with problems, you know.' With that, she turned and resumed stacking the dishwasher.

There was clearly no point in attempting to discuss my situation any further. Admittedly I had been focusing almost entirely on my predicament, but considering that I felt my life was at risk, I thought that was forgivable. Hannah was my best friend, but even she didn't want to hear about my problems, and I was feeling uncomfortably isolated.

We carried on clearing up from the party the previous day in silence, and finished in time to open for lunch. Although it was Sunday, it was too wet for many people to be going out, so the café was quiet. Hannah kept herself busy in the kitchen, baking and restocking the freezer now the party was over, leaving me on my own to think. I wanted to go to the police, but had nothing definite to tell them except that I was convinced someone was out to get me. They were likely to be even more dismissive of my concerns than my friends.

As I was worrying about my situation, and wondering whether Hannah was right to believe I was imagining I had an enemy, Norman and Maud came in. Smiling, Maud told us it was her birthday and Norman was taking her out for tea. It made a change to see her outside the Village Emporium, which was the rather grandiose name for her shop which sold all kinds of provisions, kitchen utensils, toiletries and cleaning products. Behind the counter she stocked batteries, and a variety of wines and spirits. This afternoon she had abandoned the long-sleeved gingham overalls she wore in the shop, in favour of a lightweight lilac knitted twin set and pearls. Her dyed blonde hair was neatly cut, and her beady eyes twinkled behind the rimless glasses perched on her pointed nose.

'We'll have a full cream tea,' Norman said, as he lowered himself heavily onto a chair. 'Nothing less than the full works for Maud.'

Seated, he looked even larger than when he was standing up. His legs looked as though they were too long for the chair, and he sat hunched over the table clasping a menu in his huge hands.

'Make it three,' he added. 'Maud's nephew is joining us.'

Maud smiled at him. 'Norman, you're so generous,' she simpered.

It would be madness to speak my mind in front of Maud, who was the most indiscreet gossip in the village, yet Barry's arrival gave me an idea. I didn't have enough information to request an injunction, or lodge a complaint, against an anonymous enemy. My suspicion of Virginia was based solely on the fact that she had shouted at me in public a couple of times, while she was still in shock about the death of her son. There was no way the police were going to take me seriously and my accusations would be dismissed as prompted by bad feeling between neighbours. But at least I could talk to Barry and ask his advice, as a friend.

'Are you going to The Plough this evening?' I asked him, as I brought over their order. 'Maybe I'll see you there later?'

I had to be careful. Barry had made it clear he was attracted to me, and I didn't want to lead him on. As it happened, he was a decent guy with a steady job, but I wanted more than that from a boyfriend. Despite his protruding teeth and goofy grin, he wasn't bad looking, and his personality was affable, if pedestrian. Reliable and sensible, he was someone I was keen to have as a friend, but that was all. At the same time, I desperately wanted to quiz him about what to do. He answered me with a grunt and I let the question drop, hoping to find an opportunity to speak to him before anything else happened.

That evening I went to the pub on the off chance that Barry would respond to my tenuous invitation to meet, and I saw him sitting in a corner with a pint. He looked as though he had been waiting for a while, and I felt a twinge of guilt in case he had misunderstood my invitation. He stood up as soon as he saw me, and came over to offer me a drink. After he'd been to the bar, and had made a fuss of Poppy, he asked me whether there was any particular reason why I had asked to speak to him. I was relieved that he seemed to have interpreted my approach as a straightforward request for help, with no romantic agenda.

'Well, there is something,' I told him, and hesitated.

'Are you going to tell me what it is?'

'This is strictly between us.'

He inclined his head. 'As long as you haven't committed a crime, and no one is at risk, you can be assured of my discretion. I'll treat what you tell me in confidence.'

'The thing is, I don't know if I'm at risk or not.'

Barry sat forward. He was no longer smiling. 'Go on,' he said softly. 'I'm listening.'

In a low voice, I told him about the mysterious attempt to run me over, and hearing footsteps as though someone was following me. The only detail I left out was finding Adam's watch. My relationship with Hannah and Adam was already starting to seem fragile, and I deemed it best to leave them out of my informal statement. Hannah wouldn't appreciate being questioned by Barry about the discovery of Adam's watch in my front garden. Barry listened closely without interrupting me. Other than Tess, who came over to take our empty glasses, no one approached us, and it was a relief to share my thoughts privately, with a friend. I concluded with an account of the attempted robbery in the lane when Poppy had chased my assailant away. Barry pointed out that she could have picked up any random piece of fabric from the ground, and the scrap of blue denim I had found between her teeth was inconclusive.

'Have you told anyone else about this?' was his first question when I finished.

'Only Hannah, and she seems to think I'm putting two and two together and coming up with five. She as good as accused me of being paranoid and seeing an imaginary antagonist everywhere. According to her, it was just someone from the fair who tried to rob me. But that doesn't explain the attempt to run me over.'

Barry nodded. 'It's true, we have had some issues in the past with the fair attracting people from outside the area.'

'But this didn't stop when the fair left.' I paused, seeing him frown. 'Do you think I'm overreacting and being hysterical?'

Barry was about to answer when Poppy let out a bark of greeting. Looking round, I saw Hannah and Adam entering the bar. They came over to join us, and that was the end of my private discussion with Barry. He gave me a brief nod, as though to confirm he had heard what I'd said, but I wasn't convinced he believed me.

# 33

NORMALLY I WOULD HAVE been happy to see my friends, but I would have welcomed the chance to spend just ten more minutes alone with Barry. My best friend, Hannah, didn't want to listen to what she regarded as my melodramatic imaginings. Our friend, Toby, was away for a few days on a field trip with the school where he worked. Had he been there, his girlfriend would probably have been at his side, making it impossible for me to confide in him. I tried not to begrudge him his new found happiness, but I missed our close friendship, which seemed to have faded away since Michelle came into his life.

It seemed to be a popular time of year for taking trips, because the pub landlord, Cliff, had also gone away for a week, leaving Tess in charge. She looked more stressed than usual as she rushed around clearing tables and serving drinks, but I had little time for other people's concerns. I had disturbing problems of my own. I couldn't share my worries with my mother, who was bound to fuss and badger me to return 'home'. She still kept my bedroom waiting for me in her house. I had reminded her several times that I had a house of my own now, but she only murmured darkly that you never knew what might happen. When I pointed out that my older sister's former bedroom had been turned into a study, my mother snapped that my sister was married. According to my mother's world view, a woman could not be treated as an adult until she married.

'What about Great Aunt Lorna?' I had asked my mother. 'She never married. Are you saying she never grew up?'

Conversations about my single status never went well, and my mother and I had reached a tacit agreement to avoid the topic. She was blindly convinced it was unsafe for a woman to live alone, and her obstinacy inevitably led us to quarrel. So, there was no way I could talk to her about what had been happening. Had it not been for Poppy finding Adam's watch in my front garden, and my resulting suspicion of him, I might have consulted my next door neighbour, Richard. Under normal circumstances he could always be counted on to lend a sympathetic ear to my concerns. But he was Adam's father, and I wasn't sure whether Adam and Hannah had discussed my situation with him. Even if Richard knew nothing about the watch Poppy had found in my front garden, I couldn't confide in him in case he spoke to Adam.

There was no one I could talk to about my problems apart from Barry, which made me desperate to seek out his advice. But there was nothing else for it but to smile at my two friends as though I was really pleased they had joined us. We sat chatting about trivia for a while. It felt strange to be indulging in idle gossip about our neighbours while I was convinced that someone wanted to harm me. Time seemed to pass slowly while I waited, hoping for an opportunity to continue my conversation with Barry. At last, Hannah and Adam stood up to leave. Hoping Barry would stay, at least for a few minutes, I was disappointed when he rose to his feet as well, saying he would be late for his aunt who was expecting him for dinner.

'I'm sure Maud won't mind,' I mumbled ineffectually. 'How about one more for the road?'

Barry shook his head. 'You don't know my aunt. It's more than my life's worth to be late for supper.' He chuckled.

Once Barry had turned down my offer, there was nothing more to be done. If I tried to insist he stay for another drink, Hannah might suspect me of spreading stories about Adam's watch behind her back, or she might think I had designs on Barry. Both would be equally galling. Reluctant to invite suspicion, I watched the three of them walk to the door and disappear. Still, Barry would probably have agreed with Hannah that my fears were no more than groundless paranoia anyway. My evening at the pub had been a waste of time, and it was time for me to leave too. I was growing hungry and didn't want to eat at The Plough on my own. But when I looked, Poppy was no longer curled up under the table.

I called her, quietly at first, but she didn't come running over to me. To begin with, I wasn't bothered. Assuming she had made her way out into the pub garden to enjoy the attention of one of my neighbours, my only worry was that she might be digging in one of Cliff's flowerbeds. With a sigh, I went outside and made a circuit of the whole garden area, but couldn't see her anywhere. I checked under all the tables in case she was dozing outside, but there was no sign of her. The back gate was shut, with the bolt in place. A young couple who were seated at one of the tables assured me they hadn't seen a dog in the garden that evening. Returning to the bar, I walked around, searching for her. By now I was beginning to worry.

If Poppy had slipped out of the door to the street, I thought she would be able to make her own way home but, despite my efforts to drum some road sense into her, she had to be restrained from darting out into the path of oncoming vehicles. Motorbikes provoked her, and she would pull on her lead, barking at them and trying to give chase. Looking around, I saw Tess collecting dirty glasses. She was dressed in a baggy black T shirt and faded jeans, and scratched black shoes. When I asked her if she had seen Poppy, she shook her head, scowling, and muttered something about keeping dogs on leads so they couldn't run off. I wanted to protest that Poppy never ran off, but it didn't seem appropriate, given that she had disappeared. An old man was seated at a corner table, mumbling into his glass. I never saw him arrive or leave, but whenever I entered the bar, he was there, nursing a pint. His table was near the door and he could hardly have missed seeing anyone go in or out.

'Dog?' he repeated, when I asked him if he had seen Poppy running out of the pub. 'What would I be wanting with a dog?' Bowed shoulders shrugged inside his grubby grey raincoat, and his whiskery white eyebrows shot upwards, expressing surprise.

With difficulty I made him understand that I was searching for Poppy.

'You lost your dog?' he wheezed. 'That little dog I seen running around with you?'

I nodded and repeated my question. The old man coughed, a dry rattling sound.

'I ain't seen that dog,' he croaked. 'No dog's gone out here. I would've seen.' He raised his glass hopefully.

'Lost something?' Tess asked, passing by with a few glasses chinking in her hands. 'You're not still looking for that dog?'

The surly barmaid was hardly my favourite person, but right now I needed help.

Quickly I explained that Poppy wasn't in the bar, and she wasn't in the garden, yet no one had seen her leave the pub. Tess gazed blankly at me for a moment. Then, muttering that it was hardly her concern if I couldn't take care of my own dog, she turned and began energetically wiping a nearby table with a damp cloth, as though to signal that our conversation was over.

'You don't understand,' I blurted out. 'I don't know where she is. I've looked everywhere. She would never run off like that. She just wouldn't.'

'But she has,' Tess retorted.

'Probably gone home,' the old man called out. With a toothless grin, he lifted up his empty glass and banged it down on the table.

Tess glared at me. 'You going to buy old Bert a pint, or what?' she asked.

Without stopping to answer, I hurried outside to continue searching for Poppy. Walking briskly home, I looked around all the time but there was no sign of her, and I heard no answering barks when I called her name. Fear made me feel slightly sick, but at least there was no sign of a brown and white furry body lying in the road. I kept telling myself she would be waiting for me outside Rosecroft, sitting by the gate, or stretched out on the doorstep. I would even have been happy to find her ferreting around in the garden, digging up randomly planted flowers that bloomed among the weeds I planned to pull up.

But when I reached home, the pavement was empty, and there was no small dog lying on my doorstep, nor any sound of welcoming barking. Unsure what to do, I retraced my steps back to The Plough, but there was no sign of Poppy anywhere on my route along the lane and back down the High Street, or in the pub. At a loss, I called Hannah but she didn't answer her phone. When I tried Adam's phone, he picked up straightaway and commiserated with me on hearing that Poppy was missing. He handed his phone to Hannah who was sympathetic but could only suggest I go home and wait for her there.

'I don't think there's much you can do right now,' she said. 'She's probably just gone off chasing a fox or a cat and fallen asleep somewhere. I'm sure she'll make her way back home soon,' she added kindly. 'Either that, or someone's taken her in and is looking after her until they can get her chip checked. Don't worry. I'm sure she'll be back with you soon.'

Miserably I walked home again, scarcely daring to hope that Poppy would have returned. But there was still no sign of her.

# 34

LOSING POPPY WAS THE most upsetting experience of my life. For two years she had been my constant companion, and I could hardly bear to think she might be gone for good. Of course, I could remember what my life had been like before she came along, and I had always known she wouldn't live forever, but I simply couldn't imagine a future without her. Not yet. In melancholy moments, I had pictured her growing old, and eventually passing away peacefully at the end of a long and happy life. But she could now be gone forever, without any warning, and I might never discover what had happened to her. All the same, Hannah had been right in saying there was nothing to be done until the morning. That night I slept very little, constantly waking to listen for Poppy barking to be let in. At two o'clock a fox barked, a haunting lonely sound. Other than that, the night remained silent. Opening my curtains I lay, gazing out at the stars, waiting for morning.

The next day, I dressed in a hurry and raced around the house, checking in frantic desperation, in case Poppy had fallen asleep curled up in a cupboard. Having searched the house and garden, I went out to hunt for her along the lane, walking all the way down as far as the bridge. It was difficult looking down at the river, but I saw no small furry body floating on the darkly flowing water. Hannah had promised to search the streets on the other side of the bridge, so I returned home and checked there again, even though I no longer held out any hope that she would be there, waiting for me. The time for looking in likely – or even possible – places was past. By now I was desperate enough to search everywhere.

Hoping Poppy had found her way to the café, I arrived at work early. Hannah was already there, but she was alone. Too agitated to eat or talk or think about laying breakfast trays, I was grateful when Hannah gave me the morning off to pin 'Missing' signs on trees, in Maud's village shop and in The Plough when it opened. Attached to the description of a small brown and white dog, answering to the name of Poppy, I posted grainy photos of her, taken on my phone. They weren't very clear, but many of the villagers knew Poppy, and Hannah was fairly confident that she would be found and returned to me. All morning we kept a look out, waiting for someone to walk in with Poppy in their arms. Hannah was positive she would reappear soon, with a helpful neighbour or by herself, and I tried to share my friend's optimism. Neither of us admitted out loud that the longer Poppy was missing, the less chance there was that she would turn up alive and unharmed.

Having already complained at length to Barry that someone was stalking me, I felt awkward about making a point of contacting him again, this time on a different matter. He had made it clear that he wanted to go out with me, so it didn't feel right to be treating him like some kind of private detective working for me, unpaid, as if he owed me a favour. But I didn't know where else to turn. Hannah continued to urge patience. She claimed to be sure Poppy would turn up before long, none the worse for her adventure, but as the hours passed, her protestations sounded increasingly hollow.

'Someone must have taken her in,' she said. 'You'll see. Dogs don't just disappear. She wears a collar, and she's been chipped. Anyone can see she belongs to someone.'

But her eyes failed to conceal her anxiety. All through the afternoon I waited at tables as though working in a dream. At one point, I heard a dog bark. Dropping my notepad, I dashed outside, only to see a stranger walking along the High Street with a black dog trotting at her heels. I nearly cried when the dog looked up at me and yelped, as though it understood my feelings.

There was little point in ringing round local vets, because Poppy was chipped and a vet would contact me if anyone took my dog to them. Nevertheless, I looked up contact details of vets in the area and called them all to enquire whether a lost Jack Tzu had been brought in. No one had seen her. It was beginning to look as though she had met with an accident, or been stolen. Anxiously, I discussed those possibilities with Hannah when we were clearing up for the day. I had been without my faithful little companion for nearly twenty-four hours, and it felt like a lifetime. Ahead of me lay a lonely future.

'You have to stop being so negative,' Hannah said. 'Until you know something's happened to her, there's still hope. She's only been missing for a day, and she's nothing if not resourceful. I'm sure she's fine.'

That evening I stayed in, too miserable for company. Eventually, I went to bed. Exhausted, I drifted into an uneasy sleep, only to be startled awake by my phone. It was two o'clock in the morning. Convinced that Poppy had been found, I answered at once.

'You've lost something,' the caller said in a flat rasping voice. It didn't sound like a question.

'Yes, yes. Have you found her?'

'We need to meet.'

This struck me as strange, but I was feeling both wound up and, at the same time, groggy, and didn't know how to respond.

'What do you mean? Who are you? Where's my dog?' I stammered.

'Walk down the slope towards the river. Leave now.' The voice was hoarse but clear.

'What are you talking about? It's two o'clock in the morning. I'm in bed.'

'Come alone or you'll never see your dog again. If you're not there in five minutes, it will be too late.'

'How do I know –' I began, but the caller rang off.

I tried calling back, but the number had been withheld. Even if I wanted to summon someone to accompany me, no one could possibly join me in time. The caller had given me five minutes. There wasn't even time for me to get dressed. Jumping out of bed, I put on some socks, grabbed my keys, and ran downstairs. Frantic with hurry, I pulled on my coat and shoes, and dashed out of the house. It was a cloudless night. The moon shone down, cold and white, set in a dark canopy speckled with bright points of stars. The silence felt oddly oppressive. Far off an owl hooted, a ghostly cry that hung in the air before being swallowed by silence. There was no one around as I hurried across the grass, gazing around, unable to see much. I was beginning to suspect I had been lured outside by a sick prankster when a hooded apparition emerged from the darkness, seeming to materialise out of the air. Had I been superstitious, I would have been paralysed with fear. As it was, my legs were trembling. The figure approached, and I saw that they were wearing a mask, like a balaclava. Only a glint of reflected moonlight from two eyeholes indicated there was a face watching me.

'How much money do you want?' I demanded angrily. 'I don't have much, but if you think – '

'You want your dog to stay alive?' issued from the featureless head. I recognised the hard flat voice from the phone. 'Then you're going to have to do exactly what I say. This isn't about money.'

The words were so unexpected, I almost laughed. But there was something about the threat that made me believe the speaker was deadly serious.

'You've got Poppy?' I blurted out. 'Where is she? If you've hurt her... '

'What will you do?' the voice sounded amused. 'How did that work out for you with Silas?'

'What are you talking about? Where's Poppy?' I demanded.

'There's only one way you're ever going to see your dog again,' the voice went on, expressionless yet somehow ferocious. 'If you don't want the dog to die, you need to go to the police and confess.'

'Confess what? I don't know what you mean.'

'You need to confess you killed Silas Strang.'

'I didn't kill him,' I stammered.

'Confess or the dog dies.'

'This is insane. I don't believe you,' I blurted out, horrified. 'I don't believe you've got Poppy.'

'Take your confession to the police and I'll spare your dog. Or do you want her to suffer for your mistake? You have forty-eight hours to convince the police you're guilty. After that, it's all over. She's already hungry and frightened, so you'd better not hang around.'

I opened my mouth to protest, when a shaft of moonlight pierced the overhanging clouds and I caught a glimpse of scratched shoes as the figure turned and vanished. I kicked myself for failing to try and wrench the mask off. I should have at least launched myself at my blackmailer and snatched a hair, or scraped their skin, anything to enable me to leave with a sample of their DNA. As it was, I had no idea who had kidnapped Poppy in order to force me to confess to a crime of which I was innocent. To save Poppy, I might have to accept a prison sentence. There seemed to be no other choice.

# 35

I RETURNED HOME IN a state of shock. There was no chance of getting any more sleep that night, so I brewed a pot of tea and sat down in the living room to consider my options. Uppermost in my mind was the need to save Poppy from the maniac who claimed to have snatched her. I still had no proof that she had been stolen, but she had certainly vanished without trace which suggested the hooded figure had been telling the truth. I wasn't about to gamble on the possibility that Poppy hadn't been kidnapped at all, but had just wandered off and got lost. She might even be perfectly safe at the home of some well meaning person who had not yet got around to taking her to a vet for identification, or had even decided to keep her, thinking she was a stray. But that seemed unlikely, given my night time encounter.

Assuming that she *had* been stolen, and was being held hostage, there was still no guarantee that she would be released if I followed the kidnapper's instructions. Once I had confessed to a murder of which I was innocent, the police would lock me up, after which Poppy might be mistreated or killed anyway. For all I knew, she was already dead, but I refused to believe I might never see her again. It was vital to remain positive and clear thinking. What I needed to do now was work out who my enemy was, and rescue Poppy from their clutches as quickly as I could. But without knowing their identity, it was difficult to see how to proceed.

As to the request that I confess to murder, that was really strange, whichever way I looked at it. Possibly the kidnapper genuinely believed that I had killed Silas, and was determined to see me punished for my crime. If that was the case, they should have gone to the police. Perhaps they already had. Virginia Strang had publicly accused me of murdering Silas, so she had to be my main suspect for the kidnap. If she had gone to the police and they had dismissed her accusation, she might have been desperate enough to decide to take matters into her own hands. Grief could have a strange effect on people and, revolting though he had been, Silas was her son and she had loved him. I wondered whether the hooded figure who had met me at night could have been Virginia. I tried to recall anything about the figure, but the whole episode had passed in a blur, and my recollection was no sharper than a half remembered dream. I resolved to tell Barry about it, and ask him whether anyone other than Virginia had gone to the police to accuse me of murdering Silas.

The only other explanation that made any sense was that the killer was setting me up as a scapegoat in order to escape justice themselves. So it seemed that a false confession from me would shield a murderer. It was a dreadful predicament to find myself in, considering going to prison to protect a murderer, but I was afraid Poppy would suffer if I refused. And I still had no proof that they had even taken her.

Once again, there was nothing to be done until the morning, but it was clear this situation was too serious for me to tackle on my own. It was time to recruit some serious help. Waiting for the morning, I jotted down as much as I could remember about my night time encounter, from the phone call at two o'clock arranging our meeting, to the shadowy appearance of a mysterious masked figure. At six o'clock I made a few phone calls of my own. Hannah protested at my calling her so early, but she agreed to meet me before work.

'I can't tell you any more about it over the phone,' I concluded. 'Meet me at the café in half an hour.'

'Is it so urgent that it can't wait until we open?' Hannah asked sleepily.

'Yes,' I replied firmly. 'It is that urgent. And it can't wait until people are up and about because we might be seen. Go in through the back gate and make sure no one sees you.'

'How am I supposed to know if anyone sees us?'

'Just do it.'

She promised to be there, with Adam. 'I'll have to wake him up,' she muttered.

'So wake him up.'

Toby was less easy to convince. I wasn't sure if he would turn up, or whether he would bring Michelle with him. I hesitated, but could hardly ask him to come without her. As soon as the call finished, I regretted having contacted him, but it was too late to change that.

Two hours before opening time, I was seated in the café with Hannah, Adam and Barry. A few moments later, Richard arrived. They had all expressed varying degrees of surprise and irritation on receiving my summons, but all of them had answered my request for help. I experienced a fleeting sense of gratitude at finding my friends were prepared to turn out so early without knowing what was going on, but perhaps it was curiosity rather than loyalty to our friendship that had brought them there.

We sat around a table with the lights out and the blind drawn.

'Is it really necessary to sit here in the dark like this?' Hannah grumbled.

'Yes,' I replied quickly. 'We mustn't let anyone know we're here. I don't know who is watching me.'

Hannah muttered about my paranoia, Adam scowled, and even Barry drummed his fingers on the table in irritation. The atmosphere was uncomfortable and I was relieved when Richard suggested they at least listen to me before reaching any conclusion.

'Thank you,' I said. 'If you think I'm deluded after this, feel free to ignore what I'm about to tell you and write me off as going crazy. The way things are looking, that might happen sooner than you think anyway, and not in the way you're expecting, because I'm not making any of this up.'

'Emily, what are you talking about?' Hannah burst out, sounding exasperated.

Before we could continue, Toby walked in. I was relieved to see he was alone.

'What's this all about? And where's Poppy?' he asked as

he took a seat beside Adam. 'And what are we all doing here?'

Just back from his school field trip, he had no idea what had happened.

'Poppy's gone missing,' Hannah told him. 'And Emily seems to think we –'

'Not just missing,' I interrupted her. 'Poppy's been kidnapped.'

There was a brief hiatus as my friends absorbed this news. Hannah and Adam exchanged a glance, and I suspected they were thinking my comment was a hysterical response to Poppy wandering off and getting lost.

'Kidnapped? Emily, what the hell are you talking about?' Toby asked.

Even Richard gazed at me sceptically. 'You mustn't blame yourself if she's run off,' he murmured. 'These things happen.'

'The trouble is, you're not going to believe what's really happened,' I told them as Hannah started pouring us all a cup of tea from the large pot that had been brewing on the table. 'But hear me out.' It was hard to know where to begin. 'I can hardly believe it myself.'

And then I told them about the phone call in the night.

'They actually threatened to kill Poppy?' Adam asked, looking shocked.

'If I don't confess to the murder. So whoever it is, I'm guessing they killed Silas and are hoping to get away with it by forcing me to take the blame.'

Hannah put the teapot down with a bang. 'That's outrageous!'

'You can't give in to blackmail,' Adam said.

'I can't let them hurt Poppy,' I replied grimly.

Barry agreed to try and find out who was the main suspect, as they were possibly behind the blackmail, but we didn't have much time. He assured me that he would tell the detective in charge of the murder investigation exactly what had happened. If necessary, they would go through the motions of arresting me for murder before the forty-eight hours were up, although there was no guarantee Poppy would be set free even if the kidnapper was convinced by my fake arrest. It wasn't a very satisfactory plan, but it was the best we could come up with, and we all hoped that it would at least buy us some time while we tried to figure out who was behind the murder. It was pretty clear to me that Virginia was the culprit, and I said so.

'She's his mother,' Hannah protested.

'They were both bat shit crazy,' I replied. 'And she threatened me with violence. I mean, she's clearly an aggressive woman. It's perfectly feasible she might have killed him in a fit of temper, even if he is her son.'

'Especially so,' Toby chimed in. 'Crime of passion and all that.'

For once, none of my friends doubted my story. On the contrary, they all seemed keen to do whatever they could to help rescue Poppy. Adam agreed to subtly recruit Maud to investigate where Poppy might be. It would be difficult to involve her without revealing the reason for his interest, but he agreed to pretend he was thinking of buying a dog, so he could discover who had bought dog food recently. Hopefully someone who hadn't previously bought anything for dogs had made a purchase that would offer us a clue. If Virginia Strang had bought food suitable for a small dog for the first time, that would clinch it, at least as far as I was concerned, but it was a long shot. The alleged dognapper didn't sound as though they would care whether Poppy was fed or left hungry. Other than that, we all agreed to stay alert for any sight or sound of her. A single bark from a house where no dog was known to live would be enough for Barry to investigate. It was nearly time for Hannah to open the café, and there was nothing more to say for now. I tried to feel hopeful, now that my friends were helping me, but it was hard not to break down in tears when I thought of Poppy and how she might be suffering at the hands of a sadistic maniac.

# 36

IT WAS TWELVE HOURS since my horrifying encounter with the kidnapper, and we were no closer to discovering their identity. I didn't even know whether they had been telling me the truth when they said Poppy was still alive. Sitting out of sight, in the yard behind the café kitchen, Barry quizzed me about the meeting. There wasn't much I could tell him. I was unable to recall if my adversary was taller or shorter than me, and I couldn't say whether they were male or female. In a fleeting encounter in the middle of the night, it had been impossible to notice any details in the darkness.

'Whoever it was, they were wearing a hood,' I said. 'That's all I can remember.'

'Describe the voice again,' Barry said patiently.

'It was like someone who's lost their voice and is having to force it, really hoarse, like a stage whisper, but they were probably just trying to disguise how they sounded.'

'You don't say,' Hannah muttered.

The café was empty and she had come to sit beside the kitchen door, listening out for the bell. Focused on questioning me and listening to my answers, Barry ignored her occasional interjections.

'Did you notice anything about his or her shoes?'

I shook my head. 'No. Not really. I mean, it was dark, and I was quite confused by it all.' I paused. 'I think the shoes were scratched,' I added slowly. 'But I'm not sure. And they could have been black. They were flat but they could have belonged to a man or a woman. And they would have got muddy because it had been raining in the night and the grass was still wet.'

Barry nodded. 'Possible scratches on shoes,' he muttered, tapping at his phone, 'muddy shoes'. He looked at me. 'This doesn't give us much to go on. Can you remember if the shoes were larger than yours?'

I shook my head. 'Honestly, I've got absolutely no idea.'

'And he or she was wearing trousers?'

'Yes. They could have been jeans but I couldn't really see them clearly in the dark.'

'And a long jacket?' Barry went on, reading from his notes.

'Yes, nearly knee length, I think, and dark, and it had a hood which was up and covered the top and sides of the head and under that there was a black or dark mask with just the eye holes cut out. It could have been a balaclava.'

Barry nodded. We were going over the same ground.

'And you can't recall the colour of their eyes? Try to remember. This could help to narrow it down a bit.'

I shook my head. 'I'm sorry, I just don't know. I couldn't see and even if I had, I can't remember. We weren't standing that close to each other.'

'And this person ran off in the direction of the bridge?'

'I couldn't see where they went. They just disappeared into the night.'

When I enquired about the phone call I had received, setting up the meeting, Barry had no positive news. The police had traced the call, which had been made from a pay as you go mobile bought for cash a few days earlier in Swindon. They had no way of identifying the purchaser whom they suspected had ditched the phone after the call. The number was now unobtainable. Five pounds had originally been put on the phone, with a voucher paid for in cash. Whoever was claiming to have kidnapped Poppy was being careful to cover their tracks. Barry assured me that this evidence of premeditation would count against them once they were caught. But first the police had to find them.

'If you hear from your dognapper again, use this,' Barry said, handing me a phone. 'It's preset. As soon as you hit 1 on speed dial, it will send an alert, and we might manage to trace the phone that's calling your number and locate it, if you can keep them talking for long enough. Remember, switch it on and hit 1 on speed dial, and keep them on the line as long as you can.'

'It's likely to be during the night, if they call again,' I told him.

'Any time of the day or night, let us know,' he said. 'We need to track the location of that caller. We've applied for a warrant to track the phone. Just make sure you hit the alert button as soon as you know it's them.'

Barry had arranged for a scene of crime officer to meet me on the slopes. At my insistence she would be dressed in plainclothes, in case the dognapper was watching me. If I could point out exactly where the encounter had taken place, the officer would search discreetly for foot prints on the grass, hoping to discover details of the shoes worn by the hooded figure. Barry admitted they didn't hold out much hope of finding anything useful. For the second time in twelve hours, I met a stranger on the grassy slope leading down to the river. It was impossible for me to be exact about where the night time meeting had taken place, and the officer shrugged. Regretfully she told me this was going to be like searching for the proverbial needle in a haystack.

'When you look closely,' she said, 'there are so many footprints going in all different directions. And tracks on grass aren't exactly clear anyway.'

'This is a popular spot,' I muttered.

As though to prove what the scene of crime officer was saying, a group of Japanese tourists appeared on the slope. They followed their guide across the grass towards the river, pausing to take photos of the old brick bridge. Some people alleged it dated back to the Romans but according to Richard, who was something of an expert about such matters, it had been built by the Victorians, probably on the site of an earlier bridge. After their walk around the picturesque village, the group of tourists would possibly end up at the Sunshine Tea Shoppe for a traditional English tea. Having failed to make much headway with the scene of crime officer, I made my excuses before returning to work, where at least I would be able to help Hannah.

The Japanese tourists didn't come to the café, but we had a steady trickle of customers that afternoon. At least Hannah had forgotten again about banishing me to the kitchen. Normally I would have been pleased not to have to run frantically backwards and forwards between the kitchen and the tables, but on this occasion I would have welcomed the distraction of a busy afternoon. Forcing myself to smile at strangers as I took their orders in the bright and cheery yellow café, my afternoon took on a dreamlike quality. For people to be enjoying tea and scones, oblivious to the threat hanging over Poppy, seemed reprehensible. One of the customers could be my vicious adversary, come to gloat, and I found myself paying close attention to their voices, listening for any familiar feature that linked them to the hoarse whisper of the night. But there was nothing to connect the convivial reality of life in the café with the sinister threat playing out behind the scenes.

That evening, I met my friends in the pub. We were a dejected group. Reluctant to discuss the topic that was uppermost in all our minds, we didn't stay long. All the way home, I listened out for Poppy's bark and kept looking around, hoping to catch a glimpse of her in a window. But I neither heard nor saw any sign of her. Returning to an empty house, I struggled to remain positive. 'Poppy, Poppy,' I murmured to myself. 'Where are you? You have to escape and come back to me. You have to.'

I wondered whether she was suffering, and if she knew I was thinking about her and missing her. My phone rang several times that evening, and every time I felt my heart pound with terror as I switched on the phone Barry had given me, poised to hit the speed dial number. The first call was from Hannah who was checking that I was all right.

'We felt bad about letting you go home by yourself,' she admitted. 'We should have invited you over for supper, not left you on your own at a time like this.'

I thanked her for her kind thought, and assured her I was fine. It would have been churlish to point out that an invitation for supper wouldn't bring Poppy back to me. Shortly after that, my phone rang again. Hoping it was Barry with some news about the killer, I switched on the phone he had given me, in case it was the dognapper, and was disappointed to hear my mother's voice.

'Emily, how are you?' she gushed. 'We haven't spoken for days. Weeks. And Susie says she's not heard from you either. I meant to call before now, but I've been so busy, what with one thing and another. Did I tell you I've joined an art class? It's every Wednesday, and the tutor is an absolute wizard. A genius. I mean, you wouldn't believe what he can create in seconds. He thinks I have hidden talent.' She giggled.

'That's wonderful, mum. I can't wait to see your paintings.' Once again the outside world became surreal, an arena where people conversed as though nothing untoward had taken place. I glanced down, half expecting to see Poppy curled up at my feet.

'Oh, they're just sketches at the moment,' my mother was saying. 'I'm not ready for paint yet. But Julio says it won't be long. He says he can't believe I've never had lessons before now.'

I listened to her chattering about her latest pastime, and tried to be pleased for her.

By the time she paused and thought to enquire how I was, it seemed mean to tell her that Poppy was missing. My mother sounded so happy, there was no point in upsetting her.

'I'm fine,' I said.

It wasn't an outright lie. There was nothing physically the matter with me, but my life had turned into a waking nightmare.

# 37

THAT NIGHT, MY PHONE rang shortly after midnight. I knew immediately who was calling. No one else would phone me so late. Even so, I couldn't ignore a flicker of hope that someone had found Poppy and was too impatient to wait until morning to let me know. That hope was extinguished as soon as I heard the forced whisper. I was ready. Switching on the phone Barry had given me, I hit the speed dial straightaway.

'Have you made your confession?' the caller was asking.

'No, and you need to stop this. I've never killed anyone. Why would I confess to something I haven't done? What you're asking is insane,' I blurted out, gabbling in an effort to keep talking for as long as possible. 'This isn't fair. You can't carry on punishing an innocent animal –'

'Your poor dog,' the voice rasped. 'It seems you don't care about her after all. You have until midnight tomorrow.'

'No, wait –'

But the caller rang off. I could only hope that I had kept them talking for long enough for the police to trace the call. Barry contacted me soon after to tell me the police had traced the number but not the location.

'Whoever it was, they seemed to be moving,' he said.

'Moving? So what does that mean? Is it going to be possible to track them down?'

'Not this time,' he replied.

'This time?' I repeated, with a sick feeling in my stomach. 'What does that mean? It's been twenty-four hours. We've only got another day.' My voice rose in alarm and I stopped talking, afraid of breaking down in tears.

But there was nothing more the police could do to track the caller.

I passed a miserable day, watching my phone and checking that all my 'Missing' notices were in place, in case anyone spotted Poppy anywhere in the area. That evening, Hannah insisted I join her and Adam at the pub, where my friends could do little to console me. After one drink I was ready to go home, but Hannah insisted this was no time for me to be alone.

'What if Poppy's there, expecting me to let her in?' I asked.

'If she's found her way back, she'll wait for you,' Adam replied, not unreasonably.

So we all stayed on at The Plough for supper. It was a subdued evening. The food wasn't up to the usual standard but, with Cliff away, that was no surprise. What did surprise us was that Tess didn't seem to object to our staying to eat. We had expected her to go out of her way to make us feel unwelcome for adding to her workload. She pointed out that the lad who helped in the kitchen, and was rather grandly called the chef, was working that night. Hannah nagged me to eat but I had no appetite and kept my phone on the table beside my plate, in case anyone called. Aware that I was running out of time, I was losing hope.

As Tess called last orders, Hannah glanced at Adam who nodded before she invited me to stay with them that night. I thanked them but refused. They tried to insist but I was adamant, and they left soon after. It was kind of them to offer, but I had to go home in case Poppy returned. It was possible the caller claiming to have taken her was a crank, and she hadn't been stolen at all. She might have just run off and got lost, in which case it was reasonable to suppose she might find her way back home again. I was almost afraid to go home and cope with further disappointment. At least while I procrastinated at the pub, I could cling to a faint hope that Poppy would be sitting patiently on the doorstep when I returned home. The thought of her fluffy white tail wagging at my approach made me feel tearful with longing. We had stayed late, and the pub was empty. Even the old man who was always seated in a corner of the bar had gone. I was nearly at the door when Tess came over to me and put her hand on my arm to stop me. She glanced around but we were alone in the bar.

'Have you found your dog yet?' she asked in a low voice, even though no one else was there.

'No.'

'I might be able to help you.'

Instantly alert, I turned to her in surprise.

'That is, I overheard something just now that might interest you,' she went on.

This was unexpected and I was intrigued, although I tried not to be overly optimistic.

'Shall I call Barry?' I asked, pulling out my phone, together with the one Barry had given me. 'I've got the police on speed dial here,' I explained.

Tess's eyes widened. 'Let me speak to them. I think I know what's going on.' Before I could stop her, she took both phones from me. 'Right now, just follow me. Come on. Quickly. We don't have time to hang around.' Ignoring my squeal of protest at her taking my phones, she seized me by the arm, telling me that we needed to hurry. 'You want to rescue your dog, don't you?'

Had I stopped for a moment to consider what she was doing, I would have realised how odd it was, but I was too desperate to rescue Poppy to remonstrate with Tess as she propelled me across the room.

'Where are we going?' I asked as we crossed the bar area. 'Give me back my phone.'

'I'll have to take you,' she replied, completely ignoring my halfhearted protest. 'The door's kept locked. We don't want anyone going down there and helping themselves.'

'What door?' I asked her. 'What do you mean? Helping themselves to what?'

'To booze, of course.'

Without another word, she pushed me behind the bar and led me along a dimly lit passageway with threadbare dark green carpet and stained and peeling beige wallpaper. Tess glanced around before stopping at a wooden door. Once painted white, it was now grey and grimy. I had never been behind the bar before, and was slightly taken aback at how poorly maintained it was, compared to the public areas of the pub. Keys jangled as Tess unlocked the heavy door. Hearing a familiar bark ahead of us, I forgot about Tess and rushed forward, down a wide stone slope. In front of us, I could see rows of barrels and crates of bottles, stored on racks around a dusty low-ceilinged cellar. Echoing from the shadows, I recognised Poppy's bark. In my relief, I scarcely registered that Tess was muttering in my ear as, holding onto a rail, I hurried down the ramp and into the darkness of the cellar.

Poppy jumped up at me as soon as I drew near, her tail wagging in a frenzy of joy at seeing me. Squatting down beside her, I held her in my arms and assured her that she was safe and we would soon be home. Her heart was palpitating violently against my hand as she nuzzled my chest and grabbed my sleeve in her teeth, in an attempt to prevent me from leaving her again. Not until I tried to move did I discover that she was chained to a post.

'What's going on? Someone's tied her up. Who did this?' I cried out in alarm.

Looking around, I made out the gleam of eyes and teeth in the light coming through the open door, and saw that Tess was standing in the doorway brandishing a notepad and a pen. At the same time, I noticed the hem of her jeans was torn.

'Write your confession or you can both stay here and rot!' she said, with a grin.

She put the notepad down on the ramp. As she straightened up, the light fell on her shoes and I saw that they were scratched. But I had already realised, too late, the identity of the dognapper.

'You need to confess that you killed Silas Strang,' she snarled. 'If you want your dog to get out of here alive, that is.'

Poppy whimpered and I knelt down to assess her situation, and found she was attached to a strong chain by a stout padlock. Without a key, only some kind of bolt cutters could release her. Straightening up with her in my arms I spun round, doing my best to control my growing panic.

'You're crazy if you think you can frighten me,' I said, stepping forward as far as Poppy's chain would allow.

Tess sniggered. She must have known I was terrified.

'You know what you have to do,' she replied exultantly.

Silhouetted against the open door, she turned to leave. Ignoring Poppy's growling, I put her down and raced towards the ramp, shouting at Tess to stop.

'Tess, this isn't funny!' I cried out. 'You can't keep us locked up in here. This is crazy. Cliff's going to find us as soon as he comes down here. You won't get away with this! You'll go to prison!' I yelled as the door closed.

The sound of manic laughter rang out, cut off abruptly as the door shut. Running up to the door, I twisted the handle and pushed, but the door didn't budge. I banged on it, screaming at Tess to let us out, but there was no answer and the door remained locked. No one in the pub had heard Poppy barking, so I figured the cellar must be effectively soundproofed. There was no point in wasting energy in shouting for help. A few threads of light came into the cellar through a low gap at the bottom of the back wall, but other than the street lamps it was dark outside. Returning to Poppy in the near darkness, I slumped down on the floor beside her and stroked her back. It felt bony.

Before anything else, I needed to attend to her physical needs before it became too dark to see. She must have been down there, all alone, for nearly two days. Searching among wooden crates of beer and wine, I found a cardboard tray of litre water bottles sealed in cellophane. With difficulty I tore open the packaging. We had to manage without cups or bowls, but at least we had plenty of water. Poppy lapped eagerly from a pool on the floor, and I drank a little from one of the bottles. Poor Poppy must have been starving, but there was not much I could do about that. The only food stored in the cellar seemed to be crisps and nuts. I thought I might have to try and wash the salty crisps, but then I found a stack of packets of crackers and Poppy devoured some eagerly. The urgent concern after that was to get us out of there. Neither of us could survive for long on dry crackers and water. And there was still Tess's deadline hanging over us.

Eventually, my absence would be noticed. Hannah and Adam would tell the police they had last seen me at The Plough. With luck they would carry out a thorough search of the premises, but there was no way of knowing how long it would take them to decide to look for me in the pub. By the time we were discovered, it might be too late. I wracked my brain trying to remember how long Cliff was going to be away. It could have been a week, but was possibly as long as a fortnight. Either way, he was unlikely to be back in time to save us. Poppy and I were on our own, locked in a cellar, with no means of contacting the outside world. Only a maniac knew we were there, and she appeared to have no intention of letting us go. Poppy lay down at my feet, rested her head on her paws, and closed her eyes. She was confident I had come to rescue her, but I had a horrible feeling her trust in me was misplaced.

# 38

IT WAS TIME TO take stock of our situation. Sitting on the cold floor beside Poppy, I studied what I could make out of our surroundings. The floor was unpolished wooden boards, the walls were bare brick, and cobwebs hung from the corners of the ceiling, thick with dust. It was cold and dank and, along with a powerful smell of beer, there was a stench like rotting wood. Looking around, I was surprised to see there was a low door in the back wall, which I had missed at first in the semi-darkness. I only picked it out at all because a line of light showed beneath it, casting a faint glow across the cellar floor. I guessed it led outside and was used for deliveries. A flicker of hope shook me so strongly that for a moment I trembled and was unable to move.

Forcing myself to breathe slowly, I made my way cautiously over to the back door, and found it was securely locked. I knocked on it as loudly as I could, and screamed for help at the top of my voice, until my throat hurt. Poppy woke up and joined in, barking loudly, but there was no response from the other side of the door. Clearly, no one was coming to investigate our racket. Probably very little sound travelled through the door, which I figured must open onto an alley that ran down the side of the pub and was generally deserted. Only delivery vans went along there, and it might be days before another consignment was due. With Cliff away, Tess would be in control of stock, so there was no point in my hoping to be discovered by someone making a delivery. It was down to me, and Poppy, to save ourselves.

I went over and examined the low door, which looked impenetrable. It wouldn't budge when I tried to force it open. The wheels of thousands of trolleys bearing heavy weights had worn a shallow rut beneath it, through which a thin stream of fading daylight was visible. Crouching down, I examined the gap between the floor and the bottom of the door. If I could remove a floorboard, there was a chance Poppy might be able to squeeze through the gap beneath the door, but first I would need to free her from her chain. That alone seemed impossible. Returning to Poppy, I sat down to consider our options. I couldn't abandon my efforts to escape because if Poppy remained in captivity, she would die. On the other hand, if Poppy were free, Tess would lose her hold over me. She would probably still want to silence me, given what I knew, but at least Poppy would be safe. I squatted on the dirty floor, warming my hands in Poppy's fur, and pondering.

My first task was to force open the padlock on Poppy's chain. Once I had managed that, I could try to get Poppy out of there. The ray of light beneath the back door afforded some illumination. Taking my bag over to the patch of light, I rummaged through it, looking for anything I could use as a pin. I wasn't sure how to open a lock with a pin, but I had seen it could be done in films. Tipping out the entire contents of my bag, I sifted through everything, but there was nothing there with a pin. Making my way gingerly back across the shadowy cellar, I felt for the slope leading back up to the pub and hunted for the pen Tess had left me. It was a cheap biro, easily pulled apart. I tried to push the tip of the pen into the padlock but it didn't fit. Next I attempted to shatter the barrel of the biro, hoping to find an appropriate shard of hard plastic, but it was no use. The fragments of plastic were too thick to insert in the lock.

Poppy was lying down, watching me sleepily. I was afraid she was too hungry to be curious. Spurred on by her lethargy, I carried on hunting for something to use as a pin. In the end, I tried breaking off a long splinter of wood from one of the beer crates. It was tricky, but I finally managed to prise a sliver of wood away from a slat of a wooden crate. I inserted the thin end of my makeshift pick into the padlock and jiggled it around. For a long time nothing happened, while my cold fingers fumbled to manipulate the fragment of wood. Then, with a faint crack, the splinter snapped, leaving the point embedded in the lock. I swore out loud. Opening the padlock had just become even more difficult.

I had to remove the fragment of wood that was lodged in the padlock before I could resume my attempt to open it. I fiddled around, but it was impossible to get hold of the splinter, which was firmly jammed in the lock. Using a different sliver of wood, I tried to dislodge the piece that was stuck. Several hours must have passed as I persevered, and still I was no closer to removing the wood from the padlock. Determined to keep going for as long as possible, I carried on poking at the tip of the splinter that was jammed in the lock. All at once there was a faint click, the fragment of wood shot out and went skittering across the floor, and the padlock sprang open. The sudden movement of the wooden peg had released the lock. I let out an involuntary cheer.

Poppy opened a sleepy eye and put her head on one side, as if to enquire why I was so pleased. She had a point. We were still a long way from freedom. Unless we could somehow escape from the cellar, we could do nothing but sit and wait for Tess to return. But at least I could finally release Poppy from her chain. Realising she was free to roam freely within the confines of the cellar, she leapt to her feet and started to explore. Relieved to see her regain some of her usual vigour, I watched her disappear behind a stack of barrels. She reappeared as soon as I called her, her face and paws dusty from her exploration of the corners behind the barrels.

'Poppy, we need to dig,' I told her.

Grasping the padlock, I walked over to the back door and began scratching at the gap between the floor and the door. The metal was hard, and the edge of the padlock quite sharp, but it was a thankless task. Painstakingly I managed to scrape away a fine layer of dirt and dig a few tiny notches in a floorboard. It was quickly apparent that it would take hours to make any impression on the floor, and I had no idea how long it would be before Tess returned. Poppy sat watching me. After a while, my arm began to ache too much for me to continue. I sat back on my heels and Poppy darted forward and began scraping furiously but ineffectively at the floor. Using the padlock as a lever, I tried to prise one of the floorboards up and, very slowly, it began to shift. Encouraged by the movement, I renewed my efforts to raise the board from the ground. If I could remove it completely, there might be just enough room for Poppy to squirm underneath the door and escape. We worked on, me determined to dislodge a floorboard, and Poppy scrabbling pointlessly at my side.

Gradually the light from outside changed from a faint glow to a stronger beam. The light shed by street lamps was giving way before the rising sun while, slowly, the floorboard began to rise. Poppy seemed to understand what we needed to do, and she scratched at it as I struggled to force it upwards. Finally, with a creak, the end of the floorboard lifted up. Using my sleeves to protect my hands from splinters, I grabbed hold of the raised end, and pulled with all my might. Nothing happened. Then, with a rending sound, the floorboard lifted briefly from its position. It fell back almost immediately, but it was skewed over to one side, leaving a gap large enough for my fingers, which enabled me to pull it more effectively. Several determined tugs later, the floorboard finally came away, leaving a gap where the floor met the door. This was our chance.

Before I could push Poppy down into the hole, or attempt to widen it further, there was a faint sound behind us: the scraping of a key turning in a lock. Tess was returning to collect my confession.

'Go,' I whispered to Poppy. 'Find Hannah. Get help. Go!'

She blinked up at me and whimpered softly, as if to say she wasn't going anywhere without me.

Behind me, I heard the door creak on its hinges.

# 39

POPPY BEGAN BARKING FURIOUSLY, as the door swung open to reveal a figure in the doorway. In the light from behind her, Tess's unruly hair formed a shaggy halo around a face cast in shadow. She paused for a second to register what was going on, before she switched on her phone torch, and launched herself down the ramp.

'Get away from the bloody dog!' she shrieked.

In the light from Tess's torch, the trench beneath the door looked very shallow as I thrust Poppy towards it. She scrabbled in my arms for a moment, and let out a despairing yelp. If the channel we had opened up ended in solid earth, I could only hope that Poppy would be able to tunnel her way out.

'Go on, Poppy, dig, dig!' I urged her. 'Get yourself away, survive, don't die. Please don't die!'

Past caring whether she succeeded in finding help for me, I just wanted her to escape. Poppy let out a frantic bark before wriggling out of my grasp and zooming past me, back into the cellar.

'No, Poppy,' I wailed. 'Not that way. Come back here before she traps you again.'

Tess lunged at her, but Poppy was too fast. Darting past our captor, she scampered up the ramp and vanished through the open door. I was buoyed up by her escape, but Tess was still blocking my exit. Facing her boldly, I struggled to address her calmly.

'It's time to end this,' I announced, and was pleased to hear that my voice sounded firm and clear. 'Move aside and let me go.'

'What's this? What are you playing at?' she shouted, ignoring my demands and snatching up the blank notebook that was lying on the steps where she had left it. 'Where's your confession?' The bright beam of light from her phone torch waved around wildly, dazzling me.

'I'm not going to confess to a crime I didn't commit,' I replied, speaking as calmly as I could, and hoping she hadn't come armed with a knife. 'I would have thought everyone would want to discover who killed Silas, instead of trying to pin the murder on someone who's completely innocent,' I broke off as the truth suddenly struck me. 'It was you, wasn't it?' I whispered, horrified. There was no longer any point in attempting to discuss the situation rationally. 'You killed Silas.'

The explanation for her bizarre behaviour now seemed so obvious, it was hard to believe it had taken me so long to realise it.

'You murdered him and now you're doing everything you can to force me to confess,' I went on. 'You think you can get away with it by pinning the murder on me. Well, you're completely insane if you think I'll sacrifice myself to save you from prison. You're wrong and, what's more, you're disgusting, using Poppy to blackmail me into doing what you want.' My voice rose involuntarily. 'You can just get lost and take your filthy notebook with you, because I won't write anything. No one would believe it anyway', I blustered. 'There's no point in forcing me to sign a lie. The police would see through it straightaway. I'll tell them what happened and they'll dismiss it.'

It struck me that my confession was bound to be disregarded once it was clear that I had written it under duress. Perhaps, after all, it would be sensible to write what Tess dictated and persuade her to let me out of there. That way, at least she would let me go.

Tess glared at me. 'Of course, they'll believe it. You're already a suspect because you were stupid enough to argue with him in public.'

'Me and just about everyone else in the village,' I retorted.

'There are witnesses who heard you threatening to kill him.' She grinned. 'You're the perfect person to take responsibility for murdering Silas.'

'There's nothing to stop me denying it once I'm out of here,' I replied. Even as I spoke, I realised it was the wrong thing to say.

Tess shook her head and took a step closer to me. 'But you won't be in a position to deny anything.'

Something in her smug tone made me shiver. 'What do you mean?'

She smiled. 'You won't be able to say anything, because you're going to add a suicide note to your confession.'

The full horror of what she was threatening finally came home to me. But without Poppy as her bargaining chip, she couldn't force me to comply. I tensed, preparing to push her out of my way and charge past her.

'If you believe I'd write anything to incriminate myself in murder, you're even stupider than I thought,' I said. 'And I certainly won't let you make it look as though I've killed myself. If you attack me, I'll fight back. There'll be signs of a struggle, and what's more, I'll win, and it will be you that dies, not me.'

As I was speaking, I wondered whether threatening her was the most sensible way to proceed. Tess moved across to stand right in front of me, blocking my path, and whipped a knife out of her jacket pocket.

'Put that away,' I said, struggling to hide my alarm. 'Neither of us is going to die, because you're going to let me out of here. You need to let me go, right now! Get away from me!'

I started yelling as loudly as possible, hoping that someone would hear me. The same thought clearly occurred to Tess, because she darted back up the ramp and slammed the door.

I decided to make a reasoned appeal. 'Let me go and we'll say nothing more about any of this. No one else need ever know what went on between us. We'll put it down to a temporary panic on your part. We can say you were drunk. I'll agree to whatever excuse you want. Say it was a misunderstanding. Say it was all my fault. But you must see that you can't keep me here indefinitely. And the longer this goes on, the worse it'll be for you in the end.'

Tess laughed. 'Stop babbling. It makes no difference to me. Nothing you say will make any difference once you're dead, so just shut up. Don't you see? It doesn't matter about the dog. I've got you exactly where you need to be, completely under my control. We don't need the bloody dog any longer.'

'So, what happens now?'

Slowly a smile spread across her face, but she didn't look happy.

'Now I'm going to kill you,' she replied. 'Even if I have to write your confession and suicide note myself. It really doesn't matter whether you cooperate or not. Either way, it's all over for you, so you might as well accept that.'

I watched in disbelief as she raised her knife and took a step towards me. Desperately I grabbed a wine bottle, brandished it in the air and swung it in a wild arc in front of my face.

'Come on then,' I yelled, frantic with fear and rage, 'attack me if you dare, but you can't force me to write anything, and you won't be able to forge my handwriting, so you're a moron as well as a murderer. And you'll never get away with this! Never!'

Tess began slowly descending the ramp. The light from her phone swung dizzily, nearly blinding me after hours in the dark. The blade of her knife glinted in her hand. Still waving my wine bottle in front of me, I stood my ground, yelling that she didn't scare me, which was a lie. I had never been so terrified of anyone before in my life. Tess took another step towards me. Her eyes fixed on mine, she was halfway down the shallow stone ramp when I flung my bottle at her in blind panic. I wasn't sure what my clumsy missile could achieve, but I hurled it with all my strength. By some fluke, the bottle hit her in the chest, and the unexpected impact caused her to lose her balance. The stone ramp was worn smooth, making it dangerously slippery. With a shriek, she missed her footing. Her feet slid from under her and she fell, hitting the back of her head with a loud thud as she landed in a crumpled heap on the floor.

Her phone dropped from her hand and smashed, leaving us in semi-darkness. Only a ray of light from beneath the back door enabled me to see anything. Cautiously, I approached the shadowy hump of her body. I called her name, but she didn't answer. Her eyes were closed and she seemed to be unconscious. Without touching her, I couldn't even tell if she was breathing. Close up, I could make out a thin dark stream trickling across the dirty floor beside her head. Blood. I searched for her phone, and finally found it lying at the foot of the ramp. The back had come off as it smashed on the hard floor, and the battery was lost somewhere in the darkness. Frantically, I hit the emergency key, but nothing happened.

Trembling, I hurried past Tess up the ramp but the door had swung shut, and it wouldn't budge. The key had to be somewhere on Tess's person. Cautiously, I descended the ramp again, aware that if I fell, we would both die. Kneeling beside her inert body, I began searching for the key. It felt intrusive, sliding my hand into the back pockets of her jeans. I cringed, feeling the squishy mound of her buttocks. One of her side pockets was going to be difficult to reach. I was leaning forward over her body, when icy cold fingers suddenly latched onto my wrist and clung to me with a vice-like grip. In the near darkness I saw her eyes open and gleam at me, filled with hatred.

'Where's the key?' I blurted out. 'You're hurt. You need help.'

She growled, like a wild animal. 'You'll never get away,' she mumbled.

'Tess, listen to me. You're bleeding. You fell and cracked your head. Tell me where the key is so I can get help. You need a doctor. Just give me the key and once we're out of here I'll write a confession, I give you my word.' I was barely coherent in my frenzied determination to get out of the cellar. 'Just tell me where the key is so I can fetch help.'

With a rasping sigh, Tess closed her eyes, muttering to me that I wouldn't get away with it.

'Tess, you have to give me the key,' I said. 'You need help. Give me the key.'

She opened her eyes a slit at that. 'Why?' she croaked. 'Why should I help you?'

'Because you're hurt,' I replied, as patiently as I could. 'Because you don't want to die like this, in a cold cellar, in the dark. We need to get out of here and get you some help.'

'Oh no,' she whispered. 'Don't think you can get away. You're staying right here, where you belong, until you confess.' She groaned and closed her eyes, murmuring incoherently about needing a confession.

'I'm not going to confess to something I didn't do,' I insisted, but she could no longer hear me.

# 40

REACHING FORWARD, I RESUMED searching for the key but couldn't find it. Tess was lying on her left hand side, and having checked everywhere else, I assumed the key must be in the jeans pocket that was beneath her. Either that or she had left it on the other side of the door, because she hadn't intended to close it behind her. Not knowing the extent of her injuries, I was reluctant to try and move her but I didn't know what else to do. Sitting back on my heels, I considered my options. There was really nothing else for it but to find the key and get us both out of there. It might risk causing her further harm if I moved her, but if I did nothing we might both die. Tentatively, I reached out and pushed her gently, rolling her over until I was nearly able to slip my hand into her side pocket, the one that had previously been inaccessible. She let out a wheezy groan and I let go, afraid she would grab my wrist again. She rolled back onto her side. Minutes seemed to tick by as I held my breath. She didn't open her eyes, but I dared not disturb her again.

She seemed to have lost consciousness again. For all I knew, it was already too late to save her. Not only was she in a bad way, but unless I could get out, I risked dying alongside her, imprisoned in the dark damp cellar. The prospect of Cliff returning from his holiday and coming down into the cellar to find two corpses prompted me to move. Weak from hunger, I stumbled across the cellar. My legs were stiff from sitting around overnight and I was so tired, I could hardly think straight. Remembering that I had been too stressed to eat much the previous day, I opened a bag of crisps and another one of salty nuts. The strong taste of salt and vinegar crisps revived me, and for a while I sat on the floor crunching crisps and nuts and drinking water, not thinking about anything beyond that one moment. I was tempted to crack open a bottle of wine, but resisted. I needed to keep my wits about me. The aroma of the crisps overpowered all the other smells in the cellar so that, closing my eyes, I could almost forget where I was. My hunger sated, I felt a resurgence of energy.

The shaft of light coming in from under the back door was stronger now. Looking at the shape of the lit up area on the floor, the hole appeared larger than I had thought at first. Someone might hear me if I yelled loudly enough. The alley running along the back of the pub was usually quiet, but there could be people about, especially if they were looking for me. A search was already under way for Poppy but it was still early, and overnight no one would notice my absence. In the morning, Hannah would assume I hadn't turned up for work because I was out searching for Poppy. It could be some time before anyone came looking for me. Hoping to spy a way out, I lay down and squinted through the gap under the door. The tunnel beneath the wall looked very narrow, but daylight streamed through it from the other end. Warily, I reached in and tried to claw at the sides of the tiny passage, which was wide enough for my hand to reach through. As I dislodged a handful of earth, a clump of rubble fell down, nearly trapping my fingers. With difficulty I withdrew my hand. The source of light had grown dimmer, as though a torch had been turned low. It would be impossible to burrow my way out under the wall.

Abandoning any hope of digging my way out under the back door, I reverted to my original plan of finding the key that would unlock the door. My head was beginning to pound. Ignoring the aching in my legs and the throbbing in my head, I crept back to the unconscious body of the barmaid, cursing myself for reducing my source of light. She hadn't stirred while I was investigating the door to the alley, so after a moment's hesitation, I squatted down beside her to resume my search. Unless she received help soon, she might die for want of medical attention. I wasn't actually too bothered about her, but I didn't relish the idea of being locked in a cellar with a corpse. At last, with much manoeuvring, I succeeded in raising her body slightly to allow my fingers to close on a set of keys in her hip pocket. Spurred on by my discovery, I abandoned my caution and wrested the keys forcibly out of her pocket. She didn't respond. Taking the keys straight over to the back door, as far away from Tess as possible, I studied them in the trickle of light that still penetrated the gap under the door.

There were about a dozen keys attached to a plain metal keyring. They were mostly Yale design, with a few large warded keys. I tried them all, but none of them fitted the lock in the back door. Crossing the cellar once more, I ascended the ramp, taking care to avoid Tess, in case she had recovered sufficiently to reach out and grab me as I passed her. Injured though she was, I didn't trust her. But she lay motionless where she had fallen, and gave no indication that she was still breathing.

One by one, I fumbled to insert each key in the lock. To my dismay, none of them fitted. Desperately I carried on trying, long after it had become a hopeless task. There must be at least one other key that Tess had concealed about her person. Perhaps she had dropped it and I would have to scrabble around searching for it in the darkness. But the other possibility was that the key was on the other side of the door. Leaning against the wall, I shut my eyes, worn out, when suddenly the door jolted and I leapt backwards just in time to avoid being knocked as it swung open. Staggering down the slope, I almost lost my footing. There was a blinding light. As I closed my eyes, I heard a familiar barking and felt a warm wet tongue on the back of my hand.

After that, there was a confused babble of voices, all talking excitedly at once. Ignoring everyone else, I knelt down and buried my fingers in Poppy's soft fur.

'You made it,' I murmured to her. 'You got out. You're a good girl. Good girl, Poppy.'

She let out a growl, as if to assure me there had never been the slightest doubt she would escape and come to my rescue. Then there was more noise and subdued mutterings and I felt myself being lifted up. I opened my eyes and saw that I was lying on a stretcher with two ambulance men carrying me down the corridor.

'No, it's not me you should be looking at,' I protested. 'I'm not injured. It's Tess. She's down in the cellar and I think she might be dead. She fell and hit her head. You don't need to worry about me. I'm fine.' To prove my point, I raised myself up as far as I could, and forced a smile. 'I probably look terrible,' I added, falling back on the stretcher, exhausted, 'but I'm not hurt. Really, I'm not.'

They put me gently down on the floor as Hannah came bustling over, with Poppy in her arms.

'You need to be checked,' she said.

'And you need to stop being bossy,' I countered irritably, clambering to my feet and holding my arms out for Poppy. 'There's nothing wrong with me, I promise you. I'm not hurt, just dirty and relieved to be out of there. I need to go to the loo, and then I need to talk to the police about the murder of Silas Strang.'

# 41

AFTER A NIGHT IN the cellar my hands were filthy, my fingernails black with grime. My clothes smelt foul, and my scalp felt itchy with dust and mould. I couldn't wait to go home and wash off all the dirt.

A shower followed by a mug of tea and two fried eggs on toast, with lashings of ketchup, made me feel a whole lot better. My legs were still stiff and painful, and my shoulders hurt from straining to lift up a floorboard, but my headache had gone. Hannah was worried about me but I assured her that all I needed was a good night's sleep, and I would be back to my normal self.

But my ordeal was not over yet. There was still the police to face. The inspector had agreed to question me at home, which was a relief, because it meant there was no question I would have to leave Poppy behind while I went to Swindon. Although we hadn't actually been apart for very long, it had felt like months, and I couldn't bear the thought of being separated from her again just yet. I suspected it was Barry's idea that his senior officer come to Ashton Mead, because Barry arrived at Rosecroft to wait with me, looking solemn. Without his goofy grin, he was actually not bad looking. In my rush of gratitude at being free, I even caught myself wondering whether I had been hasty in rejecting his advances.

While we waited for the detective to arrive from Swindon, Hannah told me how my rescue had come about. After dodging past Tess, Poppy had managed to escape from the pub, probably through a gap in the garden fence. She must have realised there was no point in going home to wait for me there. Instead, she had gone to the café to look for Hannah. Puzzled at finding Poppy sitting outside alone, and unable to reach me on my phone, Hannah had shut the café and set off to look for me.

'As soon as I saw Poppy on her own, I knew something had happened.'

'It's lucky you didn't have any customers,' I said.

Hannah nodded. 'I hadn't opened up yet, but I would have thrown them out if anyone had been there. Poppy arriving without you rang huge alarm bells. We ran straight to Rosecroft to look for you. I thought maybe you'd had an accident.'

When I hadn't answered the door, Hannah had used her spare key and gone inside to find my cottage empty. My phone wasn't ringing, so Hannah had contacted Barry who immediately instigated a hunt for me. Meanwhile Hannah had decided not to return to work and wait for the outcome of the police search. Instead she had followed Poppy, trusting that Poppy would find me. Poppy had led her straight to The Plough. Having taken Hannah behind the bar and along a dingy passageway, she stood scratching at the cellar door and refused to leave. Her suspicions alerted, Hannah called Barry, and before long the police had arrived and turned the key which Tess had left in the door, not intending it to shut behind her.

Hannah finished her account and was on her way to the kitchen to make another pot of tea when there was a knock at the door. Detective Inspector Langdon and Detective Constable Crooks had arrived to take my statement. They sat down on the two armchairs in my living room, while I sat on the sofa with Poppy beside me. I was pleased to have the pretext of watching Poppy, to avoid having to look at the inspector when he spoke to me. Even though I had done nothing wrong, my eyes fell before his calculating stare that appeared to gaze right through me. Unlike her senior officer's, the constable's expression seemed sympathetic. I wondered if they were in the habit of playing 'good cop, bad cop'. He might have developed a veneer of impassivity in the course of his work, or perhaps an innately detached personality had led him to rise to the rank of inspector. Either way, there was something unnaturally robotic about him.

Keeping one hand on Poppy's back as she snoozed beside me, I wondered how to explain what had happened to me during the night. It was going to sound far-fetched, but the police had found me locked in the cellar with Tess, so I hoped they wouldn't be too surprised by my statement.

'How is Tess?' I asked, putting off the moment when I would have to launch into my account. 'It was impossible to see her injuries in the dark, but I think she must have hit her head when she fell, because she seemed to be unconscious. I know you shouldn't move someone who's been injured, if you can help it, but I had to try and get the door open and fetch help. So, I figured it was the lesser of two evils, to move her around so I could find the key. Although I never did find it,' I added. 'If you hadn't come along when you did, her injuries might have been a lot worse. She would probably have died.' I paused, hoping the detectives wouldn't realise I was talking so much to avoid having to give my version of events.

The sergeant told me Tess had recovered consciousness in hospital, and had been questioned by the police. The inspector interrupted her, rather curtly I thought, to say they wanted to hear what I had to say.

'Tell us why you were locked in the cellar of The Plough,' he said.

His voice was level, his blank expression disconcerting. It was hard to believe that he was genuinely interested in anything I had to say. I hesitated, wondering where to begin.

'Why were you locked in the cellar?' he repeated, with a hint of impatience.

So I drew in a deep breath and blurted out how Tess had lured me down there and shut me in, threatening to leave me there unless I signed a confession.

The inspector checked a few points in my statement, but in the end it came down to whether or not they believed my story. The inspector asked me several times why Tess had wanted to frame me for the murder. The fact that Silas and I had engaged in an altercation in public didn't seem to satisfy him. To be fair, a lot of people had overheard us rowing. I explained that Tess had killed Silas herself, but even the well-meaning sergeant looked sceptical at that.

'It's understandable that you might want to blame Tess for what happened to you,' she said. 'Whether by intent or negligence, you're telling us she was responsible for locking you in the cellar.'

'It wasn't negligence,' I replied. 'Surely it's obvious what happened? She locked me in there.'

'Our problem is that she was locked in too, and she's telling us it was you who locked her in.'

'That's ridiculous,' I burst out indignantly. 'Why would I want to do that?'

The inspector stared at me. 'She asked us the same question.'

'She attacked me,' I protested.

'Yet she was the one who was injured,' the inspector replied. 'She said you hit her with a bottle.'

'I threw it at her. It was self defence. She had a knife.'

It was impossible to tell if they believed a word of my account. Eventually, they left. As soon as they had gone I opened a bottle of wine, and settled down in my living room with Hannah, Adam and Barry, to discuss what had happened.

'What I still don't understand is why she was so determined to pin the murder on you, of all people. I mean, you don't look like the sort of person who would go around killing people,' Adam said. 'It seems a stretch to expect everyone to be convinced you were guilty just because you had a row with this Silas character in public.

From what I've heard, everyone fell out with him, so why did she pick on you?'

'Do the police know something they're not telling us?' Hannah asked.

Barry shrugged.

'What? Like they found a knife sticking out of Silas, and it had my fingerprints all over the handle?' I replied crossly.

'If they had any evidence at all to link you to the murder, you wouldn't be sitting here now,' Adam pointed out, and Barry nodded.

I sipped my wine.

'And even if she thought you did it, why was she so interested in what happened?' Hannah added thoughtfully. 'She seems to have been determined to punish you for his death. I think she knew it wasn't you, but she was desperate to convince the police you were guilty. The question is, why was she so keen to send the police off on the wrong tack. Do you really think she's guilty?'

It was clear to me that Tess had murdered Silas, but my friends weren't convinced of that.

'It's not long since you were sure Virginia killed him,' Hannah murmured.

'Well, I was wrong then, but now I'm right. I know it was Tess.'

'Did Tess actually tell you she killed him?' Adam asked.

'Not in so many words, but I accused her and she didn't deny it.'

Hannah and Adam exchanged a rapid glance, and Barry sat staring morosely at the floor. Divided in our opinions, we all agreed to try and put it out of our minds and leave it to the police to find out what was going on. Barry grunted but didn't say anything.

'Anyway, you're safe now,' Hannah said. 'And that's the important thing.'

But I didn't feel safe.

# 42

IT WAS EASY FOR my friends to tell me to forget about my ordeal, but not so easy for me to follow their advice. After an uneasy night, during which I barely slept, I knew that it was going to be impossible to carry on as though nothing had happened. However desperately I wanted to forget about the whole horrible experience, Tess's crazy ravings seemed to repeat themselves over and over in my mind, her rasping voice telling me that I would never be free. My legs were aching, and I was stiff all over from having spent so long cooped up in the cold cellar, but my physical discomfort would soon pass. My anxiety was less easy to dismiss. One way or another I had to find out if my suspicions of Tess were justified. If she wasn't guilty of murdering Silas herself, I needed to discover who she was shielding.

As soon as I was up and dressed, I called Barry, who confirmed that Tess had not yet been charged.

'They let her go? After she stole Poppy, blackmailed me, and locked me in the cellar?' I asked.

Down the phone I heard Barry sigh. 'According to Tess, the whole episode was your fault. She claims she discovered

272

you down there and accused you of purloining a key with the intention of stealing alcohol, and you attacked her. She says she would never have shut herself in the cellar. You shut her in. It's a case of your word against hers, and the investigating officers are treating it as suspected theft. There's nothing more I can do, I'm afraid. Tess told them there's been some pilfering –'

'Pilfering? What are you talking about?'

'According to Tess – and I shouldn't really be telling you this, so you didn't hear it from me – you've been slipping into the cellar to steal alcohol for some time. She hadn't known who the culprit was, but bottles of wine had been disappearing for a while. Now she's caught you red handed, she's decided you've learned your lesson and won't be stealing from the pub again. So, she's not going to take it any further.'

'*She's* not going to take it any further?' I spluttered indignantly. 'But aren't you going to arrest her?'

'The police won't be prosecuting her. There's no evidence against her.'

'That's ridiculous!' I burst out. 'She killed Silas. She threatened me with a knife.'

'Well, yes, but it comes down to your word against hers. The police want to know what you were doing in the cellar in the first place. And they have found no evidence to support your claim that she locked you in there deliberately.'

'What about the fake confession?'

'There was no sign of it in the cellar. They found a piece of paper that had been torn out of an exercise book, as you described, but there was nothing written on it.'

'She had a notebook, and she wanted me to write a confession and a suicide note. She can't be allowed to get away with it.'

Barry sighed again, and repeated that, in the absence of any evidence, there was nothing he could do.

'What about the knife?' I asked. 'She had a knife.'

'According to her statement, you had a knife which she wrested from you.'

When I insisted she couldn't be allowed to get away with it, he warned me against trying to take the law into my own hands, and made me promise not to do anything rash or illegal. I didn't tell him that somehow I intended to force Tess to confess, as she had tried to force me.

'If only you could talk,' I said to Poppy.

She wagged her tail and gazed at me quizzically, her head on one side.

There was only one thing for it. I hurried to see Hannah and Adam before they left for work, and outlined my plan to them. Hannah was reluctant to go ahead, afraid it would put me at risk. We already knew that Tess was dangerous. Adam was circumspect.

'Are you sure she locked you in there deliberately?' he asked.

Suppressing my irritation at his scepticism, I reminded them what Tess had said to me.

'She certainly sounds deranged,' Adam admitted. 'I think Hannah might be right. This could be dangerous.'

Carefully, I explained to them that, unless Tess was convicted and locked up, I would never be safe. She might try to attack me again at any moment, and the next time she might succeed. She had only to type out a confession and fake my suicide, and I would no longer be alive to expose her deception. I had to do something to stop her.

'And I need your help,' I concluded. 'If my plan fails, I could end up as her next victim, with my murder disguised as a suicide.'

'Did Tess really kill Silas?' Hannah asked, her eyes wide with dismay. 'If she's capable of that, do you really want to be going anywhere near her?'

Adam seemed to make up his mind. He nodded and spoke firmly. 'Yes, you're right, Emily. I think you may have to do this, and you can't do it on your own. But I don't want Hannah involved. It's too dangerous. It will have to be you, me and Barry.'

Hannah sniffed. 'There's no way you're leaving me out of this. Emily's my friend. If anyone's going to be there for her, it should be me. And I don't think we ought to bring Barry on board with this. If the plan goes wrong, it wouldn't be fair on him. He could lose his job.'

No one pointed out that if my plan misfired, I might lose my life.

Cliff was due back from his holidays the following day, so there was no time to lose if I was to corner Tess on her own. We had decided The Plough was the best location for me to confront her, as Hannah and Adam would be able to conceal themselves more easily there than out in the open. So, that evening, the two of them met in the bar an hour before closing time. We had arranged for them to be the last to leave the bar. As they arrived, I slipped in through the garden and hid in the toilets, hoping no one would notice that one cubicle was occupied for about an hour that evening. At last I heard Hannah and Adam call out goodnight to Tess. I didn't hear her response. The street door banged shut as my two friends left. I listened out for them returning through the door to the garden; they came in so quietly, no one could have heard them entering. After a few moments, I slipped out of my cubicle. There was no one else in the toilets. Silently I pushed the door to the pub a fraction, and peered through the gap. Tess was standing with her back to me, locking the street door. The bar was otherwise empty. I pushed the toilet door open and stepped into the bar. Although I was doing my best to be quiet, Tess must have heard me. She spun round, startled. Her eyes narrowed when she saw me.

'What the hell – ?' she said. 'What are you doing here?'

'I want the truth,' I replied, loudly.

It was important that Adam and Hannah recorded everything we said on their phones as they stood nearby, just out of our line of vision.

'The truth is that you're a vicious bitch,' Tess snapped. 'Now get out of my pub. I'll deal with you in my own time.'

'Why are you lying?'

'Piss off right now or I'll call the police.'

'Why did you want me to confess to the murder of Silas Strang? You know it wasn't me. Who are you protecting? Tell me, who killed Silas Strang?'

'Shut up. Shut up. I don't want to hear his name on your lips.'

'I get it that you hated him. Everyone did. But why me? What have I done to you?'

'Hated him?' she screeched, suddenly losing all self control and shaken by some fierce emotion. 'You're the one who's full of hate, not me. You're the one who said you wanted to kill him. Why? What was he to you? What was going on between you and him?' She took a step towards me and let out a bark of manic laughter. 'Did he tell you he loved you? Did you think he was going to run away with you?'

Stunned by what she was saying, I barely heard a loud knocking at the front door. But I did see her pick up a bottle and wave it above her head.

'It was you, wasn't it?' I whispered, shocked. 'You were the girl who was secretly planning to elope with Silas, until his mother stopped you.' I broke off as she let out a howl.

'He lied to me,' she screeched. 'I loved him and he said he loved me. But he was just using me. He betrayed me and now you –'

'It was you,' I whispered, backing away from her and remembering just in time to raise my voice. 'You killed him.'

'Yes, yes! It was me. It was me! I killed him. It was what he deserved. I know what he was doing with you. I saw the two of you together. And now it's your turn.'

I only just ducked in time. Behind me, I heard the bottle smash against the wall, but she had already picked up another one. And then, without warning, I heard a snarl and Poppy leapt forward and grabbed her by the ankle. Shrieking in pain, Tess dropped the bottle as she lost her balance and toppled over, hitting her head on the bar. She let out a yell and shouted at me to get Poppy off her. At the same time, the door of the pub burst open and two uniformed constables burst in, followed by Barry, Adam and Hannah.

'It was her!' Tess was yelling, pointing at me. 'She set that vicious brute on me. She's a murderer! She killed Silas. Arrest her!'

Tess hauled herself to her feet and lunged at me. I was aware of her eyes glaring ferociously at me, as Poppy leapt at her again. This time she held on.

'Get that brute away from me!' Tess hollered, trying to shake Poppy off.

Poppy only relinquished her hold when Barry stepped forward and caught hold of Tess. Wrestling her to the ground, he flipped her over onto her front. She was still struggling as he put handcuffs on her.

'It's her you should be arresting, not me,' she screeched as she was taken out to the waiting police car.

Hannah went behind the bar and poured us all a drink while Adam began to relate what had happened. I hadn't heard my friends enter the pub from the garden because they had found the door to the garden locked, leaving them stuck outside. As soon as they realised they were shut out, Hannah called Barry.

'We tried knocking but no one opened the street door,' Hannah took up the tale. 'But we managed to record some of your shouting match through the letterbox.' She smiled and took out her phone.

We listened to a recording of Tess screeching. 'He lied to me. I loved him and he said he loved me. But he was just using me and –' This was interrupted by some faint mumbling, and then Tess's voice was shouting again. 'Yes, yes! It was me. It was me! I killed him. It was what he deserved. I know what he was doing with you. I saw the two of you together. And now it's your turn.'

'We heard it all,' Hannah said. 'We knew we had to get in there and help you, but it was impossible. We were afraid the police would get here too late to save you, so Adam tried to break the door down.'

Adam gave a rueful smile, and clutched his shoulder.

Hannah continued. 'We couldn't get in, but we found a small window that was loose, and we managed to unlatch it and Poppy jumped through it. We figured having her in there was better than nothing.'

I reached down to pet her. 'A lot better than nothing. She saved my life.'

Poppy looked at me and wagged her tail.

# 43

IT WAS TYPICAL OF Hannah to suggest throwing a party to mark the occasion of Tess's arrest. I should have been expecting it, but she still caught me by surprise. We were sitting in the café in a break between breakfast and lunch, and the early customers had all left, so we had the place to ourselves when she broached the subject. Tess was so clearly deranged that I wasn't really sure what there was to celebrate. We ought rather to have been commiserating with her or, at the very least, feeling desperately sorry for her. I voiced my opinion as firmly as I could, but it was pointless trying to remonstrate. Once Hannah had made up her mind, she was unshakable, and she insisted on hosting some sort of celebration at the café. Basically, any excuse for a party was enough for her to launch into enthusiastically planning some extravaganza, however inappropriate the occasion. And, after all, I couldn't really say she was wrong to want to have a good time.

'You can't close the tea shop on a Saturday,' I protested feebly, cradling my mug of tea in my hands.

'It's my tea shop, and we're closing early on Saturday,' she replied.

She patted her hair in place with a businesslike air as she spoke, as though controlling her hair was a nod to her ability to control everything else in her life. Except, perhaps, Adam. I wondered if her party planning was a kind of transference when what she really wanted was to plan her wedding, but I shelved that ungenerous thought.

'It's going ahead,' she assured me, 'so you might as well accept it with good grace. The party's in your honour, after all.'

'What if I don't come?' I asked.

But we both knew that wasn't going to happen. Before I had finished pointing out that this would be a massive overreaction to a trivial incident, Hannah was already drawing up a guest list.

'It's short notice, so not everyone will be able to come,' she murmured. 'So we'd better ask everyone.' She looked up at me, her eyes gleaming with determination. 'You can invite your family, anyone you can think of, and I'll make a list of locals. Let's make this a real bash!'

When I pointed out that my family knew nothing about what had happened with Tess, Hannah dismissed my objection with a wave of her hand. 'That's not the point,' she said. 'We don't need to be specific. No one needs to know why we're having a gathering. I mean, we can be celebrating the fact that the murderer has been caught and we can all sleep comfortably at night again. Your family don't need to know it's got anything to do with you.'

Only, of course, people were bound to talk, and my mother's ears were like magnets for gossip, especially if it was about me.

'Don't worry,' Hannah said. 'It'll be fine. Just tell her the story's been exaggerated and you weren't in any danger.'

'That's easy for you to say.'

But I had no intention of arguing with her about it. Had it not been for her quick thinking, Tess might very well have killed me. Besides, Hannah was my friend and it was very kind of her to offer to throw a party to celebrate my escape. I didn't want to be churlish, even if her offer seemed more like a command. We chatted a little more about Tess, and how surprised we both were at what she had done.

'I suppose there'll be a job going at the pub,' I said thoughtfully. 'Would you be very upset if I spoke to Cliff about it?'

Hannah gazed at me with a blank expression.

'I can still work here part-time,' I added quickly. 'I'm sure we can work something out. But it'll be better paid, so I think I should go for it. What do you think? I wanted to discuss it with you before speaking to Cliff. I mean, as long as it doesn't clash with working here, but the café closes before The Plough gets busy. Since I'm usually there in the evening anyway, I might as well be behind the bar as in front of it, and be paid rather than spending.'

Hannah nodded, and muttered that it was my decision.

'I'll think about it,' I said, and we left it at that.

By the time Saturday arrived, Hannah had invited half the residents of the village to her gathering, and to my annoyance most had accepted the invitation. Even Cliff, the landlord of The Plough, promised to join us. He had been devastated to learn that Tess had been responsible for killing Silas Strang. We had spoken to him in the bar one evening, where Tess had worked with him for over twenty years. In all that time, Cliff said, he had never suspected he had been employing a murderer.

'I guess it's something any of us might be capable of, given the right circumstances,' I suggested.

My friends stared at me. Hannah and Adam both looked a bit cross, but Hannah had been a bit distant with me ever since I had mentioned applying for a job at the pub, while Richard shook his head mournfully. Cliff just grunted and returned to the bar to serve a customer.

'It was a crime of passion,' I said, struggling to explain myself. 'She was driven mad with love.'

'Funny sort of love,' Adam muttered and Hannah agreed with him.

In a quiet moment, I went up to the bar and enquired about the job that had become vacant. Cliff asked me if I had any experience of working behind a bar, and nodded when I replied that I already worked in the hospitality industry. He agreed to think about my request. I was disappointed that Cliff didn't offer me the job there and then, but Hannah assured me it was merely a formality. She was certain Cliff would offer me the job, and she promised to write me a brilliant reference. But I couldn't help noticing she looked rather smug when she heard that Cliff hadn't rushed to offer me the job.

At Hannah's insistence, I chatted online with my mother and my sister, Susie, and told them about the Saturday gathering. To my surprise, they both accepted the invitation straightaway.

'It's about time we both came over to Ashton Mead,' my mother gushed. 'Your father hasn't seen you for ages.'

'I can't promise Joel will come, though,' Susie said. 'He leads his own life these days and he seems to have a social life that doesn't just revolve around football any more.' She sighed and I murmured that my nephew was growing up quickly. 'Too quickly,' she grumbled.

The following afternoon, Cliff paid a visit to the Sunshine Tea Shoppe. 'I just popped in to get back to you about the job,' he said, smiling affably, as he sat down and nodded to me to take a seat opposite him.

Leaning towards me, he added in a low voice that he was sorry to tell me the position had been filled. There was nothing more for me to do but thank him for considering me – which he didn't appear to have done at all – and take his order for tea and scones.

'Never mind,' Hannah said breezily when I told her I wouldn't be working at The Plough after all. 'Maybe I'll be able to give you a raise if we carry on doing well. And you don't want to tire yourself out, doing two jobs.'

At the pub that evening, I was taken aback to see Michelle serving a customer. Smiling and chatting, she looked perfectly at home behind the bar.

'It's hard to believe she's never worked in a pub before,' Cliff told us, complacently, when he passed our table collecting empties. 'She's a quick learner. You'd think she's been pulling pints all her life. And she's great with customers.' As he spoke, we saw Michelle and the customer at the bar laugh together.

'It looks like you're stuck with me,' I told Hannah, who grinned happily.

*

The next day we started preparing for the event which Hannah was calling a 'Village Celebration'. Hannah and her mother spent the next few days ordering in supplies and baking like crazy. Cliff was providing drinks, and Michelle was going to help serve. The invitation made no mention of the murder, but everyone knew what had happened. Once the village gossip, Maud, learned how Tess had dognapped Poppy and locked me up, everyone heard about it. While I was pleased my family were coming to the village, I worried that they would hear about my ordeal and make an embarrassing fuss. In the event, my mother was surprisingly relaxed about it, merely enquiring a touch wistfully whether I was ready to return to London.

The past few weeks had undoubtedly been strange and stressful, but my local friends had supported me and I was grateful for their loyalty and their trust. Whatever else happened in my life, I had no intention of leaving the village that was now my home.

'I'm not leaving Ashton Mead,' I replied, raising my voice against the babble of contented villagers tucking in to scones and cakes. 'I'm settled here, and so is Poppy.'

Hearing her name, Poppy wagged her tail and gazed up at me, her eyes bright with understanding.

'We're both very happy here,' I said.

I could have sworn Poppy was smiling as I leaned down to stroke her.

# Acknowledgements

I would like to thank all the team at The Crime & Mystery Club for supporting The Poppy Mystery Tales: Ion, Claire, Ellie, Sarah and Lisa. A special thanks to Demi for all her support. My thanks also go to Steven for his meticulous proofreading, and Steve for his lovely cover design incorporating Phillipa's brilliant original artwork. Producing a book is a team effort, and I am very fortunate to have such a dedicated team to help me.

As for the real 'Poppy', I wish you health and happiness in a life filled with treats and long walks in the grass.

## If you enjoyed *Poppy Takes the Lead*, don't miss the other Poppy Mystery Tales!

After losing her job and her boyfriend, Emily is devastated. As she is puzzling over what to do with the rest of her life, she is surprised to learn that her great aunt has died, leaving Emily her cottage in the picturesque Wiltshire village of Ashton Mead. But there is one condition to her inheritance: she finds herself the unwilling owner of a pet. Not knowing what to expect, Emily sets off for the village, hoping to make a new life for herself.

**When Emily decides to investigate the mysterious disappearance of a neighbour, she unwittingly puts her own life in danger...**

When Emily stumbles on the body of a woman who apparently drowned in the river, the other villagers suspect foul play and are quick to blame Richard, Emily's next-door neighbour and a newcomer to the village. Emily finds it hard to believe her friendly neighbour could be a cold-hearted murderer, and when she meets Richard's attractive son, Adam, her feelings only become more complicated.

**Determined to find out the truth behind the death in the village, Emily travels to London to track down the man with whom Richard's wife was having an affair.**

'Fun and heartwarming with all the mystery and tight plotting you'd expect from Leigh Russell' – **VICTORIA SELMAN**, *Sunday Times* bestselling author of *Truly, Darkly, Deeply*

**CRIMEANDMYSTERYCLUB.CO.UK/LEIGH-RUSSELL**

Sign up to The Crime & Mystery Club's newsletter
to get a FREE eBook:

**crimeandmysteryclub.co.uk/newsletter**